THRONE OF EMBERS

THRONE OF EMBERS

BLEEDING REALMS - DRAGON BLESSED

BOOK THREE

NINA WALKER

ADDISON & GRAY PRESS
WWW.NINAWALKERBOOKS.COM

To our Ivins friends,

Thank you for bringing us into the fold.

NOT QUITE MIDNIGHT

HIS MASTER DIDN'T GLARE, NOR *did he curl his lip. His hands were relaxed, not balled into fists. But his master was angry—very angry. The Occultist was sure, deep down where his blood churned with magic, where bone lay parallel to soul, that his master would never forgive him.*

This wasn't simple anger, or disappointment, or frustration… it was red-hot seething hatred. It couldn't be satiated with apologies or excuses, not even if they were true and wholly justified. All that burning hate directed right at the Occultist caused a tremor of fear to rocket down his body—a juvenile reaction. He hadn't felt this way since his long-ago days as an apprentice.

"Master," he said, bowing low and keeping his voice smooth as glass, "the dragon king is dead by his son's own hand. This

is cause for celebration."

"And what of Khali?" The master tilted his head, red eyes glowing and burgundy robe pulled so high around his face that it cast shadows over his mouth. "Is the elemental princess still alive?"

They both knew the answer to that question, unfortunately. The Occultist swallowed, nodded once, and then fell to his knees. "I have failed you. I will take my punishment."

Anticipation swept over the crowd. He wasn't alone with his master, not here, not now, not this time. Most of his brethren were in attendance tonight, as many as could be spared. This gathering was important. They needed all that bonded magic in one place—all that blood—if the spell was going to work.

He felt the heaviness of their judgement like he felt the sweat on the back of his neck, like he felt God Himself frowning down at him. Him, the failure, the son with all the favor who still couldn't fulfill the mission.

How could he have been so confident that the spell would work? Khali had been right there. For days, she'd traveled with him, her veins soft as butter, her mortal heart beating behind its flimsy cage, her neck long and elegant, so easy for twisting. He'd had ample opportunities to kill her but he hadn't because her death wasn't supposed to be at his hands. It was supposed to be Bram.

It still was. So why had Bram killed King Titus instead?

Bram. The false prince. The weak link of the Brightcaster family, the one God had given directly to him so he could spell a reaper to the boy's soul and they could be done with the dragons. But Bram failed, Bram was to blame, and one day Bram would die for it. He'd seen the hungry looks the boy had given the princess. He knew of the longing behind those searching eyes and the raspberry flush in those mortal cheeks. Whatever feelings Bram had harbored for the girl, they must have been strong enough to cause him to resist the reaper and turn his task toward another instead. Was the king merely in the wrong place at the wrong time or had the reaper chosen Titus as a second option? No matter. It couldn't be undone now.

As if reading his thoughts, his master interrupted them. "How much can you blame Bram? This is your doing. If you'd been better able to spell the reaper, if your blood had been stronger, you'd have succeeded and Bram would have, too."

He nodded, crestfallen. "Yes."

It was true. All true.

The master held his gaze for another long second, and then like a slap, turned away, his attention leveled on the encircling crowd. Maybe one of the others would be able to succeed where he'd failed. Or maybe it wouldn't take only one warlock, but all of them, collectively, to fulfill destiny.

That's why they were here, wasn't it? That was the purpose of this gathering. It was time to complete the ritual, to mend what the spirit elemental girl had broken, and to bind what was always meant to be bound.

The pale sandstone walls behind them flickered with the firelight. Flames swirled before them in the center of the dias, dancing flashes of deep red, hot orange, and bright blue. Soon the flames would be black with magic.

The Occultist fell back into the circle of his brothers, eager to blend into the sea of robes and pale unaged faces. They all looked the same; only the slightest variations set the warlocks apart from one another. This oneness was ingrained into their blood magic, and when Khali took that from him, reminding him of what it would be to be entirely mortal again, he'd nearly lost his mind. To be one small identical part of this larger whole was lifegiving compared to being a single identity without purpose. That had been torture. Punishment enough. He would not fail again.

Their master initiated the chant, his voice rolling heavy over the landscape, and they all followed in unison, growing louder, voices and faces rising into the night. The stars glistened above, paying tribute. The humid air wrapped around them in a soft embrace. The fire grew taller, wider, darker. The flames transformed from colorful and alive to black and even more vibrant.

This was it. He could feel it in his blood, in the way they were connected, stronger together. He could feel it in the blackness of the raging fire and the silent mirth of the watchful stars. The magic was growing stronger. The reapers, they were drawing closer, closer, closer.

He couldn't see them. No Sovereign Occultist could see them. But he knew they were there.

Perhaps this was what faith was, believing in the unseen things, knowing the unknowable.

Faith and obedience.

First, they would rid the earth of elemental magic—they were nearly there. Second, they would finish the bleeding of the realms, combining the mortal realm with this superior one. And finally? Finally, things would be as they were meant to be, where blood magic created an obedient race and everything and everyone bowed to the one true God.

This was their ultimate task, holy as it was. Squash the evil. Purge the impure. Combine the realms. And then the whole earth would be washed clean.

He would be washed clean—clean and forgiven.

An unknown energy snapped through them, the magic crackling and steaming—a small fire being smothered by an ocean. The shared bond fractured, releasing them from the reapers. The eerie sense of otherness that signaled a reaper was near evaporated quickly, like the thin wisps of smoke coming off of the newly departed fire. Their chanting slowed into a thick silence, like a shared drowning.

A sharp terror ran down the Occultist's body, every muscle coiled tight. A failure now could only mean one thing: the master was growing weak. They would have to strengthen their sovereign bond again, which could put everything they'd accomplished at risk. It put them at risk. Their lives. Their magic. Everything.

They needed a sacrifice.

The master screamed, his guttural voice slicing through the silence. When they all turned to look at him, and not the master, the Occultist felt the crushing weight of his failure all over again. They had trusted him. They had chosen him. And now they hated him.

"I will make this right," he vowed, speaking through clenched teeth. A sense of rightness filled his entire body. "I will sacrifice myself to strengthen the whole."

Somehow, he knew this would happen, that one day he'd volunteer himself over to the blood-bond. But he didn't realize it would happen this way—that it would be tonight—that this breath, this flesh, this moment, would be his last.

His master stepped close and before the Occultist could

react, a searing pain pierced his heart straight through. His blood ran hot and then cold. He fell to the pebbled ground, gasping for air. When he tried to beg, there was nothing left in his lungs. The last thing he saw were the red eyes of his master, moving closer. Blood magic took over, filling him with terror and then peace. The two battled within until both drifted away, until he was everything and he was nothing.

Maybe this was forgiveness. Maybe this was mercy. Maybe this was merely the price God wanted him to pay, the price that would cost his life.

ONE

HAZEL

I SWALLOW HARD AND STARE at the icy lake, my boot edging along the crusted snow. My coat is way too thin and the morning air wraps around me like a million frozen fingerprints. Dean insists that once we get through to the other side of the portal, I won't need the extra heavy stuff, so we left it behind. The Summer Forest is just as it sounds: a fae forest stuck in a perpetual state of summer. Even at night it's going to be warm. At least I won't have to worry about freezing to death when I get over there. I'll be too worried about every other little thing I see and hear and smell.

"Are you ready for this?" Dean reaches out and intertwines his fingers with mine. A wave of heat passes through my body. I smile into his fiery eyes and lean in for a simple kiss. The scruff on his chin tickles my face as I breathe in his wonderful smoky rain scent. My already thumping heart picks up a beat. I spent the night tangled in his arms and more than anything, I want to crawl back into that warm bed with him, but I know we can't.

"As ready as I'll ever be," I say, letting out a huff of visible air.

Which is to say, no, I'm not ready, but too bad—we're going in anyway!

Turns out, running away takes careful planning. We couldn't take off immediately, not when there were loose ends to tie up. Believe me, I wanted to go right after leaving the café, my mission to save my friends firmly planted in my mind. But I had to be reasonable because I also didn't want Cora and Macy's families to think something terrible had happened to them. The first thing we did after getting back to Dean's place was have him hack into their school accounts and shoot emails off to their parents. We made up some bogus story about them going with friends on a last minute Christmas vacation to Switzerland—*c'mon Mom and Dad, it's the opportunity of a lifetime*—and promised they'd be in touch as soon as they could. A terrible lie, I know, but it's better than leaving their parents filing a missing person's report. I can only imagine how my mom would react if I disappeared without a trace.

"You want me to carry that?" he asks, nodding toward the backpack I've heaved over my shoulders. I shake my head. His is even bigger.

Dean and I spent the better part of last night packing these backpacks, filling them with weapons, gear, food, and clothing. He added a few guns even though they probably wouldn't work in Eridas, as well as some sharp knives and a bunch of scary crap I have no clue how to use. And then there's his fire elemental magic, the next level of weapon. Thinking about fighting off bad guys makes my stomach feel all hollow and weird.

"Don't worry," I add. "I threw in a few candy bars last night too. You know, just in case chocolate isn't a thing over there."

He smirks. "It's not."

That seems unreasonable. "Well, what can I say? This girl has priorities."

"And you're sure about this?" It's the same question he's been asking since we decided to do this instead of going to Ohio like Harmony wanted.

Before going to sleep last night, he went over and over what I should expect in the days to come. We're going to be traveling through parts of Eridas where it might not be safe to eat the food, especially in the fae forest. We're also not going to talk to anyone we meet along the way, not unless he thinks it's okay. When we get the chance to fly, we will, but that's not always safe outside of Drakenon. And once in Drakenon, I'm not to leave his side. Not once. Trust nobody. And certainly don't fight unless it's in self defense.

Eridas. Drakenon. The Summer Court and the Fae forest…

These are all new to me and belong to this other realm that I apparently belong to as well—considering I'm a freaking dragon shifter! I can hardly believe it but there's no denying it now, not after what happened yesterday. Dean confessed that he wasn't entirely surprised; he smelled dragon on me the moment he met me, which is why he was so hostile at first. He thought I was a spy sent from one of his father's rivals. But he also smelled something else, something he wasn't sure how to describe or where it came from. And what did surprise him? The crazy form my dragon self took: a spirit dragon that seems to belong to both the spirit realm and our physical one. This is not something he's ever heard of and neither of us have any real clue as to what it means or how I'm going to supposedly defeat the Sovereign Occultists—if Harmony is to be believed.

I guess the spirit elemental runs deeper within me than any of us knew.

And I guess Harmony has secrets of her own, considering she called me from my mom's phone yesterday and we haven't been able to reach them since. My phone is now wrapped up in the waterproof backpack or I'd be tempted to pull it out and try again.

I hate this.

I want to make sure Mom's okay and I want to talk to Harmony. But I need to save my friends right now. I know for a fact they're in danger and every second I'm not going after them is a second guilt drums hard against my chest.

They'd have never gotten into this mess if they hadn't met me.

I let out a slow breath and nod to Dean. "Let's go."

Together, we leave the safety of land and run out onto the ice. It gives way almost immediately. My heart nearly explodes as we plunge under the surface. We pop back up and he keeps a tight grip on my hand, pushing the warmth from his fire elemental into my body. It helps. But I'm still terrified. I've never been much of a swimmer and images of the reaper possessing my body and forcing me into this very lake on that awful morning not long ago pierces my mind. We swim out to the middle of the lake, chunky slabs of ice floating around us. I suck in little breaths of freezing air and splashes of what feels like the coldest water on earth.

He kisses me once more. Quick.

"I'm ready," I say. I'm shivering like crazy and he shoots another blast of warmth into my body. He holds my gaze with his. He's so sure, confident and strong. He believes in me and that means the world. We take another deep breath and slide under the surface. Time to swim. Water surrounds everything, me, him, our slick backpacks, our black athletic clothing. We swim into the true blue of it until it grows darker, blacker, riskier. And then, as Dean promised, there's a glow of rainbow lights swirling along the bottom of the lake.

The portal to Eridas.

We kick harder, moving closer, and a thrill of anticipation pushes its way past the fear. *Here we go. Time to be brave.*

Something black floats at my right, catching my attention.

I stop swimming.

A reaper hovers in the water. Otherworldly, dark cloak, red glowing eyes, skeletal.

No!

I want to scream, to tell it to go away, but I can't.

It rushes toward us, and Dean pulls me after him. He can't see the things I see so he has no idea the reaper is beside us. Maybe we should have shifted into our dragon forms before swimming down here because at least then we could have talked to each other. Why didn't we do that? Oh that's right,

Dean suggested it, but I'd been too worried about shifting again, not ready to take the leap quite yet.

Stupid, stupid, girl!

Go back, the reaper urges. His voice is different than all the other times I've heard the reapers before. This one is calmer. I'd freed them from whatever spell they were under, hadn't I? I sent them back to their spirit realm. So why was one here?

Go back now! He says again, his raspy voice louder in my mind, no longer so calm.

We keep swimming. The reaper can't touch us now.

At least, I hope it can't.

The Occultists are on the other side of the portal, the reaper says again, his thoughts so clear in my mind that for a flash, I can see what he sees. Men in burgundy robes line the shore, chanting in succession. Their eyes are glowing red, similar to the reapers. Their skin is stark white and they all look the same: bald, ageless. Maybe young. Maybe old. Definitely cultish and creepy. It's one of the strangest things I've ever seen and deep down in my gut, I'm terrified. I cannot face these men.

They'll kill you the second they see you, he says, *that's what they want. You. Dead.*

It's odd, trusting a reaper, but my gut tells me I can.

Somehow, I know he's right. He's not trying to hurt me or possess me or use me. He's trying to warn me. And there's something else in his tone, too. Gratitude. Yes, for freeing him from the human spirit realm where he didn't belong.

You must go back, he hisses again, urgency rising.

We're almost to the swirling glow of colors of the portal and the air in my lungs is nearly gone. I tug Dean back with all my force, shaking my head at him when he turns to me with a questioning look on his watery face.

"No!" I scream, my voice muffled by the water and pushing the last of the oxygen from my lungs in a stream of bubbles.

Dean's eyes are wide and confused but he nods once and then swims the two of us to the surface. My lungs are pure fire, panic racing through my veins. An inky darkness edges around my vision. I don't have much time. *It hurts...* We break through the water and I gasp, letting air fill me even though it's agony, like experiencing hell and heaven all at once.

"Are you okay, Hazel?" He holds me above the water, fingers gripping my skin.

"There was a reaper," I say between gasps. "A reaper down there."

"Come on," Dean says, and we swim to the shore and

climb out of the lake. He sends another blast of heat through me as soon as we make it to shore. My hands are pressed against my knees as I hunch over, trying to catch my breath and organize my thoughts.

"What happened?" Dean asks, kneeling before me and brushing a loose strand of hair from my eyes. His compassion is a beautiful thing and I'm quick to brush my lips against his before explaining.

"The reaper down there was protecting me from the portal. He told me we couldn't go through. He said the Occultists are on the other side waiting for me." I try not to sob but the tears come anyway and my voice grows thick. "I saw them. He showed me. They're the same men in the robes I saw when Harmony and I did the blood magic. They're evil. And they'll kill us the second we get to the other side of the portal. It's what they want."

Dean is silent. He closes his eyes for a minute and then nods.

"Okay," he says, "so we can't go through this one. We'll have to find another portal."

He's mentioned there are more but I assumed he knew where they were.

"Find?" I ask. "Where's the next closest one?"

He shakes his head and stands, stretching out his back. "I

don't know."

I stand too, anxiety snaking its way down my spine. I shake it off before it holds on for dear life. "Well in that case, I guess we're going to Ohio."

"Ohio?"

"If anyone knows where another portal is, it's got to be Harmony, right?"

He lets out a little laugh, even though I know he must be as frustrated as I am. "Right. I guess the faerie called it. She said we needed to come to her first and we're coming to her first after all."

"Well, she can see the future," I sigh, leaning into him. "I should've listened."

As we hike back to the car, a pesky feeling of unease sits low in my stomach. My friends went through that portal only yesterday. Are they okay? Did the occultists get to them when they passed through? Or are they still on their way to Drakenon? Maybe they're already there. It's crazy to hope they're still with the dragons but I do, because if there is anyone worse than those dragon shifters, it's the creepy men lining the lake on the other side of the portal, who apparently, want nothing more than to see me dead.

Once we're back in the car, I retrieve my phone, slide into the passenger seat, blast the heater, and call Mom. It goes directly to voicemail. Why does it keep doing that?

I know it's only been one day and she sometimes works long shifts at the hospital, but this isn't like her. Something is wrong.

I spring from the car because I don't want to shift in a moving car and focus my mind on turning into a dragon. It doesn't work. Nothing happens.

Dean stands with his door open, gaping at me.

"How do you do it?" I ask. "I want to change so I can go through the spirit realm and check on my mom."

He shakes his head once. "I just do it," he says. "It's as natural as a thought coupled with an action. Like choosing to walk."

"It's not so easy for me," I grumble. "I don't know how I managed it the first time."

"Necessity?"

I let out a bitter laugh. "You could say that." Considering I accidentally shifted into a spirit dragon when I was trying to fight off our assailants and save Dean, his theory makes perfect sense. But I can't wait until I'm in mortal danger every time I need to shift.

"I've got to figure this out." I climb back into the car and buckle in. "Let's get to Ohio as fast as we can. I have a bad feeling."

"About what?" He starts the car and pulls onto the two-lane highway, tires crunching over the icy gravel.

Once again, I can't help but laugh. "Umm—how about everything."

I'M A MARRIED WOMAN NOW.

Royal matrimony. Sealed forever. Crowned as Queen. Silas, my king.

I still can't believe this is real.

I press my hands into my stomach and try to breathe. My corset digs into my ribcage. My lungs burn. I need to take this thing off! I rip through material, fingers fumbling to pull lace through the grommets. It slowly releases and my bones ache even more. I drop the dress to my chamber's floor and stumble to the window. My underclothes are loose, which helps, but I need more air. There's latticed iron along the outside of my window but I throw open the panes anyway to let the cold breeze in. It extracts me from the panic until I'm able to relax, breathe, and think.

This new life hasn't quite settled in yet, probably because everything happened so fast. The rushed coronation took place the very same evening as our wedding day, despite the obvious displeasure shown from most of the court. Silas didn't care. He saw to it that we were crowned as quickly as possible before anything could happen to another Brightcaster. Through the whole thing, the chanting and the vows and the hushed reverence and whispers, I didn't smile. Not one time. I couldn't fake it anymore.

The last few days have been a blur of trapped emotions and long stares. I'm boiling over from the silence instead of letting the bitter truth spill from my tongue. I can't stand up to Silas right now. What good would it do? Bram's trial is set to start tomorrow and he can't afford Silas to be in a bad mood. We both know what Silas is capable of. If he can murder his twin brother in cold blood, no doubt he can and will do the same to Bram. And me standing up for Bram? It might just lead to that.

I don't know what to do…

So I stand at the window for ages, staring out into the blanket of fresh white snow that has covered the city below and the rolling hills beyond. I stand and stand and think and think and no matter how long I do it, I still don't have any solutions. For now, Silas has allowed me to stay here in my own chamber. That won't last long. At least he's agreed to give Bram a fair trial, unlike so many others in the king's position who would have struck first and asked questions later—that's if they'd have asked questions at all.

Can anyone be trusted in Eridas? As far as I know my fae friends can, but I've barely seen or spoken to them these last few days. Silas told everyone they're our guests, but it's unmistakable from the distrustful ways people stare at them that they're not welcome. My friends are not going to want to stay here for long if this keeps up. It's probably not the safe haven they were hoping for. The betrayal of that vile Sovereign Occultist still stings as fresh as the day it happened. I've chastised myself over and over for trusting him in the first place, for believing that he would be bound to the same agreements that the rest of us are. Beating myself up about it isn't helpful, but I can't seem to stop, not when there's nobody else to blame.

This is my fault.

Frustrated, I seek my magic as I've done time and time again over the last few days. But it's still absent. And my dragon, my other self, she's still gone. Tears well up in my eyes. The sun sets behind the mountains. The sky turns dark.

Someone knocks and Faros lets herself in, as she's done a thousand times before. Today, however, her face is void of color and her large round eyes can't quite meet mine. Something is wrong. Even with her elegant gown and pretty headdress and perfectly stoic expression, I know it. *I know her.*

"What is it?" My voice trembles.

"Your new chambers…" Her words taper off and I know exactly why she's come here.

I'm not an Elliot anymore. I'm a Brightcaster. Silas and I are expected to move into the King and Queen's chambers. At least they have separate bedrooms. Connected by a sitting room and only two doors, but separate nonetheless. It's a small thing but to me it's everything.

"What about my new chambers?" I push, making her say it.

"They're ready for you," she says, her tired eyes finally looking up to hold mine. There's something else there. Something more.

"What aren't you telling me?" It's a silly question. Once again, I already know.

She squares her shoulders. "It's been three days since the wedding and you still haven't spent the night with your husband."

"Yes, that's true." I hold my breath and fight the bubble of nausea rising into my throat. So far Silas has allowed me to keep my virtue intact, not making me entertain him in his chambers.

"That ends tonight," she finishes with a small smile. "Silas expects you to go to him. Everything is ready."

I squeeze my eyes shut and let out the breath. What am I supposed to do? Fight him off forever? Give in to him even though the very thought of his mouth on my skin makes me want to scratch my own eyes out?

"Fine." My voice sounds so much stronger than I expected. I pause to look out the window one last time. The white snow is a stark line against the black sky. It practically glows under the moonlight. "I'll go now. I might as well get it over with."

"It will be fine," she says, smiling the kind of smile that doesn't reach her eyes. The usual sparkle is gone from them. Even though she's trying to make me feel better about this entire situation, she knows this was never what I wanted. And now I'm stuck. She's quick to dress me, making me beautiful as she's done for years—for a life that might kill me—and now for the very man brandishing the knife.

My hair is brushed into loose curls that waterfall down my back. She finishes with a white silk cape, tying it securely to hide the flimsy lace underclothes beneath. As she escorts me to my new chambers, the drafty hallway makes my flesh prickle. At least I tell myself it's the cold. Only the cold. Admitting to the ocean of fear raging inside feels like admitting to the loss of something I'll never be able to get back. And I don't want to think about that. I've already lost too much.

She ushers me past the set of armed guards waiting at the doors and into the king and queen's chambers. She wraps me up in a quick hug and then is gone before I can collect my thoughts well enough to say goodbye. The huge engraved doors shut me inside with a heavy thud and I spin around.

It's dark in here, but not dark enough. I'm not alone.

Silas stands near the hearth where a crackling fire gently lights up the room. It illuminates the sharp planes of his face and the lightness of his blond hair. He's dressed in loose fitting jet-black linen trousers but no shirt. The black color reminds me of the night outside, his dark cotton contrasting my white silk. The sight of his tanned bare chest makes my throat go dry and my eyes water.

I've been in the royal chambers before to sit with the queen and her ladies but I've never been in this room. It's too private for my liking.

As if reading my thoughts, Silas nods toward one of the doors. "Shall I show you around your new home?"

If I speak, I won't have nice things to say, so I shrug.

He leads the way into the queen's chambers first. The bedroom is double the size of mine, filled with expensive silks and extravagant tapestries, hand carved furniture, and gold-framed paintings of the prettiest spots in Drakenon. I catch sight of a painting of the Jeweled Forest and shiver, wanting to strike that horrid place from my mind forever. There are other smaller rooms attached to this one for bathing and dressing, and then, of course, another room beyond for her to meet with her ladies. Why do I keep thinking of the queen as someone else? It's me. I'm the queen now. Brysta has been moved to another part of the castle to make way for me, and like it or not, here I am.

"It's nice," I manage, my voice straining. Silas doesn't seem to notice because he takes that in stride with a proud expression, as if this ornate room was somehow going to make up for the fact that he murdered his way to get me in here.

There are no reminders of Titus or Brysta; it's as if they've been swept away.

He leads me back into the sitting room. "This space is just for us," he says, clearly enjoying this little tour of ours, "well, and our future children."

He's so confident, so pleased with himself. I want to slap that smirk right off his face. I want nothing more than to get out of these rooms and never ever return. Maybe I can find a way to get back to Hazel and she can help me restore the magic. Or perhaps I need to find that necklace of Silas's and destroy it. Could it have something to do with my magic's disappearance? It seems unlikely but at this point I'm growing desperate.

I need a plan. What's my plan? Realizing I have none leaves me ice cold.

But of a few things I'm certain: I have to find a way to get my magic back, figure out how to punish Silas for what he's done, make sure to save Bram, and put a stop to the Occultists once and for all.

I squeeze my eyes shut for a second, overwhelmed beyond reason.

"Come," Silas says, breaking my thoughts and striding over to the door opposite mine. "Let me show you my room."

My stomach flips. I wonder, does it still smell like King Titus? Could they have erased him so quickly as they did Brysta from my room? He hasn't even been buried yet. His body is in the chapel and won't be laid to rest for three days as his soul is blessed and his people pay their respects. Now there's a smell that will take a while to cleanse, no matter the amount of incense burned. At least elemental magic will be used to help keep his body cold.

The king's room is not much different than the queen's to look at, but it *feels* so vastly different. Suddenly, the energy between Silas and me is charged. Not only with the elemental magic storming behind his lavender eyes, but with something else too. Anticipation prickles off of him. Hatred pours off of me.

Does he mistake the hate for something else? Or maybe he likes it.

He inches closer and I freeze, unable to move. "Don't worry," he says, gently pulling the ribbon that holds my cape together. The silk robe falls to the ground, pooling at my bare ankles. I force myself to stand tall, don't let him see my fear. His eyes rove hungrily over my body. No man has ever seen me like this. "I'll teach you what to do. You'll like it."

He'll teach me because he's been doing this for Gods know how long and plans to continue to keep his mistresses even though he has me. He considers himself above the rules. And it's suddenly clear to me that he's been thinking about the possibility of this night for years. I still can't move. I hate him. I hate him for this. I hate him for Owen. I hate him for stealing what shouldn't be his. When his mouth captures mine, it takes everything within me not to bite him, to push him away, to scream. To cry.

I stand frozen, eyes closed as tight as they can possibly go. I can't force myself to kiss him back. And when his body presses flush against mine and he wraps his warm arms tight around my waist, his hands splayed out across my prickling skin, I don't match his movements. I don't raise my hands.

Don't kiss. Don't do anything. My mind is traveling far, far away. My body may have to stay, but I will not. He still doesn't know I've lost my magic. The mere thought hollows out my chest. I am an empty vessel; everything that was me, that is me, has been taken. And Silas, he is going to keep on taking until there is nothing left.

Suddenly I'm met with a blast of cold air.

"You're not even going to try?" he growls angrily.

My eyes pop open.

Silas is several feet back, raking his hand through his pale hair, cheeks flushed and temper rising. He stares at me like I've slapped him. Perhaps doing nothing is worse than a slap to a man like Silas. I can't help it, I feel smug, and it feels good.

"You're my wife," he seethes.

I don't know what to say. If I anger him too much, he might take it out on Bram tomorrow. I want to yell all the hateful things running through my mind but instead, I keep it all locked away and continue to do absolutely nothing.

"What is it?" He glares. "Do you really find me revolting? Do you wish I were Dean? Or pathetic Bram? Or is it Owen you—"

"Don't you dare speak his name!" I hiss, breaking my silence.

He tilts his head. "There she is." The usual smirk-like smile returns to his face. "I'd wondered where you went these last few days. You haven't been acting like yourself."

"And what's that supposed to mean?" I can't help the hellfire crackling through my tone. If I had my magic right now, it would be sizzling in my fingertips.

"It means that I like you with a little bit of sass." He licks his bottom lip, as if remembering the taste of me. "You're more fun that way. You're a challenge that I can't wait to conquer. You remind me of a wild horse that needs taming, you know. And I can't wait to be the one to do it." He wanders off as he finishes, standing over the little bar stand tucked into the corner of the room and pouring himself a glass of wine. He doesn't offer me any, not that I'd take it.

When he turns back, I meet his lazy smile with one of my own. "You might be able to force a claim on my body now that we're married but you will never claim any other part of me, especially my heart."

He slaps his chest like he's been wounded, but it's a mocking gesture. What does he care of love? Or of doing the right thing? He only cares about lust and power and winning.

My heart means nothing to him.

"I will not take a woman who isn't willing," he says coolly. "You will be mine, Khali. The Gods have already decreed it and you've already said your vows."

I swallow. He's right about that.

"So when you're ready—" his expression softens and he winks cruelly "—you'll know where to find me. You're welcome to walk through my door at any time, Wife, but next time you do, be prepared."

"Never."

The candlelight hoods his eyes. "Not never, Khali. Sooner than you think."

And then he begins undressing himself from the waist down, moving toward his bed as if he doesn't care that I'm still watching. Or maybe he does care and this too is part of his game. I catch a quick glimpse of even more bare skin and turn away, cheeks flaming and stomach twisting. As I stumble from his room, his savage laughter follows close behind.

THREE

HAZEL

THE SUN FLASHES ACROSS MY face, stinging my eyes. I lean my forehead against the cool glass and watch the scenery fly by. Outside the car, the forest is thick, a mix of snow and pine, and the sky is robin's egg blue. On the horizon, angry gray storm clouds gather. I blink, catching sight of my reflection. Up close like this, my hazel eyes remind me of my mom's. I've been praying that she's okay and I guess we're about to find out if God is listening. I believe in God, how could I not given my abilities? But I don't know a whole lot about what "God" is and if "He" or "She" is listening. I sure hope so and I also hope something happened with Mom's phone and I'll be hearing from her at any minute. That she's fine.

We're diving to Ohio. There weren't any flights available

on such short notice, not to mention, Dean has quite the arsenal of weapons stashed in the trunk of this little black sports car. He offered to try to fly us there himself during the night but was worried his magic would be too depleted from the battle to get us far. So it's his car to the rescue and I sure hope this tiny thing can handle well in the snow. It's only a six hour drive from my school to my house but that's with clear roads and no traffic. The storm on the forecast doesn't look good; it's going to be a bad one. But we're determined to beat it. It's either that or get stuck somewhere between Charleston, which we just passed, and Columbus, our destination. There are a heck of a lot of rural areas and mountain passes between here and there. Two places I'd rather not get stranded in during a blizzard.

"Are you hungry?" Dean asks, his eyes flashing to the dashboard where 4:50PM glows back at us. It's going to be dark soon. And start snowing. My stomach is a mess but I'm not sure if that's from my nerves, being hungry, or the haul of gas station junk food we ate around noon when we hurried out of town. We left soon after getting back to Dean's place, and normally road trip status and alone time with him would excite me, but not today. I'm sick with worry and every minute of this stretch on the freeway seems to feel like an hour.

"I'm okay," I reply. "I don't think I could eat now anyway.

Let's just keep going. I want to beat the storm."

He nods and fiddles with the music on the radio, turning the dial until it lands on a more upbeat song. He can probably sense my crappy attitude and wants to cheer me up. Truthfully, I liked the moody stuff we were listening to earlier, it was more in line with my mood, but I keep my mouth shut and hum along.

An hour later and we're in the middle of a full-on whiteout. The sun is long gone, shrouding us in the storm's darkness, and aside from the red taillights of the semi-truck in front of us, all I can see are the white snowflakes shooting into the windshield and flying all around us. The scene reminds me of a Star Trek episode, like we're going at light speed or something. And it feels like we're on a theme park ride and wondering if the semblance of safety is real or if we're about to go flying into the air and crash to our deaths.

The snow piles up on the road so quickly, I have to force myself to look away. I mindlessly scroll social media on my phone instead, but not even the funniest memes can make me feel better. It doesn't take long for Dean's fingers to curl tighter around the steering wheel and his shoulders to grow tense.

"Let's stop," I say, putting down my phone. "I give up. This is too freaky. We can get a room for the night and finish the drive tomorrow."

He keeps staring straight ahead. "Are you sure? We're only a few hours away."

"Yeah." I lean over to get a glimpse of the speedometer. We're only going 40 miles an hour and by the looks of things, we'll be slowing down even more soon. "At this rate we won't get to Mom's house until well after she's gone to work for her night shift. We can make up the time in the morning after the plows have come through."

His tense body deflates like a balloon and a few minutes later, he exits the freeway into a little town called Ripley, West Virginia. It's probably quaint and wonderful, or maybe it's a run-down forgotten town, but I can't tell either way through all the snow. Everything is covered in a blanket of white and the roads are even worse down here off the freeway where the big trucks help to create a path for all the helpless cars in their wake.

There's a motel just off the exit with a vacancy sign flashing, and rather than try to look around for something better, he pulls our car right in.

"This okay?"

"Fine by me."

I wait inside the car while he gets us a room key, and then loads our backpacks onto his back and leads us to room number eight.

"My lucky number." I smile and knock on the door for good luck.

Dean smirks.

"What? I like eight. It's like an infinity symbol. What's not to like about that?"

"I never thought about it." His lips twitch into a smile.

The room is much colder than I was hoping for but I'm sure Dean's extra warm body heat will take care of that in no time. And at least it's clean. There are two queen beds, though I'm sure we'll cuddle up in one, and a simple bathroom at the back. It's in need of a remodel, the place suspended somewhere between the 1970s and the 1980s but I decide to call it retro and be happy we're here and not stuck out on those horrible roads.

"I'll go find us something to eat," Dean offers. "There were a few vending machines back in the lobby. Anything in particular you want?"

Tacos!

But I don't say that. He'd probably get back in the car if I did.

"Anything salty is fine," I supply instead. "I'm going to take a quick shower."

Dean leaves me to it. I rummage around in my backpack, looking for my pajamas, when he knocks on the door less than a minute later. He must have forgotten his wallet or something.

"Miss me already?" I tease, swinging the door wide open. But it's not Dean standing on the other side.

The man is young, my age perhaps, but it's hard to make out his features in the shadows. Behind him the light from the parking lot shines too bright, casting him into a silhouette. He's dressed in a stylish leather jacket with a white t-shirt and dark jeans. His flaxen hair flops perfectly over his smooth forehead, like a male model in a photo shoot. He steps closer and the light from the hotel room illuminates his chiseled face. Amber eyes lock me in.

My stomach drops.

I know him. He's the strange supernatural guy from The Roasted Bean, the one who told us about Cora and Macy. I hurry to push the door closed, a flutter of nerves and shock rippling through my body, but he sticks out a booted foot and stops me.

"Don't worry, Hazel." His voice is beautiful, like a gentle caress. It soothes me and the fear melts away. I'm alarmed, but then I'm not, all at the same time. He's most definitely doing that to me. *So freaky.* "I came to deliver a message."

"Another one?" I choke out.

He nods once. I scan the area for Dean but there's nobody

out here but the two of us, the snowy stillness, and the silent night. I don't want this guy coming into our room, no matter the intense way he makes me trust him. Somewhere in the back of my mind, I know I have to be careful and that the feeling I have has more to do with whatever supernatural voodoo he has going on and less to do with my actual feelings.

I've been through enough terror for a lifetime, thank you very much.

I pull the latch on the upper part of the door open so when I step outside and close it, the door stays cracked. I shiver against the cold and tuck my arms into my torso.

"What's your name?" I ask, somehow knowing he's not going to tell me. But to my surprise, he answers.

"I am Elias," he says, tilting his head and letting the name settle over me. "But please, keep that name to yourself."

"Uh, hi." I don't know what to say. I probably sound like an idiot. "So what's the message, Elias?"

He considers me for a moment, his amber eyes intensifying as they bore into mine. "I'm not supposed to meddle in the affairs of the other realm. It is not my job or my place."

"Okay…" And yet, here he is.

"But this realm, this human world, is my concern, and right now, a bunch of crazed lunatics think it's their holy calling to cross over into my realm and take over. You can imagine why that would bother me, yes?"

I raise my eyebrows. "Of course. It bothers me, too."

"So you have to stop them."

"How? I don't know what to do."

"All the portals are jeopardized," he says, cutting my complaint with his sharp tone. "The Occultists currently have members of their cult at every single portal save for the one in Drakenon."

So there's a portal in Drakenon? Good to know…

"And why can't they come through, again? According to you, my human friends were taken through it just fine."

He winces at my barbed tone. "Yes, I have failed Cora and Macy. I would go after them, but I'm forbidden to travel to Eridas."

"So tell me something that could actually help me," I plead. The wind kicks snow at us but I don't even care, this is my chance. "The reapers warned me of the Occultists near Westinbrooke, so it stands to reason they're at other portals too. Give me something I can work with here, Elias. Help me."

"They want to kill you," he sighs.

I scoff. "Ya think."

"They want to kill you because of the spell between you and the dragon princess. If they kill you, they kill her."

"I know, and if they kill her, then I die too."

He shakes his head. "No, you won't. You can go to the spirit realm and back. She can't."

That sends my mind racing. So it turns out this spell between us is most dangerous to Khali? I guess that's kind of nice. Well, except for the fact that I have a bunch of crazies after me because of it. So not nice, after all.

I frown, suddenly unsure of everything. "This is getting weird. How do you know all this? Why do you keep showing up? *Who are you?*"

"As I said, I'm here to protect the humans."

"Okay, fine, but *what* are you?"

He smiles, and something playful flickers across his expression. "You really can't tell? You don't feel it?"

That sets me back. There's definitely something about him that's different and familiar, all at the same time, but I have no idea what it is. "Uh, no, I don't know. Sorry. This is all new to me."

He shakes his head. "My kind are certainly not new to you, Hazel."

"Ummm—"

"No matter. I only came to warn you."

"And how exactly am I supposed to fight the Occultists?" I've barely figured out what I am!

"With the sight."

"The what?"

A door opens and shuts with the clang of metal and the ring of a bell. "I must go," he says, turning and gliding away, just like that. Like our conversation is nothing. He moves quickly, never once looking back. I gape at him, beyond confused at what the heck just happened. Did he follow me here? How? And where's his car?

As he crosses under the streetlamp, something lights up around him. The air is knocked from my lungs—and shock is knocked right on in!

Angel wings stretch out of his back.

They're not the glowing white of the angels I've seen helping humans cross to the other side; those tall guys and gals never look at me and they certainly aren't in physical bodies. Elias's wings are almost white except they're tipped in silvery gray. Even so, they're downright beautiful. Is he a full-blooded angel? Some kind of nephilim crossbreed? I want to run after him and ask. I have so many questions. I shuffle forward, words rushing to the tip of my tongue.

"Hey, You." Dean's velvety voice breaks me from my stare.

I jump and turn to him.

"What are you doing out here? You must be freezing." He holds up two plastic bags full of what must be our vending machine dinner. "Are you alright?" His gaze travels down my face and then flicks out into the parking lot and then back again. "You look like you've seen a ghost."

I bark out a laugh. "Well, I see ghosts everyday so…"

All I want is to point out Elias and his angel wings to Dean, but Elias is gone. And his footsteps, they're gone, too. Dang it! I swear I saw them in the snow. How could they have disappeared already? Vanishing bootprints must be an angel thing. Their rules are different from ours, I already know that considering the things I've seen over the years.

This day keeps getting weirder and weirder.

And scarier…

"What's wrong?" Dean's voice is steeled now, with that protective edge I'm used to. Being on this side of it feels pretty nice, I have to admit.

I push back through the motel room door behind me and smile. "It's okay. Everything's fine. But I have something to tell you."

"Okay?"

"Well, one thing is amazing, but the other's actually pretty terrifying."

Dean follows me inside. "Well, I shouldn't expect anything less."

Thinking about the warning Elias delivered sends my heart racing. I already know I'm going to tell Dean everything except for Elias's name. The guy asked me to keep that to myself and I'm pretty sure betraying an angel is a cosmic no-no.

Dean tosses me my coveted bag of Funions and I rip them open.

"Okay, where should I start…"

FOUR

KHALI

THE AIR CATCHES IN MY lungs the moment Bram appears. My eyes water, tears threatening to break free, but I can't show emotion for another man so I blink them away. I already know what will happen if Silas were to suspect Bram and I have something between us—a death sentence. So I relax my expression as he's dragged into the throne room in chains. He's been beaten, that much is clear. His brown wavy hair is matted around his face and darkened with dried blood. Purple and yellow bruises circle both of his eyes and his limp is unmistakable as he's dragged behind two large jailers.

He's an innocent man. Let him go. I long to scream the words but I don't, not yet. Timing is everything during these tribunals. I've sat through enough to know the farce that they can be. Ultimately the king gets to decide the fate of the accused. I can only hope that somewhere in Silas's cold and ruthless heart is a soft spot for his little brother. He was always pretty nasty toward Bram growing up, so anything could happen today, none of it surprising.

"Be seated," Silas bellows and the members of court comply. We're in the vast throne room, seated along the wood benches that line the sides of the room with a large open space in the middle. At the head sit the thrones, one taller than the other, both carved from dark red oak. I hate them. I sit in mine, trying not to fidget. It's way too hard and being in it means way too much.

Drafty air rolls through the room. I try not to shiver, wishing I had my fire elemental to keep me comfortable. The stone walls feel like they're closing in around us, gray and cold and witness to centuries of court life. I adjust in my gown, attempting to use the fabric to cover more of my legs. This particular dress is too revealing for my taste. It's low cut around the bodice, showing off my breasts. When Faros dressed me in it this morning, she said Silas picked it out.

My eyes zero in on Bram. Nothing else matters except for the boy who stands broken in the center of the room. Not my stupid dress. Not the people seated all around, staring and whispering. Not the dragons stationed at the door, nor the guards, nor the high flames in the candlelit chandelier despite the sunlight streaming through the windows.

He won't meet my eyes. *Why won't he meet my eyes?*

The room is overflowing with the same members of court who attended my wedding and the unexpected coronation that night. Their attire of velvet and lace is rich, much like their enjoyment and anticipation. It's inappropriate and sets a hateful burn in my heart.

Except… they're not all like that.

Many watch Bram with expressions of worry and sadness and horror. And I know beyond the people here, are the thousands all over Drakenon who would never condone such treatment toward one of their princes. Well, that is if they believe he's innocent. Those that don't are undoubtedly calling for his execution.

Everyone grows silent and Silas stands, cocking his head and strolling toward his brother.

"Well, young Bram, what do you have to say for yourself?"

Bram stays silent—the room stays silent. I can't stand it.

"Nothing?" Silas snarls, his voice echoing. "You kill our father and you have nothing to say?"

"I don't remember," Bram says quietly. His tone is thick with guilt. "I don't remember any of it. I blacked out. And I'm so sorry." He peers around for a minute, as if looking for someone who's not here, those green eyes scanning the room, seeking and failing. "Tell Mother I'm sorry."

"She's not here," Silas replies. "She couldn't bear to look at you."

"Yes," is all Bram says to this. My heart twists—this isn't right.

"How does someone black out and do something like that?" Silas questions further but of course he already knows. I've told him about the reapers. I told him and whoever else was left in the room after the murder. Silas is toying with Bram. Does the boy truly not understand what's happened to him?

Bram has nothing more to say and before long the members of court start to murmur among themselves. They begin to speak the most vile words—hateful words—of how Bram should be executed, that Bram was always jealous and never of any use, always worthless, and condemned to hell. This hatred grows and grows, and Silas stands in the midst of it, a playful smile dancing across his lips. Is this all a game to him? Is he enjoying it?

My whole body grows hot, igniting all the way to my bones. I can't let this go on.

"No!" I stand, my voice ringing strong like a bell. It breaks through the noise and the room falls silent again. When eager faces turn to look at me, my knees weaken. "Bram blacked out because an Occultist spelled him to a reaper who made him do things against his will."

Even as I say it, I know it sounds far-fetched. And the complete disbelief that meets me is a force of its own, pressing me down. Silas stares at me through a hooded gaze. I can't tell what he's thinking, but it can't be good. Bram looks as if he's about to be sick. His emerald green eyes are rimmed with red and his face has drained of color.

One of the more outspoken dukes, Duke Kensey, stands. He raises his hand to me and his round belly bounces as he speaks. "Explain how this is possible, Queen Khali."

I swallow. "I don't know how it's possible, but when Bram killed King Titus, his eyes were entirely black. Did you not see it?" A few members of the court nod, their faces softening in understanding. "That's not possible without some kind of magical interference."

"We're supposed to believe that a reaper was involved? We don't even know for sure that they exist," the duke continues. He speaks to me as if I'm an insolent child, not his queen. I'm used to this kind of treatment, but that doesn't make it okay, and it doesn't stop my anger from sparking hot.

"But they do," I snap. "Just because something doesn't have a good explanation doesn't mean it's impossible. Look at who we are, what we can do. How do you explain magic?

How do you explain the Dragon Blessing?"

He doesn't have anything to say to that.

The tall oak doors open with a bang and my father appears, making my heart squeeze yet again. He's slow, using a cane to help him walk since his muscles grew weak from being stuck in bed, but the sight of him sends a smile to my face. And dare I say it, hope to my heart. Mother holds onto his arm, her eyes clearer and happier than I've seen in ages. I wonder how long it will be before she starts going back to playing her political games, but then again, she got what she wanted, didn't she? I married her favorite of the Brightcaster brothers and my father is alive.

"What did we miss?" Father asks, his face set in determination. He wears his finest jacket, the maroon one with gold inlay. His hair is much grayer than it was months ago and is combed back into a neat style. Mother's gown matches his jacket. The exhaustion underneath her expression is unmistakable.

"Lord Paul Elliot." Silas motions for them to come sit by us. "Nice of you to join us." But there's something clipped in his tone.

"I can explain why this boy is innocent." My father points to Bram with his cane. "Because the same thing almost happened to me." This is news to most of these people and they lean forward in their creaking benches, dying for an explanation, and of course the next thing to entertain their gossip circles for a while. "When I was last outside of Drakenon on business for King Titus, I was caught by a Sovereign Occultist." The room erupts into gasps, and my father holds up his hand to shush them. He leans against his cane and Mother holds her supportive stance at his side. "I thought he was going to kill me but strangely, he didn't. He cut me, spelled me, and then let me go." The room is so quiet I can hear my heart beating in my ears. "As I traveled home I started to lose bits and pieces of time. I would blackout and end up in places I never intended to be. Entire chunks of time disappeared without any explanation." A haunted tone slips into the cracks of his normally strong voice. "And that's when he started talking to me."

"Who?" Silas asks. The sharpness in his question is unmistakable. Why is he so angry about the truth coming out? Maybe he wanted to execute Bram today. The very thought of it sends bile to my throat. *Evil, evil man.*

"It was a voice in my head," Father continues. "He confessed to being a reaper and told me that the Occultist linked us together. Something was wrong with him… he was off. I don't know how to explain it. He wanted me to do bad things to the people I loved. He wanted me to hurry home and I did, even though I tried not to. I fought it, fought him, and I—" he lets out a resigned breath "—even tried to kill myself. Nothing worked. He brought me back to Drakenon and into this castle anyway."

A tear releases from my eye and splashes hot down my cheek. I don't have the strength to wipe it away.

"Just when the reaper was forcing me to make an attempt at my own daughter's life, I was able to take control over my mind and body again. It nearly cost me everything. I fell into a restless and painful sleep for weeks. I nearly died." A smile flits across his face, accentuating the wrinkles. Many of them are new. "The night the reaper left me was the strangest of all. I didn't have to do anything. He just… left. I felt this tension between us snap, and then this enormous sense of relief came over both of us. It was as if he didn't want to be stuck with me any more than I wanted him. The second he left for good, I woke up, and now I'm here. The reaper is gone and he hasn't come back." Mother hugs Father from the side and he nods, pointing toward Bram. "And I believe the same thing has happened to Bram. Unfortunately Bram wasn't as lucky as I was. His reaper succeeded in completing his murderous task before he was released from the spell."

Bram's face is pale as a ghost, his eyes wide and round. He stares at the ground.

"And how are we supposed to believe they're really gone?" Duke Kensey hollers. "If you've been spelled by an Occultist you should be locked up." The man and his family are but distant acquaintances to me, and if he deserves his title or not, I wouldn't know. But right now? Right now I'd love to strip him of his title and send him away for good. All he's doing is directing suspicion to my father and Bram.

Unfortunately, the court erupts in murmurs of agreement. I can't hold back any longer. I jump off the throne and dash to my dad, pulling him against me and glaring back at the crowd. "Nobody touch him," I growl. "He's fine. He's better. Don't condemn him for something that wasn't his fault."

"Bram could still be dangerous too," the duke goes on, completely ignoring me. He doesn't look at me, doesn't gester to me, as his voice raises higher and higher.

Silas strolls across the room and leans in close to me, his lips brushing soft against my ear. "This is why you should have kept your mouth shut. I was handling it. They didn't need to know about the reapers and now they will use it to say we're unfit for the throne."

"If that was your plan, you should have told me," I whisper back.

I don't know what else to say to him, except that he's right about one thing: the court is outraged. They talk over each other, some yelling, panicking and angry. Others are defending my father and Bram. But everyone, and I mean everyone, is unhappy.

"Enough," Silas shouts and the room fades into reluctant silence again. "We'll make sure Paul Elliot and my brother are kept somewhere they can't hurt anyone."

The court is slow to applaud and my heart is stripped in two.

"That's not fair," I gasp. The pain in my chest swells.

Silas holds up his hand. "It's not going to last forever. They will be carefully monitored and when I decide they can be trusted, they will be. My word is final." He's met with a mix of nods and glares. "But we have a bigger issue to worry about and that is the Occultists. I will do everything in my power to make us stronger and that includes finding allies wherever I can."

Silas is making all these decisions on his own and so quickly. Normally king's have advisors, leaders they must listen to and work together with, but I see none of that here. He's a fool. Truly. And I'm not only going to be seeing it all unfold, I'm going to have to stand at his side and pretend to be a party to it.

The doors open again and my fae friends are escorted into the room. At least they're not in chains. They're dressed in clean riches and groomed better than I've ever seen them. My heart and hands squeeze tighter as I hold onto my father. I haven't seen my friends in days. They look well-rested. Fed. And their smiles seem genuine, if not a little nervous.

"You're not welcome here!" someone jeers and several more clap and cheer.

"Enough," Silas snaps, his voice growing louder than the rest. "Our new fae allies have been around the Occultists far more than we have and we'll welcome our new friends into this kingdom so long as they agree to help us, which they already have."

I don't like this. I don't trust Silas.

What's his endgame? What is he really using my friends for? And of course I don't appreciate the judgemental way so many members of the court are looking at them like they're a problem that needs to be squashed. I don't know if I can take another death on my hands. These fae came to Drakenon because of me; they were offered protection here by King Titus. I can only pray that Silas is true to his word and keeps them safe.

"Now then," Silas says coolly, "let's get ready for a funeral, shall we? We must honor my father and honor him well."

As we walk toward the exit—the royals always get to leave the room first—the energy in the room shifts again. Guards surround us, eyes glued to my father and Bram, their newest prisoners. I hold tight to Father and move along, wanting to get out of here and away from this nightmarish crowd of onlookers.

"You're making a mockery of this kingdom." Duke Kensey lunges forward, pointing his meaty finger at Silas. "You're a foolish child! Not fit for King!"

Silas turns, scowling. Violet lightning zaps from his hand right to the man. It strikes him center in the chest. It's so quick, there's hardly time to react.

He falls, dead before he hits the floor.

The crack of it echoes loud in my ears. The rancid smell of burnt flesh fills the room, making my stomach twist. My heart races through deafening silence and then the cries of fear. I blink, trying to process what I just witnessed. I never saw Titus do *anything* like this.

It's hard to believe.

But I know Silas, so I do believe it.

And Silas? He needs to be stopped. Who else is going to do it if I don't? This is wrong. To strike someone dead for pointing out your failings is the mark of a tyrant. I want to glare at Silas, to say something cutting, or at the very least, go comfort Duke Kensey's horrified family.

I do none of those things.

Instead I stand there and keep calm, because one day I will have a plan, I will enact that plan, and it will end Silas. Until then, I will watch and I will gather information and I will learn everything I need to learn.

"Anyone else have something they'd like to say?" Silas calls back to the crowd, his voice sickly sweet. He ignores the dead man's family who sob next to the smoking body. "I'm not here to be your friend. I'm not here to be manipulated or bullied. I'm King Silas Skylen Brightcaster and what I say is law. You can either support me or you can leave Drakenon. But anyone who speaks ill of me or acts against me *in my kingdom* will not be shown mercy."

The message is clear and nobody rebukes him—nobody dares.

He turns on his polished leather boots and storms from the room, his palms crackling with electricity as he goes.

FIVE

HAZEL

DEAN AND I PARK OUTSIDE of my childhood home, a cute little updated three bedroom rambler built in the 1950s with an added attached garage and a decades' old oak tree taking up most of the yard. An old tire swing hangs from the tallest branch, still and forgotten. The front walk and driveway are covered in a thick layer of fresh snow, but considering Mom should be gone on her nightshift, it isn't the strangest thing to see the snow undisturbed. But what if she's not at work and what if nothing's wrong with her phone? I fumble with the seatbelt.

"That's weird," I say, narrowing my eyes.

"What?"

I point to where the garbage cans are sitting out on the curb, covered in snow. One is tipped on its side.

"Garbage day is Friday." My voice quivers. "It's Monday. Mom would never just let them sit out all weekend like that, especially not during a storm when the city needs space for the plows to come through."

I release a slow breath, trying to calm my nerves. I didn't want to believe something was wrong but of course it is. Is she okay? Is Harmony? Can Harmony really be trusted? Is someone hurt? It's a sharp and painful thought—like a bee's stinger stuck under the skin—the thought may be small but it's everything in this moment. Harmony told me I needed to come to Ohio right away and I didn't listen. That conversation was almost two days ago. A lot can happen in two days.

"Come on." I burst from the car and sprint to the front door, lifting my knees high to get through the heavy snow and trying not to biff it on the icy pavement. Luckily I don't slip. It helps that Dean is right there with me, holding me up. "Door's locked," I grumble. "Follow me."

I lead him over to the garage and enter the code I know by heart. It rumbles open slow as molasses, revealing Mom's little black Toyota sitting inside. Another thing that isn't right; this car shouldn't be here.

"She's definitely not at work."

Dean places a reassuring hand on my shoulder. "Are you okay?"

I shake my head. And I love him for thinking of me, but this isn't the time to soothe my fears. I should be afraid. I should be worried. My only parent is in trouble! My hands start to shake and my breath speeds because I don't know what I'd do if I lost her.

The inner garage door isn't locked—Mom never locks it. I throw open the door and storm into the house, first noticing how very cold it is inside, the air almost the same temperature as outside. Sure, Mom likes to keep the thermostat down to save money but not this much.

I round the corner from the back hallway and run into the living room. I stop short. Mom and Harmony are sprawled across the carpet. Our two cats, Bella and Edward, meow and pace around their bodies. Edward spooks and runs off, but Bella prances over and rubs herself against my ankles, meowing even louder. I'm frozen, all wind having been knocked right out of my lungs at the sight of Mom and Harmony like this. They're laying side by side, as if sleeping.

Sleeping, I tell myself, *they have to be sleeping.*

But what if they're not…

"Mom!" I cry out and fall to my knees between them, going for her first. Her brown curly hair is fanned out around her face and her dainty chin is tilted to the side. I cup her face. She's not cold, not like the room. Her skin is perfectly warm.

I lean in close. "She's breathing."

Dean leans over Harmony. "Same here."

I shake Mom and yell for her to wake up and then I say a little prayer, but nothing happens. They're both out cold. "Should we call an ambulance?" My voice sounds miles away.

It's what I was taught growing up. If someone is hurt, you call 911, right? Well, first you go find Mom. But as I glance about the room, taking it all in, I know that's not an option. This situation is beyond what a paramedic or a doctor could diagnose. Not to mention Harmony doesn't have her glamour on anymore. The tips of her wings are visible behind her back and her skin has that baby blue hue to it again.

A silver bowl lays between the two of them. I edge closer. It's filled with a thin layer of a dark liquid.

Blood.

My heart sinks, realizing what this means. Just to be certain, I grab Mom's hands, which are both curled into tight fists. I gently pry them open and sure enough, find the cut across one of her palms. It's a thin line of angry red. Dean lifts Harmony's hand; the same marking lays stark against her blue skin.

"Blood magic," he says, his voice growing dark. "Harmony did it again. She shouldn't have."

"It made her so weak the first time." My voice cracks, remember how she couldn't even stand after she helped me peer into old memories a few weeks ago. "Why would she do that? And why would she come here, of all places? Why get my mom involved in all of this?"

I hate these questions. Every single one.

Dean clears his throat. "Hazel, come on." His frown is so, so sad and I wonder if it's a mirror of my own.

"Come on, what?"

"Look closer." He nods toward my mom but when I don't move, he crawls over and lifts her body, carefully rolling her onto her side. I gasp. Delicate metallic wings hunch together against her back. Her skin is normal. Everything else looks like a regular human. But there's no denying that those wings are anything but normal. "Whatever happened," he says, "it took away her glamour too."

I can't breathe. What's going on? Mom's a faerie, too? But she never said a word to me and I never once suspected anything like this. How could she have kept this from me all this time? It doesn't make sense. Mom and I are all each other has in the world. She knows about me and my curse, or gift, as she likes to call it. So why wouldn't she tell me the truth?

I want to make excuses for her but can't help feeling betrayed. It opens up a chasm of emptiness in my chest, taking away my voice, my thoughts, my everything… and I just sit there. Gutted. Angry. My stomach raw. My throat empty. I have nothing to say.

I feel betrayed to the absolute core but I can't even let myself feel that because Mom is unconscious and needs my help.

"Hazel," Dean asks gently, "what are you thinking?"

I swallow down the heaviness and fight back tears. "Something went wrong." I point to their palms and the bowl. "They were obviously doing something with blood magic and it backfired. They're not dead. They're just… asleep, right? This is some kind of coma?"

"It looks that way." His mouth is thin as he peers around the room, his mind puzzling through something. A plan? I don't know. I hope so, because I've got nothing.

"Do you think they're okay?"

Dean turns back to me with calculating eyes as he considers this for a minute. "I want to say yes but I can't lie to you." He runs a thumb along his lower lip. "I'm sorry, but no, I don't think they're okay, Hazel. I have a bad feeling about this."

My hands shake. I hate that my hands are still shaking. I grit my teeth and try to shake them out. Dean catches them with his own and holds them against his warm chest, a tender move that makes me relax just a little bit. Below us, Harmony sleeps.

"But whatever this means, we'll figure it out and we'll save them." He sounds so sure of himself. I nod numbly, and he releases my hands. "Are you okay?"

I nod again. "I will be."

He glances away and I know he doesn't believe me. "How about I go get your cats a fresh bowl of food and water and then find some towels? Let's get this cleaned up and get them moved into beds and then we'll brainstorm ideas to fix this." He says it like it's important, like it might save them, even though we both know it won't.

He's being so kind and comforting, but he doesn't know what to do. I can tell by the worry in his voice that he has no idea what's going to happen next.

This can't be real. How is this my life?

This is my fault. I should have listened to Harmony and raced to Ohio the second she called. And yet I'm still angry that my mother lied to me for all these years. How did she pull it off? Why did she do it? Did she lie about my father, too? The sucky thing is I might never find out the truth.

Dean leaves and I sit there with Bella in my lap, my eyes searching the family room, my chest rising and falling as the panic rises and falls as well. There's the red brick fireplace and the white mantel with all our pictures lined up in silver frames. There's the big round ticking clock on the wall. The old leather couches that have seen more than a decade of movie nights. The happy little plant in the corner, slightly dusty. The beige carpet, freshly vacuumed, now stained with little drops of blood. I follow the trail of drops until I see it—the glint of metal tucked under Harmony's leg. It's the hilt of her silver dagger. As far as I know, blood magic is strong because it requires a sacrifice of blood, if not more. The one and only time I used it, Harmony had chosen to pay the price for the both of us, and she'd been weaker than ever when it was over. And then? Then she'd disappeared.

Maybe it's my turn to pay for this magic.

Could I wake them if I took a little bit of the pressure off?

Before I can talk myself out of it, I snatch up the dagger and slice the blade across my palm, squeezing a trickle of blood into the bowl to mix with theirs. Bella hisses and darts away just as a zap of prickling magic races through my bloodstream. It stings something fierce—*holy crap*—and I gasp. But I push the pain to the back of my mind and slide the bowl over, grab hold of both their hands, and lie down between them. My vision tunnels, going bright white, then black, then white again.

The air disappears from my lungs, like getting punched

right in the stomach. I'm falling fast. It's as if my soul is being syphoned out of my body. When I try to scream, there's no sound. There's nothing. I'm nothing. And then I'm everything and I see it all.

SIX

KHALI

AFTER BRAM AND MY PARENTS are escorted from the room, all I can do is stand there. It's like my feet are sinking into the stone floor and at any minute I'll be swallowed up. Anger burns raw in my throat. Hopelessness spreads in my belly. And guilt… guilt is everywhere. Is this my fault? Should I have let Silas handle the tribunal and kept quiet about everything I knew?

No. He can't be trusted.

And from the shocked looks on everyone staring at me, the dead body, and the fae, it's not just me—nobody wants to trust Silas right now. And yet, we all have to. These are my people, they're counting on me to save the day, or at least temper my husband, but I can't. At least, not yet.

Shaking myself free of the intense emotions, I pull my

shoulders back and stalk toward my fae friends. I don't care what the people of court think of me doing it. I can't. They probably all hate me or at least find me weak. I hope I haven't lost all my favor with those beyond the castle walls, it's the most vulnerable of our people who need me now more than ever. But what can I do for them until I get my magic back and figure out how to best Silas?

Terek stands relaxed between Maxx and Juniper, his cat-like blue eyes roaming the crowd of onlookers, a tiny smirk on his bronzed face. If I didn't know better, I'd say he was about to hiss at them just to see what they'd do.

"Hello again." I force a smile. "Why don't we get out of here? We need to talk in private."

"As if there's anywhere safe to talk in this place." Juniper rolls her eyes. Her white-blonde hair is tied back into an intricate braid, showcasing her one pointed fae ear and one doe ear. She's prettier today than I've ever seen her. No longer dressed like a warrior, she wears a soft pink gown that could rival even the most beautiful of courtesans.

"I know where we can go," I reply.

Maxx nods at me, his horns reflecting the sunlight streaming in through the windows. More than a few of the men look at him as if they'd love nothing more than to take him out, their stances wide, weapons on display, watchful eyes fixed with animosity. Maxx is huge, muscles bigger than even the biggest of the Dragon Blessed. The elf is a force of nature, to be sure, but I've seen the softer and cautious sides to him. He doesn't worry me in the slightest. Quite the opposite; having him around makes me feel more protected.

Accompanied by two guards, I lead the party to my new chambers where I have my own private sitting room. As I suspected, it's empty. I motion to one of the guards in the hallway outside and tell them not to allow anyone inside. He nods and I lock us inside. Maybe this isn't the safest place to talk but I don't know where else to go. It's not like we can easily sneak off. Times have changed.

"Nice place you got here." Maxx whistles as we make ourselves comfortable in the plush chairs. "Queen Khali," he continues, "has a nice ring to it."

Juniper shrugs, unimpressed, and Terek grins with a questioning raise of his eyebrow.

"Yeah, about that," I groan. "A lot has happened since we got to Drakenon. I'm sorry I haven't had much time to come check in with you. Has everything been okay? Has Silas honored his father's bargain to let you stay here safely?"

"So far." Terek rolls a long lock of his golden hair around one finger. It's normally tied back but today it hangs around his bony shoulders. "He's been nothing but a terrifying gentleman." He flounces into one of the chairs and relaxes into it as if he's right at home.

"He's made it clear that he's not bound by his father's word," Maxx says, standing guard at the door, "so while he's been cordial and has treated us like guests, it's only a matter of time before he turns on us."

"Did you see the way your dragon court looked at us just now? They want us gone or dead," Juniper adds. She ambles over to the window and folds her willowy arms over her chest, staring out at the gardens and the city beyond with a worried grimace.

But I'm still stuck on something Maxx said.

Silas isn't bound by the bargains his father made but does that mean I'm still bound? The magic worked two ways, binding both of us to what we agreed upon. As far as I know, if one of us dies, the magic of the vow isn't suddenly gone. Unfortunately, I'm pretty sure *I'm* still bound to *my* word. I'd agreed to marry Silas but what else had I agreed to? I close my eyes, thinking back through the mess of emotions and craziness of the last week to what exactly happened between Titus and I that day on the Drakenon border.

I agreed to marry Silas, to not fight it, and to have his children. I bend over and grip my stomach, forcing myself to breathe.

He's going to want children.

"Is she okay?" I hear Juniper question, her voice sounding far away.

I straighten. I'm next to one of the tufted chairs and have to grab onto the soft red fabric to keep my knees from buckling. My eyes zero in on the cracking fire in the hearth as my mind whirls. Okay, I can't push Silas away forever, but what if I found another way? What if he was the one to make the choice to end things between us? Or what if something bigger than both of us made the choice for him? Or maybe he could go away…

A sparkling of an idea lights in my mind and I smile faintly at the first shred of hope I've felt in ages.

Terek smacks his lips together, startling me. "Hello there, Queenie, what aren't you telling us?"

I let out a long breath and decide to let these three be my confidantes in at least one thing today. "I've lost my magic," I admit. "Nobody knows."

They offer varying degrees of shock on their faces.

"What do you mean, you lost your magic?" Juniper snaps, her face falling and fear slipping through.

"I mean, on my eighteenth birthday, the same day I had to marry my enemy, it disappeared." I sigh and my eyes water. I'm quick to blink the tears away and continue. "It had been acting strange for a while and then I met the human Hazel and it *really* didn't like her. When I left the human realm I'd hoped that would be the end of the problems but it wasn't. I think the spell must have done something to me." I'm talking in circles. They don't even know what I'm saying!

"Wait, wait, wait." Terek holds up his hands, claws glinting. "Back up, start from the beginning."

I go back to the beginning and tell them everything, answering a million questions as I go, and as we talk the heavy weight of my secrets slowly begin to lift off my body. In one sense, I feel better having friends to share this burden with, but then I have to remind myself just how terrifying this situation is, and the heavy weight of it piles back on.

"We're in deep trouble," Maxx states when I've finished. He leaves his post at the door to start pacing the room. "This is worse than I thought."

"Yeah…"

I brought them here and now I'm powerless to help them stay safe. Our centaur friend is who knows where and the two people we made bargains with, the Occultist and Titus, either died or escaped. Oh, and my husband is a tyrant. Deep trouble about sums it up.

"I'm so sorry."

"Maybe I can help." Juniper strides from her spot by the

window and I stand to meet her. Her expression toward me is the softest I've seen. She's always acted like she hates me, and maybe she still does, but now I think she just feels sorry for me. She inches closer and lays cool hands on both my shoulders. "Let me see if there's anything I can heal, alright?" She smiles, and the little spots around her maple colored eyes lift. Her doe-like face falls into concentration, and I pray she can do something for me, anything. She healed Terek's broken wrist and she helped Bram when he was hurt. But I don't feel anything change and after a few tense minutes, she steps back and shakes her head. "I'm sorry," she relents. "It's strange. You're like a vault. I can't break in."

"Thank you for trying."

"So now what?" she asks.

"I can't leave. If I could run away again, I would. But I'm bound by my word to stay here with Silas. But that doesn't mean you all can't leave. The Sovereign Occultists are going to come and when they do I don't want you here. Things could get bad. Very bad."

"Oh believe me," Maxx says, "we know how they can get."

"How they *will* get." Juniper sighs, her eyes growing haunted.

"But we're not leaving." Terek stands and folds me into a tight hug. "We're just going to have to find a way to stop the

Occultists together."

His hug feels so good. I didn't know how much I needed it until now. "I need Hazel." My voice cracks. "Or that stupid Occultist to come back and keep his word to us. If I could find a way to get my magic back, all of this would be so much more manageable."

"How exactly are you going to do that?" Maxx asks. It's not a challenge, but a genuine question.

I peel away from Terek. "Do I look like I have a plan?" My eyes fill with tears again and we all go silent. I don't have a plan for my magic, not yet. But I can't stop thinking about the little spark from earlier, about a way I might be able to get Silas to leave me alone.

"Alright," Juniper says at last. "No more feeling sorry for yourself. You may be married to Silas but that also makes you Queen. You have power too. You're walking around acting like you're completely powerless but that can't be true. You have sway over people, even your husband."

"Yeah, right."

"No," she presses. "I'm serious. We all saw it today. People look up to you. Most like you and some revere you." Her words ring true but I have the hardest time believing them. She doesn't know the court like I know them. "And anyway, nobody has to know you've lost your magic. We'll find a way to get it back before they find out it was ever gone. In the meantime, you need to get the court on your side for good, all of them, and especially your husband. And if not your husband, at least the people need to listen to you."

"But why?" I sigh. "What's the point?"

She shakes her head at me. "Are you kidding, Khali? What's the point? The point is that you can get them to take the Occultist problem as seriously as possible, and not only that, you need to convince Silas to let you go find Hazel. You said your magic didn't like her, well that's got to mean something."

"Silas will never let me leave," I challenge. "You could go fetch her, perhaps?"

"No can do," Terek breaks in. "Silas has made it clear to us we're his prisoners, even if we're not locked up right now, we've been ordered not to leave. If we leave, he'll come after us and he won't show mercy."

Mercy—the same word he threw in all our faces earlier and the quality Silas lacks most.

Angry heat prickles all over my body. I know the link with Hazel is all speculation but Silas taking that away from me is too much. And now he's threatening my friends? Of course he is.

"Maybe you could ask him to let you go get her," Juniper

tries again. "He obviously likes you."

I laugh. It seems so far-fetched that Silas would let me leave this castle again, let alone travel back to the human realm. I'm not his wife because he cares for me. I'm his wife because he wants to own me. But the word ownership gives me another idea.

"The necklace," I whisper.

"What necklace?"

"You remember. The one I used to subdue the Occultist, the one Silas used on me? I need to find it. What if I can use it on Silas to take his powers? I could blackmail him with it at the very least."

"Sounds dangerous," Maxx interjects, frowning.

"But also kind of fun," Terek purrs as he paces the room. "I'll help you look for the necklace."

"And how are you going to do that?" I scoff.

"Let's just say I like shiny things."

Juniper laughs. "And he has a certain sway with some of our guards."

Terek winks and fans himself, and Maxx rolls his eyes. "Yeah, you could say that again. We've been given a set of rooms together and we're monitored at all times by guards. There's a few who definitely have a soft spot for Terek."

"A few?" I shake my head and laugh.

"Don't look so surprised!" Terek purrs. "I'll ask around. No big deal."

"Okay, but please be careful." I study my friends, so grateful for each one of them. I don't know what I'd do if I didn't have them to talk to and hopefully help me. "All of you. You can't trust people here to be your friends, even if they're attracted to you. We haven't had any fae in our kingdom for a century and the prejudices run deep."

"We're being careful," Maxx assures me and shoots Terek an annoyed look. "At least some of us are."

"Oh, relax." Terek smirks. "I've got everything under control."

"That's what I used to think, too." I pause for a second, looking my new friends up and down. "What can you tell me about magicked items?"

Nobody speaks. "The necklace isn't the only one," I continue, "Flannery has something special with that spear and shield."

"We can't say." Maxx raises a hand. "We've been sworn to secrecy."

"About the spear, yes," Terek adds. "But what I can tell you is this. That necklace probably isn't magicked. It's spelled by a sorcerer. Magicked items are born from the land and are hidden throughout Eridas. There aren't many and it's believed all have been found."

"But…" Juniper bites her lip. "There's no way to know for sure."

That seals my idea and I smile. "So you're saying there's a chance?"

"I HAVE AN IDEA," I GUSH, infusing extra enthusiasm into each word. I sashay across our sitting room and relax next to Silas on the settee. He studies me with equal parts intrigue and skepticism. His blond hair hangs around his face, framing his jaw, and his eyes are alight with electricity. I can guess exactly what he's hoping for and my stomach twists.

"And what idea is that, Wife?" His voice is liquid fire.

I pause for dramatic effect. "We need more magicked items."

He sits back with an exhale. "And why would we need that?"

"To fight the Occultists, obviously." I raise my eyebrows. "And according to my fae friends, they're hidden all over Eridas, especially in the most dangerous of places."

"Yes, well, I already knew that." His voice is growing tired but his eyes say something else; that he's considering what I have to say. He's intrigued. I can work with intrigued.

"What about the Jeweled Forest?" My heart beats frantically as I speak it. "Bram and I traveled through there when I ran away." His eyes flash with jealousy and I hurry to finish. "It's only a day's flight from Stonehearth and if there's any place where a magicked object would be in Drakenon, that would be it."

I long to say more, to ask him about the pendant necklace with the dragon crest. To encourage him to pick up a jewel when he visits the forest. Anything that could help me. But I force myself to keep quiet and let him consider my proposition. If there's one thing I know about Silas, it's that he's willing to take massive risks if it means more power for him to claim. When he agrees to go to the Jeweled Forest a minute of thought later, I'm not the least bit surprised.

SEVEN

HAZEL

I'M SWEPT INTO THE WHITENESS of the supernatural spirit realm, and when I find Harmony and my mother standing aimlessly, I let out a panicked scream. They shouldn't be here! And yet they are and my scream doesn't disturb them. They stand motionless, looking off into the distance, eyes glazed over.

"Mom?" I wave my hand in front of her face.

She doesn't move.

"Harmony?"

Same.

When I reach out to touch them, my hand goes right through their forms as if they're ghosts and my stomach twists into knots. This is so strange—I know they're not dead. I don't understand what's happening. But why can't they see me? I take a deep breath, trying not to let the panic seize control, and stare out into the vastness of bright white. It seems to go on forever.

Something sparkles up ahead, and I'm suddenly struck by the very same image they're watching. It's a scene through a portal, similar to when I could see my loved ones from this place… but also different. There was a sharpness to the scenes before that's lacking here. I edge closer. What exactly am I looking at?

It's a woman—a faerie—walking through a glistening spring meadow at sunrise. She turns, and I'm immediately struck by her youth and flawless beauty. Her skin is perfectly unblemished, her dark curly hair is long, all the way to her butt, and her wide green eyes are oddly familiar. She can't be much older than me. She glides through a field of budding flowers as if they're her best friends. They surround her on all sides, and I try not to gasp by the ridiculous gorgeousness of it all. She stops, twisting the ends of her hair nervously in a gesture that's also familiar to me. Who do I know that does the same thing?

It hits me. I'm looking at a younger version of my mother. Her dainty metallic wings sparkle in the morning sun, the edges of them brushing against the long grass as she strolls. Without thinking, I step forward, reaching my hand out toward the scene, toward this young version of my mother.

Suddenly, I'm pulled forward until I'm no longer in the endless white room but in the spring forest. I look down at my hands. They're not my own. The fingers are slightly longer, nails painted a pretty lavender. This memory of my mother's is no longer a memory. I'm living it now. My heart beats in tandem with hers, and I can feel every emotion she feels, see every color, and smell every scent. My mother's history unfolds before my eyes.

This is the last time I'll have to wait for him and worry if I'll never see him again. A smile spreads across my face as I stroll through the field of wildflowers where we'd agreed to meet at sunrise. This is our place, we made so many memories here, and I'm sad to leave it behind. I let my fingers dance along the tops of the wildflowers instead of where I really want to put them: my belly. I've had to train myself not to cup my hands there and reveal my wonderful secret.

Our child grows within my womb.

I can already feel her kicking, silly little thing that she is. I'm probably imagining the kicks. She's too small to be felt and it's too early for me to know she's a girl. And yet, somehow, I just know she's my daughter and that she's rolling around in there at this very second, as excited for her papa to come back to us as I am to see my husband.

Jamis has been traveling for months and even when he is here; it's hard for him to stay in any one place for long. Most of the faeries hate shifters, especially dragon shifters. Our feuds run centuries deep and although Jamis has nothing to do with them, faeries don't forgive easily. And from what he tells me, Drakenon isn't much better. It's nothing like our sweet kingdom of whimsy and mirth. There are far too many rules and societal obligations.

Him and I? We were never supposed to fall in love.

And yet we did, meeting by chance when he traveled to our Spring Kingdom on behest of his king. And like a roll of thunder impossible to stop, love boomed into our lives and shook our foundations. His family disowned him. His kingdom shunned him, told him he couldn't bring me back. And so he left, choosing to live here, to marry me, and to set up our life. But it was soon apparent that my kingdom wasn't safe for him either.

So he traveled often, in search of a welcoming home for us where both our kinds could be accepted. It was no use. There's nothing here for us in Eridas. And with our child coming, and hybrids being so shunned as they are, we've already decided to leave the realm. As soon as he arrives, we'll be on our way to the nearest portal and venturing into our new life together. My heart hurts just thinking about what it could mean to leave

Spring, what it will do to our magicks to flee Eridas, and what it will feel like to never see our extended families again.

But I'll do it. For him, I'll do anything.

I've already concocted the potion that will make my wings retract into my body while I'm in the human realm. Imagining life without flying is hard, but it's not nearly as hard as imagining life without my Jamis, and so I'll do it. I must.

The sun crests the horizon and everything is bathed in that golden reddish hue of early morning. It warms my face, and I breathe in the sweet flowery scent of my home one last time. I'm going to miss it so much. I need to stop thinking about that part. It's too painful.

A speck of black crosses the sun, growing larger as it nears. From this distance, one might mistake him for a bird but I know it's my Jamis. He approaches, his dragon form as majestic as ever. The sight of him sends a blast of excitement mixed with a calm sense of grounding through my entire being and I know we're going to be okay. We're making the right choice.

He lands close and shifts immediately, turning into the man I love smiling down at me with those earthy brown eyes. I could get lost in those eyes—I have many times before. He leans in for a kiss and I give in easily, cherishing his scent and the tender press of his lips. It's been too long.

"Are you ready?" he asks, pressing his forehead to mine. I

nod. The plan is to fly to the Spring portal and pass through to the other side. He's already got our new home set up and ready to go, complete with new identities. And I'm going to school to become a nurse, which is a sort of human healer. It's the perfect trade for me. He doesn't need any glamours or potions because shifters look like the humans when they're not in their dragon form.

"Do you have the potion you need?"

"It's in here." I lift the satchel on my arm and he takes it from me.

"It's safe?"

"The faerie who taught me how to make it can be trusted. It will make my wings retract into my body while I'm in the human realm. And most importantly, it won't harm our baby."

"You're sure?"

"She swore on her life."

That settles it. Faeries don't swear on their lives, not in Eridas, not when to do so could actually mean death. But she did and she's the best in our kingdom, not to mention a dear family friend, so I am confident I can trust her.

I take his hand in mine. "Let's go."

The memory evaporates and I'm back in the endless white room. Harmony and my mother are still there, but this time, they see me. Their eyes become round as saucers and they simultaneously tackle me in a giant hug.

"Hazel, what are you doing here?" Mother asks, her breath hot against my ear.

"Am I too late?" I step back and turn to Harmony.

Harmony shakes her head, dreadlocks bouncing against her shoulders. "No, but you didn't need to come here."

"What do you mean? You called me here."

"I called you to Ohio. But you didn't need to enter into our blood bond." Her voice grows tight. Worried. "We were fine. We are fine."

"Really? Because I found you passed out on the living room floor."

She sighs and runs both hands over her tired face. "This complicates things."

"We had to find out why I lost my magic and retrieve my memories," Mom interjects. "And find out what happened to your father."

I stare at her, her shining eyes and the deep frown. "So someone stole your memories? That's why you didn't tell me the truth?"

"I thought I was a human. Everything I told you about your father being a one night stand? I'm sorry, honey, I honestly thought that was the truth. Harmony knew it wasn't and convinced me to try this magic to return my memories and figure out what's been going on."

It takes a moment for me to digest all of this, I'm shocked and sad and relieved all at the same time.

"And why would Harmony know that you're not human?" I ask, but I think I know.

"You saw the memories?" Mom asks and I nod.

Harmony smiles softly. "Because I was the faerie who helped her, the friend of the family. I taught her how to make the potion to allow her to hide her wings in this realm. Your mother was best friends with the daughter I lost to the Sovereign Occultists. I've been looking for you two for some time. I even performed a spell to get her to come to Westinbrooke, but you're the one who showed up instead."

Mom's face falls. "I'm so sorry to hear about Sariah and the others." She hugs Harmony. "She was my best friend. I can't believe it."

Harmony can't speak.

"This is all a lot to take in." I close my eyes and breathe deep, trying to relax. It's pretty much impossible. Silence falls over us as we think it all through. I open my eyes, ready to speak, when Mom's face jerks up and she screeches. She points and we turn. Fear prickles over my body. It's a reaper. His eyes glow red, his skeleton hands reach toward us, and everything turns cold.

"No!" I yell and position myself in front of Mom and Harmony. "You cannot take them. They're not actually dead."

"Our spirits are here to access memories." Harmony's voice is so much calmer than mine. "Our bodies are fine and waiting for us to return."

The reaper floats toward us, red eyes peering at us from beneath the black cloak, as if seeing into the deepest part of our souls. Finally, he speaks, "I've brought someone to you as my way to express gratitude to Hazel." The reaper pauses. "And apologies for what my kind did to you."

That shocks me, gotta be honest. "Okay…"

A form materializes and I step back as I recognize the man my mother was waiting for: Jamis.

"Dad?" My voice cracks.

He blinks at us, brown eyes mystified and then clearing. He's dressed in medieval type clothing, the same as the other dragons I've seen in visions. He's nothing like I imagined my father to be over the years, to be honest, but I don't even care. He rushes forward and wraps me and Mom into a hug. A lifetime of tears spring to my eyes. He's solid. Real. Flesh and blood. And with his dark blond hair and tannish skin and hazel eyes, he looks like me, way more so than my mom does. I always thought I'd be angry to see him, or at the very least, indifferent. But I'm not. I'm happy. And I'm sad. But mostly I'm overcome with an immense sense of relief.

"You have five minutes." The reaper's scratchy voice cuts through our shared happiness, turning it sour.

Jamis reacts by planting one on mom. To witness her melt into a man's arms like that is something I'd never thought I'd see. Mom doesn't date or do relationships. Growing up, she took care of me and rocked at her job and that was about it. She always said she wasn't interested in letting a man into her life and messing up the good thing she and I had going. Even with her memories wiped, she must have been subconsciously holding on to my father.

She's changed. Even now, I can see it. She remembers their love and is feeling the loss and it's made her a different person.

"What happened to us?" Mother begs the second they seperate. "You're dead. How did that happen?" Her voice cracks, desperate.

He nods once, his mouth turning down at the corners. "What do you remember?"

"Falling in love with you. Getting pregnant with Hazel. Deciding to leave for the human realm and that morning when we met. But then the memory stopped."

He sighs. "I'm glad it stopped. I would never want you to

relive what came next."

Mom wipes away the tears.

"We never made it to the human realm that day. We were intercepted by the Occultists. They were a new threat to both of our kingdoms and we never saw them coming, let alone coming for two travelers. They kept us prisoner for months. You really don't remember?"

She shakes her head.

"That's for the best. It was ... terrible. They did horrible things to us. They forced you to take the potion early." His eyes flash to me for a second but he doesn't expound. "Anyway, a few months after Hazel was born, we were able to break out of their prison and make a run for it. When we got to the portal an Occultist was there waiting for us. He took your memory right in front of me. I was able to get you two through the portal but I wasn't so lucky." He swallows hard. "He killed me before I could get to you. I'm so sorry."

Mom and I stare at him, neither one of us knowing what to say. Any words I thought I had have turned to ash on my tongue.

"I watched you from the other side for many years," he says. "I watched you raise Hazel. And then, well, she started seeing me. And that was too hard, too confusing for her. So when Hazel was four years old, I finally went with the reaper and moved on."

I have no memories of seeing him and I wish more than anything that I did. I don't care that it would have been confusing. It would have been better than me growing up believing my dad was a one night stand sperm donor. "You moved on… to heaven?" I ask.

He smiles. "Something like that. And someday, you'll both join me. But not today."

"Time's up," the reapers says, his voice as sharp as his scythe.

"No!" Mom and I gasp.

"It must be this way," his reply slithers over my skin.

"He broke a serious rule to bring me here," Dad relents, his voice losing it's sweet brightness. "I have to go. But don't ever forget how much I love you. Always."

We hug him, and he whispers into my ear, "Hazel, don't be afraid of who you are. You have the sight for a reason."

The sight? He must mean the medium thing, but what if there's more to it?

Before I can ask, he evaporates in our arms. Gone. The reaper, too.

Harmony, Mom, and I all turn to look at each other. Am I at peace with this? Angry? Surprised? I don't even know what to feel. Tears run down Mom's cheeks and that is something I'm definitely pissed off about.

The Occultists ripped my family apart. They spelled me as an infant. They took my mother's memories and killed my father. They want to kill me in order to kill Khali. And now? Now they're going to pay for this.

"Oh honey." Mom pulls me into her arms. "Don't let it make you bitter."

I blink, trying not to let my own tears fall, and suddenly the white room is gone. I'm back in my living room in Ohio, staring up at the ceiling fan.

"Are you okay?" Dean leans over me, his eyes blazing.

I groan and roll to my side. When I see that Harmony and my mom are both blinking and awake, relief floods my body.

"I'm okay," I say, letting out a long slow breath. "But we have a lot to talk about."

Mom's eyes catch mine and she nods once. "Oh yes, we certainly do."

We're shaky and exhausted. It's like waking up from an eons-long dream. What the blood magic did to us is crazy intense. I glance over at Harmony, expecting her to agree, but she's blanched as paper, her breath stilted and eyes pained.

"Are you okay?"

Before she can answer, her eyes roll into the back of her head and she passes out.

EIGHT

KHALI

I COUNT BACKWARDS FROM THREE hundred the moment Silas leaves me in the sitting room. He's gone to discuss the possibility of traveling to the Jeweled Forest with Bram. I can only hope Bram doesn't give too much away about the dangers there. Either way, Silas leaving has given me a chance to search for the spelled necklace.

I can't help but keep wondering about it. Is it a magicked item that was found by one of his ancestors and passed down to him? Terek doesn't think so. A family heirloom can be spelled, which is what Silas has led me to believe, too. Either way, I need to find it in case it can help me get my magic back or help me blackmail my husband.

Since he removed it from the Occultist, I haven't seen it again. He might be keeping it on his person but there's also a good chance it's hidden in his room. Okay, it's a small chance, a careless chance, but I can't stop thinking that maybe it's in there. So here I am, biting my lower lip and staring at the outside of his chamber door. Time slows but I make myself keep counting down until I'm convinced Silas isn't coming back and I'm truly all alone in our royal quarters.

There are always guards stationed in the hallway. Sometimes they will accompany us around the castle; but when we're in our own quarters, we're left alone. This is my chance. It's perfect. Except there's no such thing as perfect around here. If he catches me in his room, what will he do? What will *I* do?

I squash the questions, stroll to the door, and pull it open. *Time to be brave.*

It smells like him. Spicy and male, and it makes me want to scream because it ought to smell like all the blood on his hands. Everything about him should be awful to reflect who he is on the inside: he should look awful, smell awful, *be* awful. But at least hating him comes easy to me despite his attractive appearance and alluring scent. Not only do I hate what he's done and his callous nature, I also hate that he got everything he wanted and I got nothing. In another life it would have been Owen and me here. Or Dean.

Or Bram…

I let out a little groan and get to work, rifling through his things, careful not to knock anything out of place. I start with the intricately carved armoire, checking in any hidden areas of the furniture and the pockets of all his clothing. There's nothing. I go to the bookshelf, knowing the bed with the piles of dark bedding are next. Rummaging through the books proves to be fruitless. I was hoping to find a secret compartment in at least one of them but there aren't many to begin with and once again nothing turns up. I pad over to the bed and go for the mattress, heavy with the finest wool Drakenon has to offer. I heave at the edge to see if it's stashed between that and the bedframe.

Again, nothing.

"Hi!" a voice chirps and I startle, dropping the mattress with a thud. Bellflower Blossom pokes her tiny head out from under the bed, a dash of sparkling gold pixie dust catching the sunlight as she moves.

"What are you doing in here?" I gasp at the pixie. I haven't seen her since she helped my father feel better the night he almost died. She said she'd be around, but I'd wondered if she'd decided to take off after all.

"Helping you look for the necklace," her voice chimes happily. She smiles, showing off her razor sharp teeth. "You know I'm in your debt."

"First of all, how do you know I'm looking for the necklace?"

She does a little dance. "I'm a good spy."

I scoff. "Okay. And how long are you in my debt exactly?"

"Until you feel satisfied we're even," she replies. "Or until I decide we are. But for now, I'm quite entertained by you and your friends."

"You helped my father," I whisper. "Thank you."

"It's my pleasure." She does a little curtsy. It makes her look like even more of a flower than before. It's adorable.

"So you listened in on us earlier, did you?" I can't help it; I smile as she nods. She seems so proud of it. "Well, that's great and all but we need to get out of here soon. I've already taken way too long."

I feel as if any moment Silas is going to walk in and catch me!

"Agreed," she says happily. "Let me just finish looking under here." She slides back under the bed. The space is quite small down there so she's perfect for the job.

"Oh by the way," her little voice chimes from under the bed, "you really ought to venture down into the dungeons. You'll never believe what I found today!"

"And what's that?"

"It's probably better if I show you."

I let out sigh and turn, eyes roaming the room one last time to see if I may have missed anything, when I notice something odd about the bookshelf. Why is it inlaid into the wall like that? It's not set apart like all the other furniture. My heart skips. It must be a hidden passage leading into the castle's network of tunnels! This is the King's chambers, it only makes sense that a king would have this kind of direct access.

I rush toward it, excitement building, when the entire bookshelf swings open and Silas steps through. Surprise flashes across his face, followed quickly by suspicion, and then a sort of knowingness, and finally something else entirely. His lavender eyes flit from where I stand, to his bed right behind me, and that something is unmistakable lust.

"I thought you were with Bram?" I blurt out.

He raises an eyebrow. "I was, and then I wasn't…" I shuffle backward. "I see you've finally decided to come to me. I knew leaving you access to my bedroom would prove to be in my benefit."

He doesn't know I was here to snoop. He thinks I'm here to consummate our marriage. And that's worse.

"Yes, but I thought you'd be gone for a while. I didn't expect you so soon."

"Well, it is my room." He smirks, closes the bookcase, and strides toward me while he points. "And my bed." Another step. "And wife." His finger comes to rest against my sternum.

I don't know what to say or do, and I'm frozen because I can't make myself do what would please him right now. I don't want him asking questions or getting angry.

He's only inches from me. He gently runs his fingertip over to my shoulder and then to my hair, pinching the end of a dark curl. His lavender eyes grow dark, the storm clouds gathering, the electricity buzzing underneath his skin. It's lust. But it's also something else.

Satisfaction.

The man was angry with me earlier for not playing along with whatever plan he had for Bram, and now my father and Bram are both in some kind of quarantine situation. I defied him in front of his court, and I've been defying him over and over the last few weeks. But we're here now and clearly he thinks he's won.

He closes the distance and presses his lips to mine. So soft at first. Almost reverent. Not teasing. Not demanding. But asking. It's never been this way before with him.

I turn away.

"Let me ask you, Khali." He sounds hurt. "What are you really doing here?"

I let out a little gasp. I can't think of the right words to say.

He steps back. "You're not looking for this, are you?" He

reaches into his pocket and pulls out the necklace. The silver glints in the sunlight as it sways on the black cord.

I want it. I need it. And without thinking of the repercussions, I try to snatch it from him. I'm not fast enough. He holds it away from me as his eyes grow dark. "That's what I was afraid of. I assumed the moment you brought up magicked items you were wondering about this, too. It's not magicked, you know. It really *is* spelled. But I guess they're not so different."

"Yes they are. Magicked means it comes from Eridas's magic itself and spelled means you had some sorcerer do you a favor. If you ask me, the two are quite different."

He laughs. "If you say so."

"Where did you even get that?" I snap. "Who made it for you?" The kind of magic attached to that necklace doesn't come from dragons, not even from fae. It has to be a sorcerer but there aren't any in Drakenon. They're forbidden from our lands.

The questions get a grin out of him and what he says makes no sense. "You really don't remember, do you? Remarkable."

"Remember what?" Something tickles at the back of my mind, something I should know, should *remember*…

He chuckles. "It doesn't matter *now*, does it?"

"I don't know what you're talking about." The memory, it's

there, flitting at the back of my mind but it's been caged. "Silas, what aren't you telling me? What do you mean I don't remember where you got the necklace?"

He shrugs. "Maybe I'm not at liberty to say or maybe I just don't want to."

"I'm done with this." I step past him and hurry toward the door. But he catches my wrist and drags me back so fast that I trip. He uses the momentum to push me onto the bed and then he's on me, his lips hot against my neck. His silky hair falls around my face. The scruff on his chin scratches my skin. My heart pounds. My breath catches. Fear is as hot as his breath.

"You know what I told you before," he whispers between his kisses. "If you came back here, you'd better be prepared to act like my wife."

Once again I'm frozen but there's an anger building inside me, seconds from exploding. He takes my silence as a yes and presses himself onto me, his smell overwhelming, his body hot. Part of my body responds in the way my emotions don't want to accept.

But…

But would it be so hard to give in—to give up? He could get what he wants and I could use it to get what I want. If I go along with this and offer my body to him, I'm sure he'll be kinder to me. And maybe he'll be kinder to the people I love. And maybe things will get better.

But then the memory of Owen's dead body flashes through my mind. And the blood. The rain. The cold. All the tears. They ran down my cheeks, tasting of salt on my tongue. And I see it clearly again, all over, the self-justified look Silas had on his face that night. He didn't regret it. It didn't hurt him. And he would do it again—all over again—if he had to.

No. I'm not going to let him win so easily.

I hold my hands against his chest and heave. He doesn't move an inch. I try to say the word "stop" but I can't get it to come out; it's like it's stuck in my throat. So I shake my head, my eyes filling with tears, and begin to cry.

He stops, an angry growl reverberating from his throat as he rolls off of me. His breath is heavy, eyes electric. "You can't keep pushing me away, Khali. You're my wife, for Gods' sake! You have a duty to me as your husband."

"But—"

"And you have a duty to this kingdom," he continues. "You made vows. You're bound to bear my children and that means *this*."

"I know." My voice is twisted. I can't breathe properly. "But I don't want to."

He jumps up from the bed. "Well, too bad. I don't care about what you want anymore. I care about what I need." There isn't an ounce of compassion in his voice. "And I need to get you pregnant as soon as possible. You saw those people today? They don't want us here. We have to make them accept it. So you need to get yourself together, get over whatever prudish nonsense is going on with you, and let yourself enjoy what I know you'll like if you just give it a chance."

I want to laugh. Or cry again.

"It's not like that. It's not about being a prude and how dare you even say that to me." I run from the bed and make for the door.

"Oh, really? So are you trying to tell me that it's just me, then? That you'd happily sleep with someone else? Maybe Dean? Or is it my other pathetic brother you want? Maybe Bram should be executed but well that doesn't work because then I'd still be competing for your affection with another dead brother."

"Stop," I scream. "You're being cruel!"

"No! I'm being realistic. I'm doing what needs to be done. Nobody else was willing to do it, none of my other brothers. Well, guess what, Princess? I am. I get things done. And you'll see that when the Occultists are gone, because of me, and this castle is filled with another line of Brightcaster Dragon Blessed children, because of me, and you're living in luxury and don't have a care in the world, because of me." He glares, his voice growing dangerously low. "You'll be thanking me."

"I'll never thank you." I wipe away the last of the tears. They've been replaced with a cold hard hatred and I welcome it.

He laughs and I pull open the door. I'm so done with this.

"Hey!" he yells. "Give that back!"

I whip around, my heart leaping with hope. Bellflower Blossom hovers in the center of his room, his spelled necklace wrapped around her arm and she zips toward me with a brazen smile.

"Khali," she squeals. "Catch!"

She tosses it at me with way more force than I would have thought possible for her tiny body. It shoots like a little silver arrow and lands neatly in my hand. Silas roars, and I expect him to come after me but he doesn't. A flash of lightning shoots from his hand and strikes Bellflower. She drops to the ground with a thud, exploding into a pile of glittering pixie dust.

I fall to my knees. "No!"

"Give it to me," Silas seethes, stretching his hand out. "Give me the necklace now."

"How could you?" I choke on my words. "She wasn't bad. She was my friend."

"She was a thief and a pixie and wasn't where she belonged," he scoffs. "What value does she have to us? She got what she deserved."

"You're horrible." My body is numb. The guilt, it's too much. "You didn't even give her a chance."

That only makes him laugh bitterly. "Give the necklace to me," he demands again. "Give it to me now or I'll execute more of your ridiculous fae friends. See if I care about them, Khali. I don't."

I hold out the necklace. So much for having a plan. I really thought if I could destroy it, I could somehow free my magic. Or maybe use it against Silas. But that's stupid isn't it? This necklace isn't the problem. My spell connecting me to Hazel is, and she's not even in this realm. And Silas? Silas isn't easy to outmaneuver.

"That stupid pixie is how you got it off the first time, isn't it?" He laughs but I don't nod or say anything. Why should I give him the satisfaction? "Their teeth are sharper than anything else in Eridas. Did you know that? Well, if you didn't, you do now." He says it like it's no big deal, like we're having a regular old conversation, like he didn't just murder her.

He snags the necklace from me and instead of dropping it into his pocket, he unties the ends and gives me a pitying look. "This is for your own good."

What?

"No!" I scramble back but I'm not fast enough. He's on me, his weight pressing me down, legs straddling me and one hand pinning my arms together. My skull bangs against the doorframe and I cry out.

"Hold still," he sneers.

I feel something snap against my neck and it's over before I can fight him off, his cursed necklace tied tight around my neck, branding me. I don't know how on earth I'm going to get it off a second time now that Bellflower's gone. But then again, does it really matter? My magic is gone anyway. Silas doesn't know and now that this necklace is around my neck, he'll continue to be kept in the dark. Maybe this is for the best right now because I can have an excuse as to why I'm not using my elementals.

Except he used the necklace before to syphon magic from me if I tried to use it. And when he kissed me while I wore this stupid thing, he was able to take my magic by force. Now what is he going to think when he kisses me?

I'm in so much trouble.

He's going to find out the truth sooner rather than later. I can't avoid kissing him forever. I'm not even sure if I can avoid kissing him another week by the level of his threats.

And Gods, it's more than kissing—he wants to get me pregnant!

My stomach twists once again, bile rising. I crawl out from under him and stumble from the room, heading for mine. I don't look back to see his reaction. I want nothing to do with him, want nothing more than to shift into my dragon self and fly far, far away, but instead I'm going to have to settle for emptying my stomach. I got the necklace and all I have to show for it is a pile of pixie dust and another friend's death because of me…

No. Not because of me. Because of Silas.

NINE

HAZEL

"HARMONY?" I SCRAMBLE TO MY knees and lean over her. "Are you okay?"

But it appears she's right back in that endless sleep state again. With her human glamour, she always looked like an older woman. But in her true form, she appears middle aged, even though she told me she's much older than any human walking the earth today. Faeries are practically immortal and age very slowly. But now to look at her, it wouldn't seem that way. Her skin is that same pale blue and her wings are visibly flattened between her back and the carpet. Deep age lines have appeared around her face, eyes, and mouth that I've never seen before.

I glower at Mom. "How much blood magic have you two been doing?"

Mom is completely still, the guilt stretching across her expression. "I didn't know the toll it would take on her. Not until I got my memories back and by then it was already done."

Dean sighs. "Come on. Let's get her into a bed. It might be awhile before she wakes up. Blood magic comes with a dark price and it looks like she's the one who's taken it on for all three of you."

I remember the alarm on Harmony's face when I'd first joined them in the spirit realm. Did she know then that she was going to take this one for all of us? For me, too? She didn't have to do that. Had it been my choice, I would have taken on some of it too. But then again, I wouldn't have known how.

She's clearly too weak from all of this. "What is going to happen to her? Is she going to die?" I brush her hair aside and run my fingers along her cold skin. "Please, wake up," I whisper. But she doesn't.

Dean gathers her into his arms as if she weighs little more than a bag of feathers, and Mom leads him to her bedroom. He lays Harmony across the paisley printed comforter and she tosses to her side, fitfully.

"She's freezing," Mom says, pulling thick covers over Harmony's shivering body.

"She's moving though. That's a good sign, isn't it?" I ask.

"I can help." Dean places his hand on Harmony's arm. "I can give her a boost of heat and then we should turn up the thermostat."

Mom nods at Dean with a grateful smile. "I think she'll be waking up soon." She places the back of her hand on Harmony's cheek. "I had healing magic before I came here. It's mostly gone now. I wish it wasn't."

"That explains your career choice." My voice trails off.

The room falls into silence, and I'm suddenly overcome with this unbelievably awkward feeling and I'm pretty sure they can see it written all over my face. How do I introduce my mom to my boyfriend? Is he my boyfriend? Yes, definitely. But still, it seems such a silly thing, to discuss my relationship status right now considering all the crap we're up against. There are so many more important conversations we need to have.

"Let's let Harmony rest and I'll make us up some hot cocoa," Mom offers. We follow her out and she gets to work while we hover around the little kitchen island.

Just as I'm about to make the introductions, Dean beats me to it. "I'm Dean." He extends his hand and she's quick to shake it. "It's nice to finally meet you. I've heard so many good things."

Mom raises an eyebrow but I can see the twinkle of amusement in her green eyes. She's actually quite pleased to meet Dean which makes me feel better about it. "Let me guess. You are a dragon, too?" She smiles broadly and looks pointedly at me. "I know a dragon when I see one. What is it with our family and falling in love with dragons?"

My cheeks flame and my heart flutters. "Mom!"

Dean clears his throat and changes the subject, asking if he can help her with the cocoa.

"Actually," I interject, "Mom, there's something I've learned about myself that you should know."

Mom turns on me, her face falling. "What is it?"

"Nothing bad!" I think back to Harmony in the bedroom, hopefully in a pleasant dreamland, and wish she could help me explain everything—understand it. "This might take awhile."

We carry our drinks to the table and sit down. Once I get started, I can't help it, I tell her just about everything. I fill her in on the situation with the reapers, to which she was horrified, and then tell her about how I turned into a spirit dragon. That part makes her smile. Now that her memories are back, it's like she's complete again. I never knew she was missing something but now the stark contrast is abundantly clear. She didn't know her past the same as I didn't know my ancestry.

"Like I said," she teases, "our family falls in love with dragons. I fell in love with you, didn't I? From the moment I knew of your existence, I knew you were mine and the love was instant. And to think, you're a spirit dragon? That's remarkable!" She pulls me into a hug and I practically melt into her, the stress of the last four months practically erasing. "I'm so proud of you, honey."

"I should have told you the truth from the beginning. I hope you can understand why I didn't and forgive me."

"I understand why you didn't." She rolls her eyes. "I'd have demanded you return home and wouldn't have taken no for an answer."

"And I wouldn't have blamed you."

Dean leaves us to check on Harmony and comes back with a smile. "She's doing better," he says. "She's starting to warm up. I think she might wake up on her own soon."

"Actually, that reminds me of when we first walked in the house. It had been super cold then too, but the air is almost back to normal now."

Mom nods. "It was the blood magic. It was very... demanding."

The thought of it makes me shiver. "I'm going to go sit with Harmony for a while."

"Good idea," Mom adds. "I'm coming, too."

In the end, we all go in there. I bring a throw blanket and sit on the floor at the edge of the bed. Mom sits in a chair at Harmony's side. Dean hovers by the door, saying he'd rather stand. It's hard not to stare at Harmony, so we all do. We're exhausted, the blood magic and the day catching up with us, but we stay there for what feels like hours.

Eventually, her eyes flutter open, revealing those strange solid white eyes of hers, and I almost scream with excitement. I do jump up and lean over the bed to get a better look. Her eyes remind me to ask Mom why hers are normal and Harmony's are not even close. Maybe faeries are all different. Maybe different *is* normal for them. Mom looks pretty human, excluding the metallic wings sticking out of her back. I've been trying not to stare at them but that's hard!

"Are you okay?" Mom slides in closer, grasping Harmony's hand.

Harmony swallows hard, like she's dangerously close to falling back under the weight of sleep, forcing her eyes to stay open.

"I'm okay," she confirms. I don't believe her. How can I when she looks like she's aged overnight and can hardly breathe?

"You took on the brunt of the blood magic, didn't you?" Dean asks gently, kneeling on the floor beside her.

Harmony doesn't answer but her eyes say it all. She did. Nor does she regret it.

"They're gone," her voice finally croaks.

"Who's gone?" he asks.

She struggles to sit up, and in her wake, a pile of blue ash rests on the white sheets. I gasp, my stomach turning to stone. "My wings," Harmony sighs, her eyes filling with anguish. "They're gone, aren't they? I felt them disintegrate while I was laying there."

She picks at the ash. "And now…"

"I'm so sorry," Mom's voice cracks, "there's nothing left."

Harmony nods. "My magic is gone too. The second I woke up, I knew it had left me. I can't see any paths anymore. I can't feel anything in my blood. It's all empty."

"Blood magic can do that much?" I growl, suddenly angry. "You didn't deserve that. You were helping us."

"Blood magic is costly," Harmony replies softly. "I knew that. The more people involved in a bond of magic, the more powerful it is, but the more sacrifices must be made. Why do you think the Occultists are so powerful? They bring their victims into the bond and then sacrifice them, literally taking all their blood to feed the magic. It's what happened to my family, my children." Her voice catches. "Losing my magic is nothing compared to the pain of losing them."

I don't know what to think or what to say. This is beyond tragic. Harmony knew though; she knew what she was risking. The fact she'd risk that for my mother and I seems extraordinary.

"Why?" I ask. "Why would you sacrifice so much for us? What are we to you?"

Harmony's eyes flash from mine to my mom's and back again. "Because it's my fault."

"What is?"

She turns to my mother and gathers every ounce of strength she has left. "I saw your path before you fled Spring and I didn't warn you. I thought we could change it with the potion. I didn't realize what I'd done until it was too late. I was foolish. It cost you your husband and later it cost me my family." A tear slips down her cheek. "I'm so sorry."

Mom doesn't stop to think. She leans over and wraps Harmony into a tight hug. "It's not your fault. It never was. You are not responsible for what those warlocks did to our people."

Dean and I exchange a look, passing a small smile between us. There's a lot these two need to talk about and we should probably give them their space, but Harmony stops us the moment we start to tiptoe toward the door.

"Wait." Her voice is urgent. "I wanted you to come to Ohio

because you needed to learn of your lineage before going into Eridas. Now that you know the truth and that your father is dead, you must go to Eridas. You must stop the Occultists from making it into this side of the portal. You have to destroy their blood magic bond before it's too late."

"Well, that's the plan, except we ran into a bit of a roadblock." Dean and I go on to explain to her what happened with the portal in West Virginia and my warning from the nephilim Elias about all the portals having Occultists stationed on the other side of all of them now.

"I know where you can go." Harmony shakes her head. "It's a lesser known portal only used by a few of the winter fae. Even if the Occultists are waiting there, they won't expect you to go through at this place. You'll have to be careful but it's doable."

"They can't!" Mom interjects. "No way. She's not safe there."

"She's not safe here either," Harmony relents. "Please, we have to let them try. If we don't Eridas will fall and then this realm will follow soon after."

Mom frowns. "There's no other way?"

"No."

Mom deflates. "I don't like it."

"Nobody likes it but we'll be careful," I promise, "and Dean is going with me. He can fight."

Mom points at Dean. "You put her safety first, do you hear me?"

"I always do." And when he says it, I wonder if he always has. I was so angry at him countless times but now I can see why he was pushing me away as an attempt to protect me. And when he brought me close, made me live with him, it was for the same reasons. I want to go to him, to pull him into my arms, and kiss him. But my cheeks flame and I look away. Not in front of my mother.

"And I have weapons," Dean adds. "A trunk full of them."

Harmony laughs bitterly. "Oh boy, you know those will never work in Eridas. No technology, not even the most basic, has ever worked there or will ever work."

"But—"

"I know what you've been trying to do." She cuts him off. "It's a fool's errand, unfortunately. I saw all your paths, Dean, and I can promise you, taking electronics will only slow you down and cause you problems. You have to leave them here. They will never work in Eridas."

"But—"

"Never."

"Why didn't you tell me?"

"You didn't ask, for one. And for two, I needed you to stay

in Westinbrooke long enough to meet Hazel."

The room grows hot. Dean is pissed. And frustrated. And probably a million other negative emotions about this. He had told me this work why he got himself exiled from Drakenon in the first place, and now this news? He's not taking it well. But he nods. "Fine."

And then he looks at me, his expression softening. "It wasn't a waste to meet you."

My heart does a little happy dance at that.

"Take some time with your mother." Harmony looks at me, her eyes trying to say something I can't quite read. "Get some rest. I'll give you instructions tomorrow."

I nod, letting it all sink in. A night or two in my childhood home and then what? The future is so unknown that not even Harmony can see it anymore. I can only hope I make it out of this thing alive. Given the pointed look in Harmony's eyes, I wonder if maybe she thinks I won't.

TEN

KHALI

THIS ISN'T MY FIRST VENTURE into the Jeweled Forest. Before I'd been awed by the beauty only to be quickly horrified by the cost. This time, it's all horror, and we haven't even landed yet. This morning when Silas pulled me from slumber, demanding Bram and I accompany his party to the Jeweled Forest, he'd refused to let me stay behind. So now I'm draped across his black scales, clinging to his neck and desperate not to fall off as he flies us through the clouds. I peer over to where Bram is slung across one of Silas's guards. We hold gazes for what feels like ages. His emerald eyes are charged with worry and bow-shaped lips are set into a grim line, but still, he watches me. And I watch him. Eventually, his dragon ride zooms ahead of Silas, breaking our charged stare.

We land in a clearing similar to the one Bram and I used

weeks ago. It might even be the same spot but I can't be sure. Either way, the sight of sparkling jewels sends a chill over my entire body. Everything in me is lit up with warning. I hop off Silas's back and brush out my rumpled skirt, pulling my velvety cape tighter around my body. A light dusting of snow coats the ground and ices the jewels on the nearby trees, giving the forest an ethereal aura. I swallow down a bubble of fear and ball my hands into tight fists.

I *really* don't like this.

Silas shifts to his human form, his grin cocky as he surveys the area, eyes alight with excitement. They finally settle on me. "You don't look so thrilled to be here considering this was *your* idea."

It was my idea because I'd hoped he would get his murderous self trapped here, not because I wanted to witness it happen. This place is horrid and one visit was enough for a lifetime.

I shrug and smooth out my expression to one of aloof indifference. "I don't love jewels I can't touch."

Offering this information is pure strategy. I'm sure this crew already knows all about the risk of touching these jewels, but I hope this helps them to trust me more.

Silas laughs and rakes his eyes over my body, resting them on my tight bodice. I pull my cape closed and he chuckles.

"You always did like pretty things."

And so does he, which is why I hope the voices here will get to him, that he'll try to take something he shouldn't and get trapped. Rotting away for ages—without fully dying— sounds like the kind of punishment someone deserves for murdering their twin brother in cold blood.

I tug at the dragon pendant tied to my neck and raise an eyebrow. "Do I now?"

It's another bet. I need him to think I hate wearing this. Normally, I would.

"Be good and maybe I'll take it off," he says, lips curling into a hungry smirk. It's full of double meaning and supposed to be flirtatious but it only serves me with disgust. I don't show it. I need to be patient, to string Silas along until I've got him where I want him. So I respond with a simple, "We'll see," and turn away to find Bram watching us with a rueful expression. My stomach dips and shame washes through me.

"Don't look so jealous, brother," Silas quips. "We'll find you a woman soon enough."

Bram says nothing.

Two guards stand at his side. They're the same elemental Dragon Blessed who handled me roughly on our way back from the human realm. I shoot them a glare, hoping they know not to harm Bram, hoping they know that I remember all too clearly how badly they treated me. I'm Queen now, but their loyalty still lies with Silas.

"Oh, calm down," Silas sighs, catching onto my glare at his men. "Bram is supposed to be under lock and key, remember? These guys are just doing their jobs."

"They were doing their jobs when they dragged me through the portal, threw me into a tent with you, and then forced me to continue our journey against my will." And with bruising hands if I tried to protest, is what I don't add. I continue to glare. The men aren't affected.

"Let's get on with it," Bram says, voice already sounding bored. "We're here to search for a magicked item, right? So let's do that."

"Where should we start, Oh Wise One?" Silas laughs.

Bram shifts his gaze away. "I seriously doubt we'll find anything, but let's head to where the forest is the densest. If there's something hidden in here, it's going to be where there's the most danger."

Which is exactly what I was counting on.

But I didn't want Bram and me to have to be here for this part. I sigh, lifting the long hem of my pink skirt as we head out. My leather boots crunch against the snow and I'm careful to keep my eyes pinned right in front of me, as not to get distracted by the glittering jewels and the dazzling temptations they possess. It's not the gems themselves that hold the temptation, because even though they're gorgeous and worth a fortune, I already know the cost of taking them is impossible to pay. No, it's that this entire forest seems to have some kind of numbing effect on my judgement. There's dark magic here, dark and ancient and begging to be unbridled.

I'm struck with a startling thought: what if the forest *is* protecting something? What if there really is a magicked item here and I'm about to lead Silas right to it?

"Do you hear that?" one of the guards yelps, his voice alarmed.

I strain my ears, but I hear nothing save for the breath in my lungs, the heart beating in my chest, and the trickling of winter wind against the glimmering tall trees.

"I can hear it, Sebastian," Silas says. "It sounds like a fae lyre."

The wind kicks up a notch.

"Don't pay it any attention," Bram says, "ignore it. It's dangerous."

"Maybe we should follow it." Sebastian sounds hopeful. He turns away from us and steps toward whatever sound is luring him in. "The strings, they're beautiful."

"No," Bram snaps, grabbing Sebastian's massive bicep.

Bram jumps back, hissing and shaking out his hand. It's been burned with what looks like frostbite.

"What did you do?" I gasp, rushing to him as Silas and the other guard grab Sebastian and pin him down. The man must have used his air elemental to zap Bram. Luckily, it's not strong enough for Silas and the other dragon. They hold him back. He's lucky. He might not deserve to be held back if the way he treated me is any indication to his character.

"Snap out of it," Silas growls into Sebastian's ear, "or I'll electrocute you out of it."

Sebastian deflates, his entire body going still. "It's just so—"

"No, whatever you think it is, it's not." Bram scowls. I take his hand in mine, wincing at the patches of red. The skin isn't dead. I let out a sigh of relief. This will heal. "Unless you think something that wants to kill you is beautiful."

Silas shoots me a knowing look.

"When we get back to the castle"—I turn on Bram—"you need to have this looked at." What I don't add is by Juniper. Silas still doesn't know her secret and I can hardly stand to think of what he'd do with her if he knew the truth.

Bram pulls his hand away and puts distance between us. "Come on."

We continue down a path that winds us through the trees.

They grow thicker, more alive, more jewels of every color, shape, and size—each begging to be touched. Held. Taken. The blue sky peeks at us from between the trees. It lessens the deeper we go, until there's hardly any blue left through the thick canopy.

That's when the voices start.

"Come to me."

"Help me."

"Where are you?"

They call to us, begging us to free them, offering our wildest dreams in exchange for freedom. We huddle together, the five of us no longer individuals but one united form, slowly winding our way through the dense foliage. Anytime one of us tries to step off, the others pull them in. It happens to each of us at least once. In the back of my mind, I want Silas to go and never come back, but he seems to have control over his faculties better than anyone.

Stubborn dragon.

Every few meters, a living corpse reveals itself. These poor people all seem to hail from different times, but they have one thing in common. They don't decay and they can't move. The trees grow from their flesh, connecting to appendages. Sometimes roots or entire trunks burst from their stomachs or the sides of their heads. I try not to look, try not to vomit or cry or scream.

We continue on.

Something long and white catches my eye. "What's that?" I squint, piecing together what looks like the bones from a forearm and ribcage.

"Skeleton," Bram says. "When the thousand years are up, the body finally decomposes and the souls are released."

"That must be an old soul then," Sebastian deadpans, eyeing the skeleton.

"Maybe this means we're getting closer," Silas says.

Do I hope so? Maybe. Because if he tries to touch it, whatever it is, and the forest may be able to claim him. But what if magicked items don't work like that? What if he's able to take whatever it is? Either way, at least I could get out of here. Because I don't want to be here anymore. My breath is shallow, my hands are shaking, and my heart skips angrily against my ribcage.

And my inner voice, it screams that this isn't right. We aren't meant to be here.

"We need to go," I whisper. "This was a terrible idea."

"No," Silas says, "we're almost there. I can feel it."

That's the problem. I can feel it, too.

We're nearing *something*.

The forest is almost as dark as night, it's become so thick.

We continue, huddled close, until we come upon the largest tree I've ever seen. It's gnarled and black, the trunk the size of fifty regular trees, the branches beastly and so intertwined that they outstretch in a roof of black and jewels over our heads.

"There," Silas says breathily, pointing to the center of the trunk. I squint and step forward, trying to understand exactly what it is that I'm seeing.

A long staff is pressed against the trunk. It's embedded with glowing jewels of every color. Jewels that don't simply glitter like all the others. *They glow.*

"A sorcerer's staff," Bram adds. "Unbelievable."

Silas laughs softly, his entire face alive with greed. "Better believe it." He nods at Sebastian who is as equally giddy as he is. "You wanted to be the hero," he says, "go pick it up."

Sebastian's grin falls. "I can't."

Electricity zaps between Silas's fingers. "Do it."

Sebastian gulps and then shuffles forward. It's surreal to see the broad warrior frightened, but he is. When he stops in front of the staff, I expect him to protest, or at least to hesitate, but everything goes quiet and the man seems to become overcome again by the lure of the forest. He speaks, replying to a voice none of us can hear. "Yes," he says hungrily. "Yes, I will." And then, "Mine."

The moment his hands curl around the staff, he releases a blood curdling scream and falls against the tree trunk, convulsions raking his body.

Before we can do anything, the black bark twists and pulses, bursting with life and magic. It wraps him in its woody embrace and sucks him into the tree. Here one second, gone the next.

I scream, nearly falling to my knees.

Bram doesn't move.

The other guard doesn't move.

Silas rolls his shoulders back and sighs, his voice calculated when he says, "Leave the staff."

I have to admit, his admonition wakes me from my stupor. "You're just going to leave it here? You're not going to try to take it?"

Silas turns on me, the smile disappearing from his handsome face. His eyes turn cold. Dead. "You're not going to get rid of me that easily, Wife." His jaw clicks and he steps forward, leaning down close. "But thank you for this." He waves toward the staff. "It's exactly what I needed to find. Aleeryrick will undoubtedly agree to help me now."

"Aleeryrick?" I question. I've never heard the name before. *Or maybe...*

He stands back up and sighs. "No more questions." He

spins in a slow circle, taking everything in. The heady magic in the air intensifies, as if to meet his ambition. He turns to me again. "You're going to have to trust me on this one."

ELEVEN

HAZEL

DEAN AND I ARE IN my backyard where I'm attempting, and failing, to shift. The midday sun beats down on my head and the snow beneath my feet is beginning to melt. I unzip my hoodie and tie it around my waist. We've been at this for over an hour already and so far absolutely nothing has happened. I even removed all my obsidian jewelry, which has brought on some ghosty lurkers, but no spirit dragon magic yet. One of those lurkers is Owen. He's in his dragon form, as if to cheer me on. Whatever, it's not working.

"It will be easier in Eridas," Dean assures me. "The magic there is strong, not weak like it is here." He motions around our little yard and shrugs. We have tons of trees lining the old wooden fence and since none of my neighbors have second levels, all that's visible are the varying rooflines. It's given us some great privacy for this activity, too bad nothing is happening.

I sigh and close my eyes, taking a deep breath and letting it out slowly. "I really hope you're right."

The door squeaks open and Harmony's face appears between the frame and the door. Her blue skin is gone, as are her all-white eyes and her younger faerie glamour. Still no gossamer wings, either, not that anyone expected them to grow back. Hiding the rest of her faerie appearance was her and Mom's mission this morning and I guess whatever they were up to, it worked. I skip over to her and gather her papery hands in mine.

"You're not blue anymore. How are you feeling?"

"I'm alright." But there's a crackle of sadness in her tone and regret behind her eyes that tells me she's actually *anything* but alright.

"I've been trying so freaking hard to shift," I complain, changing the subject, "but it's not working."

She nods once, white dreadlocks stiff contrast against her bright blue sweater. "I heard, and Dean is right, it will be easier in Eridas than it is here. I believe you were able to before because you had so much at stake and were fighting for your life. You don't have that right now."

"I really hope you guys are right about this." Something

she said gives me pause. "Wait, can you see it? Can you see me being able to shift in Eridas?"

She squeezes my hands and leads me to the outdoor loveseat. It's under the porch so even though it's ice-cube cold, it's not wet or anything. "We must discuss the plan."

"You didn't answer my question." I point out as we settle into the padded seats. Dean towers over us with a look of sheer concentration on his face. I raise a brow at him and eye one of the chairs, but he just crosses his arms over his chest. He can be such an alpha-male sometimes.

Harmony frowns. "My elemental magic hasn't come back. I believe it was sacrificed to the blood magic. I'm lucky to be alive."

"I'm so sorry."

She shrugs. "I can't see your paths anymore or anyone's for that matter. But I saw them before this happened and still believe you'll be able to shift in Eridas. What's important now is how to get you to safety once you cross over."

"So you do know of a portal we can use?" Dean asks.

"I do." Harmony nods, her lips twisting as she considers her next statement. "But it's an extremely dangerous portal. You'll be catapulted into an open field right in the middle of the Winter Kingdom, which is now the center of the Occultist's territory." Just the thought sends a shiver up my spine that has nothing to do with the crappy weather. "You'll have to seek shelter and perform a spell once you're on the other side that will take you to safety."

Dean nods. "We can do that."

"We can?" This is news to me.

"You can," Harmony confirms.

"We're not witches though. But… I guess neither are you. So how did you do it?"

"There are many elemental spells." Harmony smiles softly and her eyes fill with memories. "It's different magic than sorcery. Would you like to learn?"

I nod enthusiastically. I want to learn anything and everything I can about magic, especially the kinds I can access.

We spend the rest of the day talking through everything, going over the landscape of the Winter Kingdom, discussing the spell we're to perform, and the plan to get to Drakenon from there. That's when I'll bust my friends free. Harmony still insists I'll be battling the Occultists before I head home. That's the part I'm having trouble coming to terms with. Truth is, I don't know how I could possibly stop those guys. I'm a spirit elemental dragon. I'm not filled with fire like Dean. Or four elements like Khali. I don't have control over my abilities and I've only shifted once.

Everyone may think I'm going to save them all, but right now, I'm only concerned with saving my friends and getting the heck out of there.

It stays on my mind all through dinner, and as we're cleaning up, I still can't stop thinking about it. My arms are elbow deep in a sink full of bubbles because our old dishwasher is broken again, when Mom comes to my side.

"Are you sure about this?" Her voice is as earnest as her expression.

"Saving my friends? Yes. The rest of it? No."

"Yeah, me either." Her voice trails off.

"There's a 'but' in there, isn't there?" I tease. "Spit it out."

"What if the Sovereign Occultists succeed." She massages her bottom lip between worried teeth as she considers her fears. "It won't only be Eridas that's in trouble, it'll be this world. I can glamour myself and Harmony and keep us safe for now. You can be safe here, too. But for how long?" She closes her eyes and a tear slips loose. "I don't want to lose you."

"So what you're saying is if I'm not successful in everything, not just freeing my college friends but eradicating the most powerful cult of warlocks Eridas has ever known, then we all might lose everything and die terrible deaths."

Mom lets out a laugh. Dean appears behind me and begins to massage my neck. I try to let myself relax, to melt into his touch, but it's difficult. "We've known this for a while, Hazel."

"I know. But why has it been so hard for me to accept?"

"Because you don't believe in yourself," Harmony joins in the conversation from where she's resting at the dining table. She stares at me with complete determination in her watery eyes. "But you must. And if it's any consolation, we believe in you, and I've *seen* you succeed."

I fake a smile and lie through my teeth. "Don't worry, I'm going to figure this out. And before you know it, we'll all be back together."

Mom's eyes gleam. "Maybe even by Christmas."

I laugh, the very idea ridiculous. "At the very least, New Years." I wink.

"Why don't you two go to a movie or something?" Mom suggests. "Go enjoy a night out before your big trip tomorrow."

A huge smile lifts my cheeks. "That sounds amazing, thanks, Mom." I dry my hands on the towel and turn into Dean's arms. "And actually, I have something else in mind instead of a movie." I grin up at him. "Are you game?"

"Game?"

"Yes, pun intended."

He doesn't get the joke but he will! "Always." His dark eyes twinkle with little sparks of orange. And a half hour later as we're walking into the town arcade, those sparks turn red.

"What is this place?" Dean asks, eyeing the digging games, flashing lights, and screaming children. It's a lot to take in, but for me, all I feel is happy and excited.

"That's exactly why I brought you here." I wrap my arms around his torso. "I figured you've never been somewhere like this." I point to the skee-ball. "We'll come back to the arcade games later. Right now, you and I have a date with the laser tag room."

His eyebrows raise. "Laser tag? Is that what it sounds like, because it sounds intense."

"It's exactly like it sounds and it is awesome. Come on!"

I tug him after me, pay for our wristbands, and before we know it, we're on the blue team getting briefed by a bored looking teenager. The other players are a mix of families and highschoolers, nobody I recognize, not that I wouldn't mind showing off my hot boyfriend to all the kids who bullied me growing up.

The worker opens the door and we race into the laser tag room, heavy plastic vests with fake guns attached bouncing against our rib cages. We find a good hiding spot behind a paint splattered pillar and huddle together in the darkness. The blacklight makes Dean's teeth glow crazy white as he smiles down at me. "This is actually pretty cool."

"Just you wait."

The countdown ends—three, two, one—and we're off. The techno music is head-pounding, kids are running everywhere, and we're shooting like complete maniacs, half taking this seriously and half laughing our heads off. We shoot our lasers, Dean with practiced skill, me like a girl who knows her way around a video game, and in the end, Dean and I lead the blue team to victory.

"Let's play again!" Dean laughs.

So we do. We play three more times, and then spend another two hours in the arcade, collecting a bazillion tickets that only buy us a bunch of stupid crappy toys and random hard candies at the prize counter. It's glorious. And it's also the most I've ever seen Dean relax and let himself have fun. It's kind of hard to imagine the scary, mean, threatening guy I first met back in August. It's also kind of hard to imagine this guy is an exiled prince, the kind that comes from an intense royal family and a whole dragon society.

That part I try not to think about too much, because when I do, I can't help but wonder what will happen if his people decide they want him back. Where will that leave me? Hybrids aren't welcome in Eridas, right? No way they'll think I'm good enough for a full-blooded dragon prince. It's one thing to be his girlfriend in the human realm and laser tag partner for a fun date night. But what happens down the road? Dean and I belong to two separate worlds and I want to live in this one, however great Eridas might be. What if Dean gets back to Drakenon and feels the same way about *his* home?

My heart hurts just thinking about it.

TWELVE

KHALI

EARLY THE NEXT MORNING, I join my parents for breakfast in their chambers. Father doesn't eat much, picking at the food, then going back to rest on his bed. I follow him and sit on the edge, running my hand along the oak footboard. He's still a little pale and has a long ways to go in getting his full strength back. He hadn't used his muscles or eaten properly in weeks while he was sick. "Don't you worry about me, Khali," he says adamantly. "At least I'm not stuck in some dark corner of the castle somewhere. I'll be fine here."

"I'm taking good care of him," Mother adds, coming to stand at his side. She cups her hand to his forehead and smiles gratefully. "He hasn't had a fever since he woke up and it broke."

"I still worry…" My voice trails off.

"Don't," he presses, "not about me anyway."

Mother shoots him a warning look, the kind I'm usually on the receiving end of, that gives me pause.

"I'm tired," Father is quick to supply.

"Fine." I slip off the bed and give them both a hug, finishing with a kiss on Father's cheek. "But I promise I'll be visiting as often as I can. I'm sure it won't be long until life will go back to normal."

I leave before they can see how hard it is for me to believe my own lie. But also, I leave because it's hard to be around them.

I don't feel like myself anymore and I don't wish to tell them just how unhappy I am in my marriage. What good would that do any of us? They can't help me now. Nobody can, not really. And besides, I don't want to get them involved in this mess any more than they already are. I know father would want me to confide in him. I suspect he can sense something is wrong with me and that he's worried. But at least for now, I vow to keep it all locked inside.

The same feelings come up around Faros. She's still my lady's maid and we have a history that will never be erased, but it's hard to consider her the kind of friend I could confide in. It's not like how it was before, and certainly not like how it was with Owen. I never had a friend like him before his death and worry I never will again. Things simply aren't what they used to be. I've been through so much and can no longer tolerate idle chat about court gossip and affairs and what fashion will be in style next. I know it's not Faros's fault—she hasn't been through what I've been through—but the fact still remains that there aren't very many people in this castle who I can relate to right now.

As I exit their chambers and find myself in the stone hallway I know so well, with the light streaming through the windows, with the dragon army practicing drills outside, and my old room only next door, all I want to do is find Bram. It's startling, this pull I have to him, but I can't deny it. I want to make sure he's okay after what happened yesterday in the Jeweled Forest. And I want to be near him, simply to talk to him, to see him, be with him, even though I shouldn't.

The hallway is quiet, it's still quite early. Something is different.

My guards.

They're not here. Silas has had at least two on me whenever I'm outside of the queen's chambers but now they're nowhere to be seen.

This is my chance to explore the tunnels more, except the entrance Owen and I used leads to a dead end now and the only other one I know of is behind Silas's bookshelf—no way I'm going there. And once again, it's Bram's face that flits across my mind.

Is he locked in his room right now, same as my father? If anyone sees me going to him alone we'll become the center of gossip. One thing I've learned about this place is that if people have the opportunity to spread the lastest news, they will. But the guards aren't here right now and I have no doubt that won't last. I have to do something with my sudden freedom.

I'm safe to do as I want.

Except…

Except I don't have magic anymore.

Except my husband has spies everywhere.

Except there is an Occultist on the loose somewhere, possibly still in Drakenon, and even if Silas has swept that fact under the rug, I still know it. But he knows the truth. So why isn't he being more careful? There's got to me something more going on here—something I'm not seeing. *Something secret.*

Does it have to do with what Bellflower Blossom was trying to tell me? Is it something to do with the sorcerer's staff and that strange name, Aleeryrick?

No matter what, it's my job to figure it out, to stop Silas from hurting more people, and to figure out a way to save this kingdom from the Sovereign Occultists. I may not be able to control my set of circumstances but I certainly can work toward those goals. The warlocks are coming for us; they have to be. It's only a matter of time before they show up for battle and if we're not prepared we will die. So I'll make allies and convince them to get ready, to take this seriously. And I'll spy on Silas, find a way to figure out what he's up to, and hopefully, even restore my own magic in the process.

I let out a breath and turn on my heels, striding fast, trying not to let a million doubts follow at my heels.

Enough of that. Juniper was right. Stop feeling sorry for yourself.

As I walk to Bram's chamber, I notice the way the few people awake at this hour look at me, both the servants and the courtesans. It's the way they looked at Queen Brysta, like I have something important to say, like I should be admired and sought out. I run my hand over my loose curls and try not to fidget with them. Faros met me early today and managed to create a perfect crown braid around the top of my head and secured sparkly ruby pins into the braid all before the sun had completely risen. Add the matching dress of glossy red, cut tight around the waist and low around the bodice, and I look exactly how a Queen of Drakenon should look. Silas's awful necklace holds tight around my neck but Faros layered strings of pearls over it to cover it up.

I don't feel like a queen on the inside but I look it and right now, that's all that matters. Nobody stops to question why I'm alone or where I'm going.

Maybe Juniper is right about that too and it's time I start acting like a queen, because apparently I can get a lot more done with this attitude. Would a queen fear walking into her brother-in-law's chambers to check on his health? Of course not.

I walk right past the sleepy guard stationed outside of his door, noting it's a different man from the one who survived the Jeweled Forest, and waltz in like I'm an expected guest. I don't know if Bram will be sleeping or eating breakfast, but I'm not surprised to find him the same as I've always found him in these chambers over the years, in his library with his nose stuck in a book. The pink color in his cheeks is strong and his hair is the same usual curly shag around his face which I suddenly find so endearing. I used to think he was messy and unkempt, boring and too serious, but now I don't think any of those things. When he catches me staring, there's still that haunted expression behind his eyes, but he smiles and for a second it's as if all the bad things never happened, like we're back to doing our weekly visits.

But no. This isn't mandatory and it won't be weekly. *And* … I want to be here. And besides, this is nothing like all the other visits. It can't be. I'm married.

"Hi," I say brightly, closing the library door behind me. It's just the two of us now. Another thing that never happened with our previous visits. Does he notice it, too? Does he care? And does it make his heart beat wildly like it does mine?

I stand frozen, chest rising and falling with heavy breaths, as I realize just how much I've changed. Him, too.

"Hi," he replies slowly, his voice like molten honey, and then he does the last thing I expect him to do. He stands, strides right over to me, and pulls me into a full-bodied hug. He smells earthy and wonderful, feels stronger and taller than I remember. Relief floods my system.

The contact is like a soothing balm and creates the first moment of clarity I've had in days.

I want Bram to be safe. I want him to be happy. And I care about him far more than I ever thought I did. He's so much more than a friend to me now. *I like him.* I might even love him. But it's too late to tell him these things and certainly too dangerous to act on them, so I peel myself out of his arms and step back, clearing my throat.

"How are you?" I ask. "Is everything okay now? Do you feel better? I wanted to ask you yesterday but…"

He searches my eyes like a dying man searching for life. I can't help but admire the vibrant green of his irises and I have to look away before he sees too much truth in me.

He can't know. He can't know. He can't know.

"I'm okay," he finally answers. "Devastated about my father, among other things." He swallows and his cheeks redden. "But I'm okay."

"Yeah… devastated is a good word for it." I let out a long sigh and grasp his hand in mine, holding on tight. "I'm so sorry."

"You're sorry?" He shakes his head. "No, Khali, this is my fault. If I hadn't killed my father, you'd not be queen yet and I thought maybe we could find a way to annul the wedding before the coronation but now everything has gotten so—"

"Stop," I hiss. He's already said too much.

Panic rises in my chest and I have to force myself from speaking too loudly. "You have to stop. This is treasonous and if one word of it got to your brother, you'd be dead, just like Owen, or exiled like Dean. You can't ever speak like this again."

His mouth thins into a peckish line.

"Do you promise?" When he doesn't immediately reply I can't help it, I have to push the matter. I squeeze his hand even harder. "Seriously, Bram, I mean it. I need you to promise."

"Fine." He squeezes back. "I won't speak of it again after I say this one thing."

"Bram…"

He holds up his free hand, fisting the air as he speaks. "The reaper had me and I didn't know it because I couldn't see it. But I could hear him sometimes. I thought it was my thoughts but I couldn't control them and that scared me. I don't know how to explain it."

"Bram, what happened wasn't your fault."

"But I need you to understand something." He steps closer and takes my other hand, pulling both of them against the planes of his chest. His hands are so soft and warm and envelop mine so perfectly, like they were made to rest there. And his chest, it's so hard, with a heart pounding underneath. "The reaper didn't want me to kill my father. It wanted me to kill you."

I swallow hard, letting the revelation sink in. I don't know what to say.

"That's why I was trying to distance myself from you and why I was hoping Juniper could heal me. I've never wanted to hurt you but then I'd get these images or these thoughts and I knew something was wrong. When I killed my father, it was only because I made the creature direct his hate toward whoever was standing closest to me in that moment." His voice cracks, pain breaking through. "That moment when

I was going to kill you." His hands start to shake. "It could have been anyone. My mother. Silas. The Priest. Anyone could have died that day but it happened to be my father who was closest to me. Once it took over my mind, I blacked out. I don't remember everything. Only the start of it and the end when I was being dragged from the room and you were yelling about the reapers and my father was surrounded by a pool of his own blood."

"I'm sorry." A tear splashes down my check. "I should have figured out what was going on sooner. I could have helped you. I made so many mistakes."

"Listen to me, Khali," he whispers. I look up to focus on him. We're standing so close now. "I hate that my father is dead and that you're married to my brother. I hate that he's the king now, but I can't regret that you're still alive. I could never regret that. If I had to choose, you'd be the last one to get hurt."

"What are you saying?" I whisper back.

His smile quirks. "I thought it was obvious."

My heart skips and his confession settles over me. "But you've never seemed interested in me," I blurt. "Or seemed to care."

He's silent for a long minute. We're closer than ever now and still holding hands. His thumb gently caresses the back of my hand and my knees grow weak. "I couldn't be honest but that doesn't mean I haven't loved you since I could remember, because I have. But then we all grew up and I wasn't Dragon Blessed and my brothers were. There was absolutely zero chance for us."

"You loved me?" That word, love, it means everything. And I want to say it back so bad that it's like a physical thing squeezing my chest, this overpowering desire to reciprocate his feelings.

"I still do," he whispers. "I love you."

It's everything… but it's forbidden.

"Bram don't." It hurts to stop him but I can't do this. It's too dangerous. My eyes burn. My heart rips in two. "We can't."

"Everyone thought I was resentful because I didn't have magic but really it was because I knew I'd never get to have you." He swallows, searching my face. "Can I have you now? Just this once. And then I'll fade into the background and we'll go back to the way things were before."

I should run away. *I need to go.* But my feet and my heart aren't listening to my mind and before I know it I'm inching forward and letting him wrap me into his arms. Our lips are so close but we don't close the gap, not yet. We just look at each other, everything revealing itself without words. He smells like life, like florals and sandalwood and earth and everything that is so, so alive—*I am so, so alive.*

He kisses me.

And it's gone. The fear and confusion and anger. All the bad things evaporate into nothing but him. Only him and me and this one moment in my life that makes sense. I could stay here forever and he could too. I know it because I deepen the kiss and he moans and we're up against the wall now and I suddenly understand so many things I didn't understand before about why people do careless things for love.

But then someone is knocking on the door and we're flying apart and I'm wiping my mouth and Bram's cussing with frustration and I get it.

Again, I understand.

Juniper strides through the door. Juniper … and Silas.

My breath catches, and I straighten my spine, smiling absentmindedly like I haven't a care in the world. But all I can think is if Silas saw us what he would do and why is he with Juniper? What is he going to do next? Silas's piercing gaze zeros in on me before shooting to his brother and back to me again.

No. He can't know. Not for sure. Stay calm.

"Hello, Silas," Bram says, his voice as smooth and relaxed as ever. He wanders over to his bookshelf and straightens a few volumes before turning back to us.

"What is she doing here?"

Bram shrugs. "Khali came to check on me, worried that the Jeweled Forest may have brought the reaper back, but nothing has changed. I'm fine. Is that what you two are doing here as well?" He looks away, staring out the window with a frown. "You already know I'll never forgive myself for what happened to our father. Feel free to keep me locked up in here as long as you'd like. I deserve it."

"Oh, no." Silas smiles coolly. "Give the courtesans enough time and they'll have someone else to gossip about and you can go back to whatever it is you do around here." He waves at the bookshelves like they're filled with things for children. His blond hair is tied back and his clothing is tailored to perfection. He looks amazing, like a king should look, but there's zero comparison to my stunning Bram. "I couldn't help but notice the sweet little relationship you have with our little fae elf friend here," he says to Bram. His tone is meant to sound playful, but to me, it's anything but.

Juniper smiles, her big brown doe-eyes softening when they reach Bram's fallen expression. She doesn't look at me.

"And I also couldn't help but wonder if you two ought to become more than friends," Silas continues, his words turning wicked and proud. He raises his eyebrows suggestively and smirks. "It would smooth things over with some of the courtesans, I think, to have some kind of alliance. And anyway, you're not a eunuch, are you? You ought to enjoy yourself. So I asked Juniper if she'd do us all a favor and give you a chance. Luckily, she has agreed to date you."

Bram's face burns bright red. I can't tell if this is something Juniper wants or simply something Silas wants and is demanding of her. She's become my friend, sure, but I've sensed her desire to be close to Bram. Not that I blame her.

But it can't be about diplomacy and court politics. Silas is lying about something and this must be part of his scheme.

Everyone is still as the implications set in, my heart twisting under Silas's cruelty.

"Great idea," Bram says at last. He strides to Juniper, then gives her a little bow and a soft kiss to her hand. My eyes water and all I can think of is what we were doing just minutes before. "I would be a lucky man. Anyone would."

She smiles faintly and arches a perfect brow. "We'll see. You haven't won me over yet."

Everyone laughs, though it's stilted, and Silas pats Bram on the back. "Don't screw this one up, huh? It's about time you're useful for something around here."

He turns to me, a violence in his movements I can't trust. "Khali, I'll escort you back to your room. Wouldn't want anyone to think you were in here alone, would we?"

"No." My voice croaks and I hate myself for it. Why aren't I stronger?

"Don't let it happen again." The threat is clear.

"Of course, not." My smile is sickly-sweet as I go to him, threading his arm with mine.

As he escorts me from the room, I catch Bram's eyes. They're filled with so much pain and I can only imagine they're an exact mirror of my own. And then it's Juniper I see and she's studying my neckline. Her face falls as she spots Silas's necklace underneath all the pearls. Just as well. This way she can tell Maxx and Terek to call off the search. I smile sadly at her and she frowns back. What did we really think was going to happen? Did we really think we could change things? That we'd beat Silas?

No. I'm a caged animal—locked in with a monster—and so are they.

THIRTEEN

HAZEL

"SO WHAT DID YOU LEARN?" Dean asks as I skim through the article on my phone.

"Well, in 1862, part of the Sioux Indian tribe, called the "Dakotas" got into a conflict with the United States government along the Minnesota River. It was a bad winter and the tribe was starving to death." I skip ahead. "It looks like some agents of the government had promised to give the tribe payments but they were late or never turned up at all." I click my tongue. "Geeze, this is horrible."

"What?"

"It escalated to the point of an all out bloodbath. Settlers and their families were attacked and murdered and then thirty-eight Dakotas were sentenced to hanging. Yuck—it was the largest mass execution in US history."

"That's pretty bad." Dean maneuvers our shiny new rental car that we picked up after our flight into a parking spot and kills the engine. I peer up at the weathered brick building with its mounds of snow on the roof and I'm reminded of our own little Main Street in Westinbrooke.

"It was not a great moment, that's for sure," I say. "And not something I remember learning about in history class as a kid."

"It also explains why there's a ley line portal here."

"Yup." I let out a breath. "Welcome to Minnesota."

Dean says that ley lines are energetic pathways that run all over the earth. In the areas of intense emotional events, the land will hang onto that energy forever. If there also happens to be a ley line in the same spot? Bam! Portal.

Which is exactly how Dean and I have ended up flying to freezing Mankato, Minnesota, only five days before Christmas. Harmony said she'd never been to the portal herself but knew it was here, and we should go to where the hangings took place to look for it.

"Remind me again why people live here?" I ask as soon as we get out of the car, only half joking as I bury myself into my fur-lined coat. We pop open the trunk and I heave the backpack on my shoulder. It hangs heavy, filled with everything we could possibly need for our trip to Eridas. "It's only thirteen degrees out here today," I add, "but with the wind-chill factor it's so much worse."

I borrowed this particular coat from Mom before we left. The woman hates the cold even more than I do and I knew I'd need something extra warm for where we were headed. Nothing screams bitter cold like the Winter Court! Dang, if only the Summer thing had worked out but I guess you can't win them all.

"Get used to it," Dean teases but immediately wraps an arm around me and shoots some of his elemental warmth into my limbs. I relax into it, my body melting. *Ahh, that's nice.*

"Heaven," I sigh.

Dean kisses my cheek. "The Winter Kingdom is in a perpetual state of icy winter and besides that, the Occultists have taken over, so it won't be a very safe place for either of us. We're going to have to be extra careful and move quickly to the Drakenon border."

"Good thing Harmony's got contacts for us, right?" I think back on the plan she gave us to find them, worried it won't work, but trusting that it will.

"Yes, of course," Dean says. "But either way, we can't stay for long."

"I hope it'll be the pretty blue skies and sparkling icicles kind of winter weather," I muse, trying not to let my nerves get the better of me and staying on the topic that doesn't freak me the freak out. "And not the 'colder than a freezer and blocks out the sun' kind of winter."

Dean laughs, shaking his head.

Mankato is a cute little town on the farthest outskirts of Saint Paul, Minnesota. We're near the river where there are fully grown trees everywhere and quaint historic buildings. This close to Christmas, it's dripping in holiday charm. I half expect a gaggle of carolers to come barreling around the corner. I peer at the different colored brick buildings stacked right next to each other with their welcoming stoops and neat awnings, and I almost wish we could stay here until this evening and see what it looks like lit up with Christmas lights.

Almost.

My friends are counting on me. Not just my friends—everyone. We need to keep moving.

"Reconciliation Park is this way," Dean says and we hurry across the road, ice melt crunching under our boots as we try to beat the flashing crosswalk sign before it changes to a red hand. All the info we could get from the locals at the airport is that the mass hanging took place near where the park was built in the 70s, but nobody was sure if it was the *exact* spot. As we step into the small park, we spot a memorial monument erected in dark stone and rush over.

My eyes rove across the script. It's a prayer to the tribes of the area, to the north, south, east, and west, to the Great Spirit and Mother Earth. The words are so heartfelt, but also sad, and I know that they're going to stay with me long after I leave this place.

"Wow. That's a nice tribute," Dean says softly.

"I can't pretend to understand all that went on here," I say, "but yes, it is."

Together we press our hands against the icy stone; maybe it will somehow transport us through the portal. Nothing happens. We peel away from it and wander around the park, which is actually pretty small, but loaded with something everywhere you look: the memorial monument, a few statues, a water fountain feature, a green area that's currently covered with snow, and a short path that leads to a river overlook. In the middle of a cold day like this, nobody else is milling about. I imagine this place will get busy when the Christmas lights come on though.

"I don't know, Dean. There's nothing even remotely similar to the other portal around here." The sparkling swirl of colors would be unmistakable, and even if regular human eyes couldn't see it, we would be able to. "I mean, I'm sure Harmony was right that this was the event that created the portal, but do you think it's really right here? Maybe it's nearby or somewhere else along the river."

"Maybe. Wherever it is, we'll find it," Dean assures me.

I eye the flash of sparkling river water with trepidation. "You don't think it's under the water, do you?"

"Could be." He furrows his brow, worry crossing his features. "Some portals are."

The thought of jumping into a lake is bad enough, but it's colder here than it is in West Virginia, and rivers have currents. Strong ones. We may very likely end up dead if we even attempted to swim in that kind of water, even with Dean's fire to keep us from freezing. It's not like we can shift into our dragon forms out here in public and I'm obviously not able to do that right now anyway. Harmony told us her contacts in the Winter Court might be able to help me learn to control my abilities. The plan is to dodge the Occultists, find Harmony's friends, learn as much as I can about my magic in as short of a period as I can, then go to Drakenon, and convince them to not only spare Dean's life, but to let my friends go, oh and then we're all supposed to defeat the Occultists together.

No big deal.

I shake my head, focus returning to the matter at hand. *One problem at a time, Hazel.* "We're not water elementals. It's too risky to go near moving water like that. If the portal is under there, we're going to have to find another way into Eridas."

Dean pulls me into a hug and I relax against this chest. "We'll find a way. Let's keep looking around, okay?"

I nod and gaze around again, this time focusing on the few spirits mingling about the park instead of the scenery. Ever since my birthday, I haven't had any problems with the spirits bothering me. Maybe they know what I truly am now and they're afraid of me. Or maybe I have more control over this gift when before it was a curse always spiralling out of control. I can't say one way or the other, but I'm hopeful and trying super hard not to get too excited about it or too comfortable.

We amble around the park, Dean sending me blasts of heat every few minutes, which I know isn't the best idea. He needs to get back to Eridas to restore his fire elemental magic and shouldn't be using it for my comfort, not when we might need it for a better reason. But I can see the worry growing on his face and if this is one way he can ease the tension, then I'm going to let him have it. We end up walking down a side path shrouded with trees on both sides. The leaves are long gone and the branches stick out in a chaotic pattern. No streams of sunlight bursting through; it's too cloudy today.

A Dakota warrior stands in the middle of the path, his presence unlike anything I've experienced. It stops me dead in my tracks, and a frosty chill runs through me that has nothing to do with the weather.

"What is it?" Dean asks. But I'm lost for words.

This spirit is so unlike the other spirits I'm used to seeing. There's no way he's from this modern age, which means he hasn't crossed over from the spirit realm to whatever next place waits for him. Ancient ghosts are incredibly rare. Even Westinbrooke, with its civil war history, didn't have anyone sticking around to haunt it—at least not that I saw. It's like he stepped out of a black and white photo from the past, brought to life in living color. His layered clothing is made from thick wool in every color of the rainbow and tan elk hide. Large feathers stick out the back of his headdress, and long dark braids cascade down his back. Around his neck hang more feathers, beads too, and in his right hand, rests a wooden staff with intricate carvings and more feathers adorning the top. He's magnificent, and terrifying—and staring right at me.

Dean steps forward and the ghost slams his staff into the path to block him. It's not as if Dean couldn't just walk right through him, but I pull him back anyway. "Stop."

Dean stills. "What do you see?"

"A Dakota warrior." I swallow hard. "I think he's protecting something."

"The portal?" Dean whispers and I nod. Maybe the portal,

maybe not, but this man is definitely protecting *something*.

The Dakota warrior begins speaking in a language I can't even begin to understand, his voice sharp angles and deep resonance.

"Can you help us?" I ask him as soon as he pauses.

He slams his staff into the ground, harder this time, and I scramble back. I'll take that as a big fat *NO and get the hell off this land right now, white woman!*

"It must mean the portal is nearby," Dean states and I shush him. He can't see what I'm seeing. I don't want him to mess this up, not when we're so close.

I try to connect again, this time keeping my mouth sealed and reaching under my coat to remove one of the obsidian necklaces. I keep the one Cora and Macy gave me for my birthday hidden and hold out the string of black round beads. Harmony gifted me it all those weeks ago and I hate to part with it but this is a worthy enough cause. I don't know if it's possible, but if anyone can pass an item from this world into the spirit one, it would be me, wouldn't it?

I bow my head and peer up at the warrior, hoping he can sense that I come in peace. Am I being disrespectful for looking in his eyes? Should I look down instead? Is the small gift enough? Am I being pretentious to even offer it? Maybe I should try to learn how to ask for help in his language and come back later? The questions race through my mind and I feel foolish and inadequate, trying to understand something that is so far beyond my comfort zone and life experience.

But his stony face softens, the flicker of a smile turning the corner of his lips, and he reaches out for the necklace. It works. One second it's dangling from my fingers in the mortal realm and the next he's holding it in the spirit realm. I smile, too.

Dean growls under his breath and squeezes tighter where he's holding my other hand with his. He may not be able to see what I can, but we're in this together, and thank heavens for that because my knees are starting to grow weak. I need to do this right.

The Dakota warrior runs his thumb along the black beads before depositing them into an inner pocket. Then he slams his staff into the earth again and this time, the sound of it takes on an echoing quality—unearthly. Dean tightens next to me, pulling me close. The sky flashes, turning pitch black for a second and then lighting in a swirl of sparking color. It surrounds us, spinning faster and faster as it goes, like a tornado of pinks and red, blues and greens, yellows and oranges. My hair whips around my head. Dean hugs me to his body. It grows even colder. Impossibly cold.

"Do you see this?" I pant.

"Yes," Dean says into my ear, his voice tight.

The Dakota warrior is unaffected. He slams his staff into the path one last time and then he's gone... and we're gone too. The world flashes dark again—bright white, so bright, before returning to normal. We blink.

"We're here," Dean whispers.

Eridas. The Fae's Winter Kingdom.

It's far more beautiful than I'd imagined. And far more deadly, too.

FOURTEEN

KHALI

I STARE AIMLESSLY AT THE smoke as it billows from the fire, a misshapen line of gray streaking the blue sky. It takes me back to Owen's funeral and the pain of his death stings all over again. The recent blanket of white snow reflects the bright midday sun and I try not to squint or look uncomfortable—or worse, disinterested. To appear anything other than sad during King Titus's funeral wouldn't be wise. And in a way, I am sad. He wasn't always kind to me but he was an important part of Drakenon and loved by the Brightcaster bloodline. He did a lot in recent years to make life better for the non-Dragon Blessed. And his absence will change history—he will be missed. But it's Owen who occupies my thoughts right now. He was my best friend, and I wonder what he'd say about me and Bram? What he'd make of everything that's happened with Silas. I wish I could talk to him. I'd give anything for one more conversation with my favorite person.

We're all outside, eyes glazed by the funeral pyre as it slowly burns. These kinds of goodbyes aren't easy, and Silas and Bram are visibly upset; but it's Brysta who makes my heart hurt. She loved her husband. I always wondered if maybe she didn't, or maybe he did something to her to make her so compliant to his wishes, but the raw pain on her face is unmistakable and I'm certain that she really did love him. Maybe that's why she didn't fight him more on his stance toward her magic and toward my future. Perhaps she was happy to go along with whatever he wanted because of how much she cared about him. Or it could be that she actually agreed with all of his staunch opinions. It is the way things are done, after all.

She catches me watching her and stares right back. The one brown and one blue of her eyes is hard for me to look at. I don't want to be like her. I never wanted this life, never asked for it. Does she see the resistance etched across my face? Letting her grieve in peace, I offer a kind smile and then turn back to the crackling fire even though the breeze has shifted directions and the smoke burns my eyes. I let them water, a few rogue tears falling down my face. It looks better this way.

The formal part of the funeral is long over and after a while, most people leave, couples arm in arm, long gowns brushing the snow and mud. Bram is escorted back to his chambers, Juniper at his side. I don't look at him, not even once. It's too hard knowing that we can't be together. I stand by Silas for what feels like hours, shivering under my cloak, legs aching, toes pinching in my boots, stomach growling, but I don't dare complain. He's going to be extra emotional after this and I don't want him to take any negative feelings out on me. For now his expression shifts from stoic and cold, to broken and angry. I'm not sure what to expect from him next.

The ground shakes and my knees buckle. Silas catches me before I hit the ground. Someone screams, her voice echoing across the open field. Confusion is a hot knife slicing right through my center. Are the Occultists here? Is it an elemental doing this? Something booms and crashes, and on the horizon, trees split and fall, making way for a shrouded figure emerging from the forest. Silas is yelling and his guards are circling in around us. Brysta bursts into tears which is so unlike the normally composed woman. This day is going to break her down even more than she already is.

I turn back to Silas. "What's happening?" He grips my hand in his; mine are shaking. We need to get back to the castle but…

"I can't shift."

His eyes flash to the necklace and I think maybe this is my chance to get it off but he frowns and returns to watching the field. His hands are now crackling with power. I squeal and jump away to avoid the shock. A horde of our men and women surround us, shifting into dragons. They're quicker than I expected, quicker than I remember. They must have been training more since I left. Many of them take to the skies, black scales reflecting the sun, and a few charge forward on foot, animalistic warcries booming. The rest stay behind as our protectors.

The figure continues to stride toward us. Is that all? *One person is creating all this power?*

I don't know what I expected, maybe a swarm of Occultists in their red robes and with black magic swirling about them. But no. It's only one man—one man who is most definitely *not* an Occultist. He's far enough away that I can't make out his features exactly, but he's not wearing red, his eyes aren't glowing, and he has hair, which none of the Occultists do. It's long and white, coupled with a long white beard. He's got a staff in one hand and is dressed in a silver reflective cloak, the likes of which I've never seen before.

Silas stills, his face forming an unreadable mask. He stares for a long hard minute. One of the dragons swoops in, claws outstretched, but all the man does is nudge the staff toward the dragon and the creature goes careening away, slamming into the ground. I'm not sure what's happening here but fear slips into my thoughts and I wonder if this is the end of Drakenon and by an enemy we never even knew we had.

Except… do I know him? Something about this old man is vaguely familiar.

The staff glints in the sun and my stomach drops *because I definitely know that staff!*

"That's enough," Silas belts at the dragons. "Call off the attack." When they don't immediately, he responds with a barked, "Now!"

They must relay the orders through the telepathic link we have in our dragon forms because they're quick to back off. Silas returns to holding my hand, squeezing. I wince and he pulls me forward. We cross through the line of dragons, toward the wizened man who glides across the snowy field like he's here to save us all.

Either that, or kill us.

By the time we meet in the middle, I'm holding my breath. Something doesn't feel right. I can't quite place what it is, save for a knowningness deep in my gut. I study the old man, his deep brown eyes and the hard line of his thin mouth, his white hair and beard and aged skin. He looks powerful and there's a magic unknown to me here. Different and powerful. *But wait, am I sure I don't know it?* That sense that I should know creeps into my awareness again.

None of that scares me as much as the staff in his hand does—the same one we left in the Jeweled Forest.

"Aleeryrick." Silas smiles. "I hoped you would come. I didn't know if you'd take me up on my offer."

The man bows to Silas. "Of course, Your Majesty." His grip tightens on the staff, like it's the greatest of treasures. "I am at your disposal."

Then he peers at me and my entire body goes cold. "Ah, nice to see you Queen Khali." He holds out his hand to shake mine and so I do. When our fingers touch, crackling magic travels up my arm and into the necklace at my throat. I stumble back, yanking my hand from his.

"What are you?" I don't trust him.

Silas smirks. "Aleeryrick is a sorcerer. And he's come to save us all."

I blink, trying to take this information in. This must be the sorcerer who magicked Silas's necklace. And now Silas thinks this man is going to save us? No, that can't be right. Nothing about this man or his magic feels like it's going to save us, in fact, it feels quite the opposite. His presence comes with an emptiness in my chest, a burning in my gut, and an animalistic desire to either run away or destroy him.

"Nice to meet you," I say to the man, forcing a queenly smile.

It makes Aleeryrick laugh, a knowing and terrible laugh. I still hate it—hate him and fear him—and I need to figure out why.

FIFTEEN

HAZEL

WHATEVER SLAMMED INTO MY BACK knocked away both my backpack and my breath. I blink up, expecting the blanket of clouds from before, but they're replaced with endless blue. I roll to my side to find Dean—thank goodness. We've landed in the middle of a glistening field of snow that's hard as rock, as if it's been frozen for ages. Perhaps it has! It's the bright white of untouched snow but with the softest of blues glowing from within. Is this actually ice? A glacier? No, I don't think so because—

"Come on," Dean whispers, jumping right into action while I'm still busy marveling at our new surroundings. He grabs my hand and tugs me up after him and toward a bunch of boulders that look like small jagged mountains. Some are solid white, some gray, and a few are clear blue ice.

They're all taller than us and instead of being rounded off, they're covered in razor sharp edges. I don't have much time to consider why Dean's so intent on hiding us right away until we're crouching behind a boulder. He lifts a finger to his mouth and points back out to where we were.

Of course...

Across the ice field a line of men stand along a river. It's not just any river; it sparkles like it's made of countless diamonds. And these aren't just any men; they're dressed in long burgundy robes with wet hems that brush the snow. They face away from us. Raising their hands, they chant in their guttural language. My heart races, burning fear exploding through my veins.

"Occultists," I breathe, the word barely a whisper on my lips. To see them in person, to know that they're real and they're right here, makes me want to go back through the portal and never return. Except, where is the portal? I look all around, fingertips clinging to the rock, desperately trying to find that rainbow color again, but it's gone. It's clear blue sky and jagged rocks and white snow and nothing else...

So the angel Elias was right that there would be more occultists at the portals. When we found the Dakota warrior and he brought us through, I'd been so awed and distracted that I'd almost forgotten about the very real threat waiting for me on the other side. It's a good thing Dean is better suited for this stuff or I'd have been dead within minutes of arriving.

"No matter what, I can't let the Occultists capture us because they will kill us," Dean whispers. "Especially you."

I nod and attempt to steady my ragged breath. "What's the plan again?" I know we have one, Dean and Harmony talked it through a million times, but my brain is sort of fritzing out.

"We have to get out of here." His voice is so quiet I have to strain my ears to hear him and something about that freaks me out even more. What was I thinking coming to Eridas? I'm not ready for this. I thought I was, I'm not.

I'm so not!

"But first," he whispers. "I want to know what they're doing."

Umm—what!? Shouldn't we be running for our lives?

But we stay and watch for a minute more, trying to understand what the Occultists are up to. This whole area is essentially on a giant slab of ice or snow with the pointy boulders on one side and the river on the other. A group of gray tents are erected near where the warlocks chant. There are no trees to be seen. It's so different from the cute little city of Mankato, so barren and cold.

So freaking cold…

I shiver and Dean runs his hands down my arms, flooding

me with warmth. Already I can tell his magic is stronger here than in my world. And speaking of magic…

I can feel mine, actually *feel* it alive within me. Before it was this thing I cognitively knew was a part of me, but I couldn't physically feel it. Well, I did a little on my birthday. Now I couldn't not feel it if I tried—it's like an electric current buzzing under my skin. I'm not sure what to do with it. At the moment I don't see any supernatural spirits but that doesn't mean things won't change soon. I only hope that whatever happens with this spirit elemental, I'll be able to handle it.

I count the men on the river banks—thirteen. Are they trying to get through the portal? That's what Elias had said and Harmony confirmed, but how exactly are they going about it? I'm so naive to the ways of magic.

A woman screams, a wail so charged with terror, the sound magnifies my fear tenfold.

"What's that?" I whisper so low that it hurts my throat.

My question is immediately answered. A girl is dragged from a nearby tent by two more men. She looks young, younger than me for sure. Her skin is icy white and her hair is the brightest cotton-candy blue I've ever seen. Even from all the way across the field, I can tell the color is like that of a precious gem. I catch a glimpse of pointy ears and bite my lip.

"Elf," Dean whispers. "One of the High Fae."

"What are they going to do to her?"

All at once, black tendrils of magic shoot from all thirteen of the Occultists' palms. The elf falls to her knees, screams wildly, begging for mercy, and just when I'm about ready to run out there and fight for her, she goes limp. The black magic transforms, going from the darkest of dark, to blood red. My stomach turns. It is blood. *Her* blood. And it flows into the Occultists' hands. They chant louder, happier, jovial, as if welcoming the new blood.

"They sacrificed her," Dean seethes, gritting his teeth. "They can't go through portals, probably not even with an elemental to accompany them, so they're trying to steal her magic for themselves. Either that, or they're using her magic to make whatever spell they're working stronger."

"Do you think it will work?"

"Maybe. Give them enough time and enough blood to grow the bond and it's possible."

I think of the bond and how Harmony had taken on the sacrifice of it for herself the few times we'd used ours. In this case, it looks like the warlocks are using an unwilling third-party sacrifice by entering them into the bond and then stealing away all of her power. What will happen to the elf? Will she lose her powers like Harmony?

No. She is gone.

The cult has surrounded the girl now, who I'm sure is already dead because her body is so limp and broken. They chant for a minute more and then utter silence descends. The only sounds are the rumble of the river, the soft breeze as it scatters bits of snow across the white field, and my heartbeat reverberating in my ears. The group steps away from the girl and all that's left are her simple clothes. Her body has turned to a sparkly pink ash, similar to what happened with Harmony's wings. My stomach hardens, bile burning its way up my throat.

This is what happened to Harmony's family. I saw it, the reaper showed me, but now that it's confirmed with my own eyes I can't help but think this will one day happen to me and maybe the people I love. My heart aches for the young elf girl and for a split second, I imagine Dean in her place. Tears well up and blur my vision.

Something dark swooshes above, racing toward the scene. A reaper. My heart clenches. Is the reaper here for the girl or is he here because the Occultists are binding the reapers to them again? I don't think I want to know. But I must know. I need to figure out the truth.

Even though they can't see the reaper, the Occultists must sense it, because they turn in our direction. One points directly to where we're standing.

"Time to go," Dean growls.

He takes my hand and points behind us. The rocks aren't so tightly packed together and we'll be able to navigate through them—but with an Occultist on our tail? Because I swear that guy just saw us.

I look back and the warlock is storming toward us, red eyes glowing bright.

I squeal and we take off. This might turn into a bit of a maze and we may get lost, but I'm not ready to shift yet and we have to get away. Maybe Dean could shift and carry me on his back? But with the sun bright and centered in the blue sky and enemies after us, it seems too risky to take to the skies.

Sometimes the unknown danger is a better choice than the known one.

We're quiet and quick, maneuvering through the spiraling boulders and mounds of ice. They glisten in the sunlight, catching little rainbow rays that add to the beauty of this place. It's a cruel beauty—a sharpness that looks like it could kill you but first it wants you to admire it. We continue on like this for a while, sometimes having to turn back and take a different route. Each time that happens, I swear we're going to run into an Occultist, but we never do. I don't voice my fears as Dean leads the way.

We turn a corner and a face stares out from one of the ice spires. I stumble backwards and hold my hands to my mouth.

"What?" Dean whispers. He ducks next to me in a fighter's stance.

I point to the face.

"I don't see it."

But it's still there, as if frozen in time and ice. I look closer, studying the green eyes and the pointed ears. Is this a spirit? My imagination? I take a deep breath. "It's a spirit trapped in the ice… I think."

"There's so much about this place we don't know." Dean's voice is dark. "This court was never very forthcoming with the dragons. It might be a spirit trapped in there or it might be something else." A haunted expression takes over his normally pensive face. "Let's hurry. Don't touch anything."

This isn't the first time he's told me not to touch anything while I'm here in Eridas but now I'm beginning to understand why. About an hour later, we pass more frozen faces, more that Dean can't see, and a few that he can, until we reach the other side of this horrid landmark. I'm happy to be free of it, hoping to erase it from my mind as soon as possible. My stomach is a mess, curdled with fear, and my chest feels like it's an empty cavity, my heart frozen back with those people.

Holy crap, I really hate this place.

We're not met with another field of white or sparkling river, nor are there any more warlocks. This time, it's a forest and perhaps the most beautiful one I've ever seen. I have to keep myself from gasping aloud. It's fully in bloom, unlike the winter forests of my world. Flowers of all shapes and sizes and colors that seem to be made from ice and the leaves on the trees are every shade of green with a frosty layer, giving them a pastel quality. The trees are tall and generous, like they've been growing here for a century or more. Maybe they have. They remind me of the California Redwoods, not quite as big but close, and definitely magicked for year-round winter weather.

Icicles hang off many of the branches, longer than my entire body and probably deadly sharp from the way the end points are little more than a needle. It's all so fantastic and terrifying and exactly what a magical realm should look like if I have all the books and movies I've consumed to compare it to. I immediately fall in love with this enchanted forest but I'm equally terrified, too. At least Dean's hand is still in mine. At least I'm not alone out here. There's a clear path leading into the forest that's made entirely from glistening ice crystals.

Oh, boy… this is not what I had in mind.

"Remember not to touch anything," Dean speaks of the warning again and I nod. "And don't talk to anyone, don't eat or drink anything, and stick with me. We can't get separated."

Our backpacks are still slung over our shoulders, so at least we have that. Food from home. Change of clothes. Matches. Water. Chocolate. We're going to be okay. We have to be.

"Here goes nothing." I say it sarcastically but the truth is, for the first time since arriving in Eridas, I actually feel like I'm on an adventure, like I'm the hero of one of my favorite books. A determined smile pulls at my lips and all I can hope for is that I'm actually the hero and not the geeky sidekick who ends up getting killed off in the second act.

SIXTEEN

KHALI

"THIS HAS GOT TO BE the strangest dinner I've ever experienced in my twenty years at Stonehearth's Castle." Silas laughs and takes another bite of his food, slouching across his chair like he hasn't a care in the world.

"Strange would be one way to put it," I reply.

We're at the head of the room, long tables and at least a hundred members of court stretch out before us. I fidget in Queen Brysta's old throne-like chair and try not to glower at Silas's half-witted comments. The food is much the same, buttery and rich, well seasoned and heavy. The smells of spicy meat, yeasty breads, and hearty vegetables permeate the room. Outside the black sky is sprinkled with stars.

Oh how I long to fly among them…

I study the people instead, with their buzzing background

chatter, fake smiles, and questioning eyes. And it hits me again that these are *my* people. Who else is going to protect them but their queen? The energy of the room is charged with speculation and fear. Many of the guests are the same as always but my fae friends have joined the funeral dinner tonight. I can already tell that while most people here still don't believe they belong, many are starting to get used to them, and a few seem excited by the prospect of fae at their dinner table.

Juniper sits next to Bram, a perfect match to his good looks. Her hair is down and so blonde and smooth that it reflects the candlelight. Terek and Maxx are seated farther down, flirting with a few of the courtesans who respond with both scandalized and seduced expressions. But it's none of these people that are getting to me.

They're not Aleeryrick.

The wizened sorcerer sits on my other side, magicked staff from the Jeweled Forest leaning against the table while he tackles his dinner like he hasn't eaten in ages. Who knows, maybe he hasn't. The immense magic wafting off of him is so suffocating that I can hardly eat a single bite. Not only does it remind me of the magic I've lost, but it seems to invade my space, and it especially likes Silas's necklace. The thing is freezing cold again, any colder it would burn my throat. I breathe through the sting of it, trying to focus on the conversations going on around me, especially the ones including Aleeryrick and especially not those between or about Bram and Juniper. I don't want to hear them flirting, even if it's for show.

To see them together hurts me but the idea that something real may come out of it absolutely breaks me. Even though Bram and I can never be together. Even though I've already decided I'll never be alone in a room with him again. Even though I know he deserves to be happy and Juniper is beautiful and spirited and can offer him all her attention. All that, and it still leaves my heart scattered across this castle like broken glass.

Bram is drawn to Juniper because of her healing abilities, but what if it turns into more? What if it turns into lust? Love? Marriage. I'll have to witness every stage of their relationship.

By this point I'm staring at the couple and Bram catches me, his eyes growing pensive. I can't look away. But then Juniper turns to me too and I force myself to refocus on my food.

Juniper isn't so bad. This isn't her fault. Gods, I wish she'd been able to help Bellflower Blossom. I'd love to see my feisty pixie friend here too and my heart still hurts every time I think about her. Silas didn't even care when he murdered her, it was like she meant nothing to him. More than anything I'd love to yell at Silas and embarrass him in front of everyone here, but I daren't. My fae friends might mean as little to him as Bellflower Blossom did. Not to mention, my parents aren't far away. He could blackmail me with them anytime he wants, just like his father did.

I scoff to myself. It seems Bram's been allowed to show his face lately but my father still hasn't. Not that I care to have my father embedded in this mess; he's safer in his chamber. But his absence is one more strike against Silas, and proof that he'll manipulate people and situations to better suit him, and cares little for the benefit of others.

"How are you enjoying your roasted beef, Your Majesty?" Aleeryrick asks, raising a bushy eyebrow. A ruthless glint flashes in his muddy eyes as he studies me. "You've barely touched it. Has something stolen your appetite?"

The necklace burns even colder. He knows it's him, doesn't he? He knows how much he scares me and this is his way of letting me know that he's fine with frightening me. He has no problem with it at all, in fact, he enjoys it.

"I can't eat when I'm sad," I respond.

"And what are you sad about?" His mouth thins.

"King Titus's death and the funeral, of course."

His eyes narrow. "Of course."

Dinner continues, stilted, uncomfortable, with surface level conversation and everything I want to say left brewing underneath. It goes by too slow and once it's finally over, Silas asks Aleeryrick to join him in his parlor. He doesn't ask me; in fact, he encourages me to visit my parents.

So I smile and agree with Silas like the sweet little wife he wants me to be, but I don't seek out my parents. After the guards and Faros have walked me back to my chamber, I close myself inside, and hurry through to press my ear to the door leading into our shared sitting room. It's quiet; nobody's there. I creep in and find the room empty so I go to Silas's room next, also empty, then his own private parlor, but still nobody is there. Knowing what I have to do, I sneak to the bookshelf. It's already open a crack so I slide it back a little more and slip inside.

I haven't been in these tunnels since Bram and I ran away from Drakenon weeks ago and I've been wanting to pursue what Bellflower said. So much has happened in the last few months but the tunnels feel the same. Now they're an old friend I'm not sure I can trust anymore. They're low and winding, some built into the castle, like this one, but many run underneath the castle itself and out into the town or beyond the village wall. I am convinced I don't know them all. Owen and I were fantastic at journeying through them but the one I'm sneaking through at the moment is entirely new to me.

And it's also pitch black. I don't have elements at my disposal like so many times before. I can't just light a flame in my hand. It hurts my heart to know that my favorite part of myself, the thing that made me me, has disappeared.

Don't give up, Khali, I tell myself.

I'm forced to use my hands to navigate my way down the dark tunnel, hoping I don't injure myself or run into someone or worse. The risk is worth it if I can find Silas and that creepy sorcerer. I don't know how to get my magic back yet, but putting one foot in front of the other is better than not taking any steps at all. So I wind my way farther and farther through the tunnel, and when I nearly miss a step, I catch my breath and find stairs. Down, down, down I go as my heart thunders in my ears and my limbs shake. I've never been so vulnerable in my entire life but I keep going. My eyes stay open despite the darkness and I listen attentively despite the sound of my heartbeat thudding in my ears.

Finally, I hear voices ahead. The unmistakable smooth timbre of Silas's demanding drawl and the gravelly tone of Aleeryrick's intonations. I let out a sigh of relief and I freeze, the relief evaporating because now what?

I sneak closer until I'm at the opening to a room forged

from the stone like a man-made cave and lit by torches on the walls. And then I see them.

"What can I do to get you to undo my father's bargain?" Silas asks.

"Your father and his father and many before that have kept me hidden away," Aleeryrick says bluntly. "They told me I'd prefer it that way but in actuality they wanted their secret hidden. It was always better that the bordering wards were shrouded in mystery, it gave them more of an edge over the other dragon clans."

"So you want prestige?" Silas asks with a sly smile. "Done. Live here. Work at my right hand. I would be happy to welcome you into my family."

The sorcerer scoffs and there's a stretch of silence. "Have you collected the assets?"

"All but one," Silas replies, "but it will be here soon."

"Soon had better mean within days," Aleeryrick snaps. "The Occultists are close to taking down the border. I can feel it."

"Your magic is superior to theirs," Silas is quick to placate. "But yes, she'll be here soon."

She?

The sorcerer clicks his tongue but says nothing more.

"So what about if I have a daughter..." Silas seems nervous.

"How can we negotiate a better deal on her behalf?"

Confusion wraps around me in a vice at this question and my breath catches.

The sorcerer laughs. "Maybe we should ask your wife about it?"

I shudder.

"She doesn't remember and she doesn't need to," Silas growls.

"Really? Because I'd like to enlighten her."

"No."

Something snags me—an unseen hand. I cry out as I'm dragged forward from the darkness and into the light of the caverned room. The sorcerer gazes at me like he knew I was listening in on them all along. I come to a halt a mere foot away from them. I still can't move. It must be his magic that pulled me in here, that's binding me now. Silas's stormy eyes are round and anger thins his mouth.

"Khali," Aleeryrick purrs. "It's so nice of you to join us."

"No," Silas snaps again. "She doesn't need to know. And you made a bargain with my father. You break it now and you break all of it."

The sorcerer only shrugs and says, "Sorry, Silas, but I don't see it that way. You know how bargains work, don't you? It doesn't matter that your father is dead. It still holds."

And then I'm surrounded by bright white. I shield my eyes as my memories, the ones I didn't even know had been taken from me, come flooding back like scorching water being dumped over my body.

It was a few years ago, right before Dean was exiled. There had been a tournament to join the king's army and I had entered myself under an alias and tried to win it. But things had gone wrong, *really wrong*. My powers were so much stronger than anyone had anticipated and I'd revealed myself in a way that undermined the throne.

King Titus was beyond furious. He'd dragged me, along with Dean, Owen and Silas, north to see Aleeryrick. It was there that Titus and the sorcerer made a bargain to erase the memories of my show of power from myself and from all the people of Drakenon, except for the few others who were in the room that day. In exchange, if I ever had a daughter, she would become Aleeryrick's apprentice. I'd fought against the bargain, tried to get away from the spell, but everything had gone blank the moment my memories had been stripped from me. We'd returned to the castle and that was that.

It's not until this very moment that I remember what happened to me—remember how my memories and choices had been violated.

But Owen? Silas? Dean? *They all knew…*

It was shortly after that experience that Dean was exiled. And then Owen had asked me to sneak out with him so I could train and get stronger. He'd risked everything to help me. And Silas? He'd gone right along with keeping me from knowing the truth of my abilities, even at the expense of my future daughter, someone he wanted to father.

"I remember it all now… and the looks on your faces." My voice is hollow. Titus, satisfied. Aleeryrick triumphant. And Owen? He'd been horrified, while Dean was sickened, Silas was unfeeling, and Bram wasn't even there at all.

"Khali—" Silas warns.

I blink and the whiteness and hot pain of the memories clears, making way for savage anger.

"How could you!" I snarl at the sorcerer, pointing at his smug expression. "You can't have her."

The vile man raises a white eyebrow. "I can and I will."

"Over my dead body," I hiss. "That wasn't King Titus's child to bargain away."

"And besides," Silas adds more calmly. "You don't have a deal anymore now that you've returned her memories. You broke your side of the bargain."

"Titus never said I couldn't return the memories." Aleeryrick smiles ruefully. "He only said that I had to take them away in the first place, which I did."

"You disgust me," I snarl.

He slams the staff into the dirt floor and the gems embedded into the wood light up like how they were in the Jeweled Forest. "You two act like an apprenticeship with me won't be an honor to your future child. Believe me, it will. Don't you want the most powerful child in all of Eridas to be yours?"

"No," Silas and I say in unison.

I gape at Silas, expecting to see the same outrage on his face as mine. But outrage isn't what I find there. It's fear and intimidation and jealousy. My mouth goes dry. Silas doesn't want anyone to be more powerful than him, not even his own child. What would he do to her? Would he hurt her? The answer is yes, I know it deep down. *I know it.* Lust for power can damage a soul, and Silas is the prime example.

"It's no matter," Aleeryrick sighs. "What's done is done and can't be undone. And anyway, you have to worry about the Occultists now, don't you? They're close." He turns to me, eyes narrowing and expression becoming accusatory. "And you, my dear, don't actually have the magic needed to stop them."

Silas gazes at me with a question in his eyes but I don't know what to say or what to do. I stand there, hopeless, because the sorcerer is right.

"What do you mean?" Silas questions.

Rather than let Aleeryrick explain, I decide to confess. "My magic and my dragon disappeared on my eighteenth birthday." I lock eyes with Silas and let out a bitter laugh as I step forward, our faces inches apart. The drafty room grows unimaginably still. "I wonder, Dear Husband, if you'd known you were about to wed a girl who was no longer Dragon Blessed, would you have gone through with it?"

For once in his life, Silas can't think of anything to say.

SEVENTEEN

HAZEL

AS SOON AS NIGHT FALLS, we find a clearing of trees and get to work building the altar. Every few minutes I turn and peer into the darkness because that prickling feeling that someone might be watching us refuses to go away. The Occultists are looking for us—I can feel it like I can feel the bitter air nipping at my skin.

We don't speak a word, moving as quietly as we can. The plan is to pay homage to the four directions, as well as Father Sky and Mother Earth, and the elements. In doing so, our spell will hopefully spark to life. Dean piles round, icy rocks on top of each other like Harmony had instructed. Once he's done, I start with the elemental items—the dash of water, the long thin feather for air, the little flame of fire, the handful of earth; and for spirit—a piece of charcoal that once Dean lights with his magic, smokes and crackles. I stare at the items atop the stones and turn to Dean.

He clasps my hand and I speak, my voice barely above a whisper. The words feel silly at first, foreign and ridiculous, but I push through because I need to get it right.

"North, South, East, and West. New beginnings with the rising sun. Peaceful endings with the dusk. Mother Earth and Father Sky, Ancestral spirits, and all the elements, I ask thee to lead me to my closest family."

Family…

What a loaded word. I've only ever considered my mom to be my family. I don't have any *real* family here in this strange place, but Harmony says Faeries are one big clan and my blood is half fae so I'll belong and I'm theirs. I hope they see it that way. I'm also half dragon, a hybrid, different, grown up in the human realm. What if they turn me away? Or what if the spell doesn't even work in the first place? I quickly banish the thoughts. Harmony promised. We can trust her. Right now, I need to stay focused, to believe this will lead me to the help we desperately need.

We didn't come to this kingdom without a plan and I have to cling to that. The locator spell is ancient magic, linked to the elements, and only works for those who don't wish ill on those they're trying to find.

And my heart? It beats wildly, begging to find that help—
help for me, for them, for all of us.

The smoke billows and grows, forming a long line of whitish gray, with little sparkles of magic. They remind me of stars. We watch, mesmerized, until it veers off in a strange direction, taking on a life of its own.

"This is it," Dean says. "Let's go."

He releases my hand, steps back, and shifts into his dragon form so suddenly, I don't have time to voice my fears. In fact, I don't have time to react other than grab our backpacks, climb on his scaly back, and hold on tight around his neck.

This is the plan. It's going to be okay. Breathe. Just breathe, Hazel.

He jumps into the air, wings flapping, and follows the smoke. It's so dark out, I'm surprised he can even see the smoke anymore. I keep losing sight of it myself. But that slight starry sparkle is visible to my human eyes and Dean said his eyesight is better in dragon form. They have night vision. I wonder if I will too.

I catch sight of something in the forest below us, making chase. A flash of deep red. *An Occultist!* My heart thunders and I call out to Dean, who flies even faster—impossibly fast.

The warlock is losing ground. He won't be able to keep up, not with someone as fast as Dean.

The icy wind slices past and I burrow into his back, pressing my face against his warm skin, finding his scales to be surprisingly soft compared to how they appear. I think of how Harmony told me about the spell before we left the house. It started with more history—her history. Her backstory got more and more tragic. Honestly, it was hard for me to keep it together, but I'm glad I did, I'm glad I trusted her, because so far her plan is working.

Before she left Eridas, after she lost everything and everyone she loved, she fled from the Spring Court to the Winter Court. The court hadn't fallen to the Occultists yet and they welcomed her and any other fae refugees with open arms. But did that mean they listened to her warnings? Unfortunately not.

She didn't get too far into the specifics of what happened, only that she'd had to go into hiding with a bunch of others when the Occultists came sacrificing anyone linked to elemental magic that they could find. They didn't limit the deaths to the High Fae as they'd done with other courts. No, here it was anyone and everyone, all kinds of creatures, not just the ruling class. She'd barely gotten out alive and had escaped to Summer, begging them too to heed her warnings. They'd set up a lot more precautions by then but not enough to make her feel safe, so when the Autumn Court fell, she left. By the time the Occultists arrived in Summer and had started their slaughter, she'd already gone through the portal and had her new life set up with the humans. Hers is a tragedy, a story of losing love and home, of becoming a refugee in an entirely different world, completely alone. And I can't help but wonder if we will end up the same way.

Harmony kept her secrets from me—she knew what happened to my father for one thing—but I understand her better now and why she did the things she did. Her life experiences taught her to pay closer attention to visions of the future, to stop trying to change things but to instead use her gifts to keep those she loves safe by any means possible. She's cautious about what she does, says, and when she says them. *Perfect timing*, she'd said to us last night, *is its own kind of magic, and is often more powerful than anything else in this world.*

From the way Dean follows the camouflaged smoke in the darkness of night, the locator spell must be working. A rush of nervous excitement takes over my body and I get the craziest temptation to look down. But I refuse, squeezing my eyes closed instead. We're going so fast that the Occultist doesn't have a chance of keeping up. Does he? I brave a look behind me but there is no forest. We're high in the clouds! My stomach just about drops out of my butt at that moment because *oh my heck!* This flying thing would be different if I was in my dragon form; I wouldn't be quite so freaked out. I vow here and now to try to shift again soon. I've got to get the hang of it and Harmony was right, Eridas is connecting with my magic in a way I've never felt before. It calls to it like an old friend, so natural and easy.

But this flying on Dean's back thing? Oh, this is terrifying. Almost as terrifying as going to see a bunch of fae who may hate me or may love me. But I need help and definitely need someone to train me. Harmony said the Winter Court was known for having spirit magic, far more so than any of the other kingdoms in Eridas. If there's going to be someone out there who can help me with this magic, they're probably here in this frosted world.

We race after the smoke, dropping out of the clouds and zooming right down toward a snowy forest so thick I can't imagine sunlight can make it through the branches, let alone us. The Occultist from before is long gone.

Dean speeds forward, going headlong right into the thicket of branches and I'm sure we're going to crash. Smoke may not be solid but we sure are! I squeeze tight and hold back a scream as we zip through the trees.

Wait.

Through the trees? But I didn't feel a single thing. It doesn't make logical sense. Then again, magic rarely does.

There is no forest here.

None at all.

In the darkness I can make out the outline of a village, complete with sprawling farm fields and even an old stone chapel covered in ice. This place must be surrounded by magic to make it appear as a dense forest to disguise what it truly is.

"Amazing," I murmur. And then I smile—*we freaking made it!* My smile is quickly replaced with a slice of white-hot worry *because we freaking made it* and now what? What if we're not welcomed here like we're hoping?

Dean lands in a wide open space between two homes, quiet and stealthy in his maneuvering. He crouches and I vault off his back. He shifts, smiling and pulling me into a hug. "Wow," he whispers, "That was exhilarating."

"Was it now?" a gruff voice barks from across the darkened field. We startle and turn to find a man glaring back at us as he traipses through the snow. It's pretty dark out here and he's cloaked so I don't get much of a look at him, plus I'm too distracted by the spear with the super sharp pointed end he's got a few inches from Dean's face. *Oh, crap!*

"Please," I gasp, "wait."

"We're here in peace," Dean says carefully, his voice low and even. If needed, he could wreak fire elemental havoc on this dude which would not be a good way to introduce ourselves.

"You're not welcome here," the man snaps.

I squint, trying to make out his features, but it's impossible in this light. He towers over us, his hood casting his face in shadows. But what I can tell is that this guy is broad shouldered, insanely huge, and seething mad if his fighter's stance and gritted teeth are anything to go by. Oh and the scary-sharp spear isn't too fun either!

I see all that *and* I see something else—*someone else.* Off to his right stands the ghost of a woman. She is tall and gorgeous, with bright smiling eyes, pink skin, and long flowing red hair. She nods, sending me a series of images so quickly it's like she's downloading her entire life story directly into my mind. My breath catches—she's this man's beloved wife. He lost her to the Occultists and even though the reapers are back in the supernatural spirit realm, she hasn't moved on, she won't until he's ready to let her go. Until then she refuses to leave him.

And now she wants to help me.

"Please," I try again, forcing myself to be brave. "I have a message from Penelope."

He stills, his voice growing dangerous. "What did you just say?"

I still can't see him well enough to make out his features and I have to swallow the frog that jumps in my throat. I really freaking hope I didn't sign our death certificates.

EIGHTEEN

KHALI

A FINGER TRAILS DOWN MY back and I roll toward it. My eyelids strain to open because the heaviness of sleep is too much. The glorious unconsciousness from moments before presses down and I give into it, surrendering myself to be swept away. I want to sleep, to forget everything that's happened lately. But then the finger from before becomes an arm, rocking my body in tight against another. It's so warm—*he's* so warm. I burrow against his lean chest, relaxing into him. I'm so tired; I need to sleep. I'm back in the Summer Forest with Bram and we're laying in a bed of pine needles and he's protecting me. He's—

"I need you." His voice is soft velvet against my ear.

But it's not Bram's voice.

Silas is the one holding me now. And I'm not in the forest.

I'm in my new bed.

I jolt awake.

He presses a kiss to my shoulder, then to my cheek, his lips brushing the corner of my mouth.

I rear back. "What are you doing in here?"

"What do you think?" he murmurs, moving in and pressing another kiss to my shoulder. I push him off and scramble to sit up.

"You can't sneak into my bed in the middle of the night." He shushes me with another kiss. "What did you think was going to happen?" I pull back even farther.

A long strand of blond hair falls across his eyes but he doesn't brush it away. It's too dark to see much but I know he's staring at me. He doesn't answer my question.

"And another thing," I continue, "this sorcerer friend of yours thinks he's got free reign to our future daughter, if we ever have a baby. When were you going to tell me about this?"

"*When* we have a baby." He tries to sound endearing but really he just sounds like the arrogant boy I've always known. "And he doesn't get free reign. Our first daughter would be his apprentice but you know Brightcasters rarely have girls so it's unlikely to ever happen."

Wait—*that's* his excuse?

"You believe that? This is a sorcerer we're talking about. If

I get pregnant, he'll probably spell me to have a girl."

Silas shrugs.

"Ugh, I'm serious. Get out." I ball the blanket into my fist and hold it over my chest. My nightgown is too thin for comfort. "This is supposed to be my safe space. It's my bedroom and you can't just come in here whenever you'd like. You weren't invited."

"How many times have you gone into my room uninvited?" He chuckles low.

"This is different." And it is different. "You woke me up by kissing me!"

He waves me off. "I have a proposition for you."

I know I shouldn't hear him out but there's something about the way he says it that leaves me curious. "What?"

He sits closer until his knees are pressed against mine through the silken blanket. He likes being close to me, likes pushing my buttons and making me uncomfortable.

"Give me a child," he says, "a son. Secure our bloodline, and I'll not only do whatever it takes to help you get your magic back, but I'll give you your freedom too."

"Freedom?" I scoff. "What does that word even mean to someone like you?"

"It means you can do as you please around the castle. You can fly, shift, use your magic, I don't care. You can be who you've always wanted to be."

I pause, rolling the proposition around in my head. "Why? Why do you want a baby so bad?"

His eyes flick across my body. "More reasons than one."

My stomach hardens. Even if his bargain is enticing, I can't imagine going through with it. Not with him. "I should be able to do all those things anyway and you know it. Flying, being myself, using my magic, it's all part of my birthright as Dragon Blessed!"

"Correction, you were Dragon Blessed." He talks like this is all one big game to him. "And yet I'm the one with the power to help you or stop you."

And I hate him for it.

I grit my teeth. "I don't believe you. You won't let me do as I please. That's a lie."

He scoffs. "Well, you can't touch Bram or any other man if that's what you were hoping for."

"It wasn't." But the mere thought of being with Bram sends warmth curling through my entire body.

Silas smiles and the whites of his teeth and eyes glow in the dark. Any other girl would kill to be in this position but I know better than to trust the snake.

"Good girl," he whispers.

He acts as if I'm as physically attracted to him as he is to me.

But he's got it all wrong. The thought of being with him makes me want to claw my eyes out or vomit or a million other terrible things. I hate him. I truly do. That hate isn't going to magically turn into love or even lust just because he's good looking and an expert flirt. He can't bribe me into having children with him, even if his promises prove to be true.

"You know you want to." He edges closer.

But I don't. I really don't. Even if this is my duty as queen, even if I'm bound by oath, and eventually, I'm not going to be able to say no anymore. This standoff can't last forever, not with a man like Silas.

"What about the sorcerer?" I ask. "We can't have a child and risk it being a girl. You need to find a way to get rid of Aleeryrick before I could ever agree to this."

"Hmm, you and I think more alike than you realize." He runs a finger along my bare knee. "We're good for each other, you know."

"And why's that?"

"We're powerful. We're intellectually matched. And guess what?" He leans forward and whispers. "I hate that sorcerer too, but unlike you, I know how to play the long game."

"And what game is that?"

He cups my chin. He's so close now. He smells of citrus tonight, and of an impending storm. "I have a plan to get what we need from him and then get rid of him for good."

"How very Silas Brightcaster of you."

He laughs and lets me go.

"I'm not making this deal. You can leave now."

He tilts his head at me, unconvinced. "And what about your magic? How does it just disappear overnight like that? Poof! There's something you're not telling me."

My body grows cold. I don't want to tell him about Hazel because somehow I know if he believes she's standing in our way, he'll find her and kill her without a second thought. So instead I tug on the necklace. "Don't you think this is making things worse?" I hold it up. My eyes have finally adjusted to the darkness enough that I can make out the glint of the dragon engraved on the silver. My bad human eyes are one more reminder of the dragon self that I've lost. "You have this thing on me. Aleeryrick made it, didn't he?"

It's a guess, but I know Silas had someone make it for him and he swore it wasn't an Occultist back when I challenged him on it in the Summer Forest. This is the best explanation. Silas reaches for my face, and I think he's going to try to kiss me again, which I'm not going to allow. I tense, lips sealed. "Just hold on, will you?" He grabs hold of the necklace, not me, and leans in closer. The cord strains against my neck.

"One kiss on the lips," he says. "One kiss and I'll take it off."

I turn my head away. "No."

I expect him to be angry or to laugh, what I don't expect is for him to remove the necklace anyway. It falls from my skin and I gasp, leaning back against the bed frame, rubbing my neck.

"Consider this a measure of my good faith," he says, "and my trust in you to do the right thing."

My hands clench into fists against my chest because what does he know of doing the right thing?

"Thank you." I force myself to say, voice hoarse. I don't know what this means except that Silas is trying to buy my trust and at least for tonight, he's not going to force me to try and make a child with him.

"But remember I can put this back on you anytime I need." He squeezes the silver pendant into his palm. His voice turns to liquid silver. "It's mine. Don't try to take it from me again or more than a useless pixie will get hurt."

He wants me to trust him, to sleep with him, to go along with his plans, but he doesn't want me to ever forget that he can control me. Not only me, this kingdom. "What a cruel thing to bring up right now. She was my friend."

"Sometimes cruelty gets things done."

"And sometimes so does kindness."

He shrugs. "Maybe, but I prefer guarantees. Speaking

of which," he continues. "You and I are going to have to work together whether you like it or not. And I'm not just talking about children, I'm talking about the Occultists and Aleeryrick. They think we're a weak kingdom but we're two of the last ones standing for a reason. I intend to take it all."

"Take it all? What does that mean?"

But I think I already know…

He pauses for a second, his eyes filling with lust and greed. He wants to tell me something but it's as if he's trying to talk himself out of it.

"Tell me, Silas," I say, "you know I'll figure it out soon anyway. Wouldn't you rather be the one to tell me what you're planning?"

That does the trick.

"Drakenon will conquer all of Eridas and I will rule…" His eyes grow hungry. "And you, Wife, will be at my side."

Silence stretches between us. I want to say the right thing, the cunning thing, but I can't speak anything other than the truth. "I always knew you were a greedy bastard but this is too far."

"You'll understand one day," he sighs. "Besides, if we don't take care of Eridas then the Occultists will eradicate it."

"Nothing will ever be enough for you."

"The Sovereign Occultists did the dirty work but I'm

going to finish the job. And you'll see, Khali, when all is said and done, *that I was right.*"

"Right? You're talking about reigning over the fae kingdoms."

"Their royal lines are all dead," he replies simply, "and it only makes sense that we step in and rule. We'll be fair to them and it will be for the best. The Gods want this, Khali, I can feel it."

This is crazy. He's talking about the very thing that has made the Occultists evil. I let out a slow breath. "Let's say you're right and we are meant to rule over Eridas, which I don't agree with, by the way, how do you actually think you're going to pull that off?"

He leans in and plants a quick kiss on my forehead. "Have you ever known me to not have a plan?" He gets up then, climbing from the bed. "If I'm going to trust you, it's your turn to trust me." He leaves my room without a backwards glance or another word. But he's right, he's never been someone to not have a plan, and that's exactly what scares me the most. That and the fact that he seems to think I'm going to help him accomplish his selfish goals.

My fingers trace the space where the necklace used to be and I suddenly feel more lost than ever. Silas brought up Bellflower Blossom which reminds me of what she told me before she died; that there's something in the dungeons, something Silas is hiding. Whatever it is, I need to get back to the tunnels, find my way to those dungeons, and figure out Silas's secret.

NINETEEN

HAZEL

"TELL ME! TELL ME HOW you know her name," the man growls, prodding his spear at me now instead of Dean. Dean growls, moving his weight to shield me.

My throat goes dry but I force her name out anyway. "Penelope wants me to give you a message. And she wants to make sure you're okay."

He juts his head back and the hood of his black cloak falls. The moonlight catches the planes of his face, his pointed elf ears, his graying black hair tied back in a knot. "How dare you speak her name? What do you know? Who are you?" With each question his spear gets closer and closer. Dean tenses and I know it won't be long until there are fireballs in his palms. I have to stop this.

I raise my hands, deciding to be as honest as possible.

"My name is Hazel Forrester. I'm a hybrid between a dragon shifter and a faerie. I was born with the spirit element and can see some of the people in the spirit realm. Your deceased wife is here right now."

The spear wobbles and he lowers it ever so slightly. Nobody speaks. A gust of wind kicks up snow, in the distance an owl hoots. The cold wraps itself around me but I don't dare move. "C'mon then," he says at last, his voice still guarded. "What's the message from my Penelope?"

I can tell he doesn't quite believe me but he wants to. He won't let himself, which is understandable for anyone. I probably look like a crazy girl, what with my black jeans and puffer coat, hair pulled back in a basic ponytail. I'm not from here, that much is clear. Either way, I must prove myself to him right here and now or else things are going to get bad real fast.

I clear my throat. "She wants you to know it's not your fault that she died and you need to stop blaming yourself."

His mouth hardens. "I'm not going to listen to this crap."

The woman sends another image to my mind and then I hear her voice telling me exactly what to say.

"She says that whenever you see an ice butterfly, she wants you to think of her. She knows you already do, but she wants you to know that she knows."

An ice butterfly is exactly what it sounds like from the image she's showing me, all crystalline and fluttery. I'd love to see one in real life but considering this memory is rather spectacular, I'll take it.

The elf steps back, his face clearing of anger and filling with something else entirely: grief, despair, hope... "You really can see her, can't you? How does she look? Is she okay?"

I nod and study the woman hovering next to him. She smiles. "Yes, I can and she's okay. If they're not able to move on because of something bad in their lifetime, I can usually see that by how they appear to me. But she looks great. She really does. She's beautiful, for starters. Super tall. Rosy cheeks against pink skin. Deep brown eyes. Long red hair. It's so pretty, the color of a candied apple."

"What's a candied apple?"

"Oh sorry." I smile. "This is my first time in Eridas since I was a baby. I grew up in the human realm and it's something they do there. They take like this liquid sugary stuff, it's bright red candy, and they pour it—"

"Hazel," Dean cuts me off.

"You're from the human realm?" The man's voice turns sour once again. "Well, I guess that explains your attire. But then you better have a good reason for why in the hell you'd come here?" He raises the spear. *Oh crap on a cracker,*

I overshared!

Dean growls.

I can hear Penelope and the sass in her voice. It makes me smile. I repeat what she says word for word. "Your wife says to tell you, Gregory, cut it out, leave the poor girl alone. It's not like you aren't a refugee yourself now. You have no right to judge her…" My voice trails off and my cheeks warm.

"You know my name?"

"Your wife does," Dean interjects. "Hazel's already explained."

Desperation washes over me. We need help—refuge. We need to be welcomed here. The gusty wind builds and I begin to shiver. Dean immediately grabs my hand to warm me.

"Please? What do I have to do to convince you?" I beg. "Penelope showed me everything. You met when you were children, you and your father used to travel to trade with Spring where she lived. You fell in love with her and when you were old enough, you went back on your own and convinced her to marry you. You lived here in Winter. You never had any children, though you both wanted them, and maybe given enough time it would have happened, but the Occultists came and took her away. You blame yourself but she doesn't want you to do that anymore. She says they caught almost everyone and you couldn't have known they'd get her too. She's so glad you're alive and wants you to be happy."

"I think I've heard enough." Gregory's voice is hollow. He's closer now, close enough that I can see tears have welled up in his wide eyes. "I believe you. Follow me."

He turns and traipses toward one of the little houses, throwing open a door like he's taking out all his sadness on the poor rusty hinges. "It's been empty for a while. Sorry about the dust. You can stay here tonight and in the morning we can work out what to do about you. The others aren't going to like this, you know."

Relief settles over me. This is a start. "But you believe me about Penelope?"

He sighs. "Unfortunately, I do. And you can tell Penelope to stop telling me what to do. If I want to go on blaming myself for the rest of my life then I damn well can do as I please."

Penelope stands behind him and she laughs, throwing her head back, her red curls dancing as her body shakes.

"She's laughing at you, like full body laughing."

He shrugs, the corner of his burly mouth slipping into a smile. "Yeah, I'm not surprised. That girl always had the loudest laugh. It was annoying." She shoots him a mocking look. "But cute. I loved it. I loved her. Still do."

Dean and I study the small one-roomed cottage, taking in the dust and mildew, the sparse furniture and tiny windows.

Gregory throws the door closed, locking us in. Not that I'm worried: what's a lock going to do against a couple of dragons? He probably already knows the lock isn't worth much. Maybe the lock isn't to keep us in but to keep others out? I shiver at the thought. Not to mention, it's nearly as cold in here as it is outside but Dean makes quick work of the fireplace and before long we're toasty and at least the wind is gone.

Penelope still hangs out in the corner, watching me with curious eyes. I set down my backpack and let out a strangled breath. "Why are you still here?" I ask her. "In the supernatural spirit realm, I mean. Why haven't you moved on to the next place?"

At first I couldn't move on, she sighs, her voice filtering through my mind. I still find it strange that the spirits can talk to me now, it's going to take some getting used to.

But she's also… different.

She's so real compared to the spirits I see in the human realm and all I can think is the magic of Eridas must have something to do with that, too.

None of us could move on for a long time because the reapers were gone and the Occultists… She pauses for a while and I almost expect her to disappear, but then she looks back at me, brown eyes shining. *Anyway, now that the reapers are back, I suppose I'm still not ready to go. I need Gregory to stop blaming himself before I can leave him.*

I scoff but offer her a grin and a raised eyebrow. "Well, I don't think that's going to happen. He seems way too stubborn."

She shrugs, her white gown glinting under an unseen light. *Oh he is, but so am I. If I have to wait for him to pass on before I go, that's just as well. Honestly, I'd rather go to whatever is next with him than without him.*

I nod, because I get it. It would be hard for me too. But I also think it would be too hard to stick around watching people live a life when you can't have one of your own. "You don't know what's next?"

No. Do you?

I shake my head. "Heaven, maybe? I don't know. I hope it's good."

She full body laughs again. *Same!*

"How am I going to win these people over?" I ask.

Same as you did Gregory, she replies. *Help them communicate with whoever is still waiting around for them. They'll love you for it.*

"I don't think you could call that winning Gregory over."

She raises a delicate eyebrow. *Oh no? Because I would. If he didn't like you, you wouldn't be here right now. You'd have your memories wiped clean and would be off wandering around Winter until the Occultists found you. You probably wouldn't even be able to remember your own name.*

My face falls and my body goes cold. The very idea that someone could magic me to forget who I am makes me want to get out of here. My family has been through enough of that kind of tampering, thank you very much! "Well, I guess that means you trust me if you're telling me all this."

She shrugs a round shoulder. *Who else is going to help me?*

"What's wrong?" Dean asks, his stance growing protective. "What is the spirit saying?"

It's okay, Penelope says, *you can tell him.*

So I repeat what she said about Gregory's magic.

He's worried, I can see it in the way his black eyes spark with flames and the room warms by another few degrees. "It's a rare magic and obviously useful, probably the same thing used to protect this little village from the outside world and keep it hidden."

"She says I can win these people over by doing the same thing I just did for Gregory."

"And you can." Dean wraps me in a warm hug and presses a kiss to my forehead "But if it doesn't work, I'll get you out of here before they can hurt us."

He sounds so confident but I know he's not. How can he

be? If someone wipes our memory, we're as good as dead.

But it turns out that Penelope is right.

The next morning Gregory takes us around the enchanting stone village to meet a myriad of fae: elves, faeries, pixies, a few guarded centaurs, and a handful of creatures that I have no clue what they are and I'm too polite to ask. We introduce ourselves over and over again as I work my magic on anyone who has a hanger-on in the spirit realm. Turns out a lot of these people lost loved ones to the Occultists. It doesn't take long for news of us to spread and Dean and I are welcomed into the community.

After many hours of this, I'm emotionally exhausted and physically worn down, but I don't stop until everyone has their chance. We go from house to house, Gregory at our side. Finally, on the way out of the last house, I confide in Gregory about why we've come here. "We needed a place to hide out for a few days. But there's more…"

He looks at me sideways, the lines around his eyes deepening. "Out with it," he says gruffly.

"I need to train with someone who has spirit magic. That's why Harmony sent me here, she said the Winter Court was known for it."

"Harmony?" He stops abruptly, his brown eyes widening and his mouth turning up at the corners into a happy grin.

It's the lightest I've seen him all day. Dean and I exchange an optimistic glance. "You know Harmony? Why didn't you say something earlier?"

And then, he does something I never expected. He pulls me into a barrel hug, lifting me off the ground as I squeak.

"You should have started with that!" He laughs.

Well, I guess we're idiots because that sure would have been easier than a day spent communing with the dead. But then again, it was worth the hard work to see the looks on people's faces when they realized I was for real.

"Knowing you're friends of Harmony means you're friends of ours. A lot of us knew Harmony when she lived in our court. And let me tell you something about that faerie, to know her is to love her."

I grin, thinking back on all that she's done for me. "I would have to agree with that statement."

"Everyone is going to be pleased to hear she's still alive. We assumed she'd died like so many others."

We talk about Harmony for a while and about all their good times together. This carries on as we walk from one end of the village, to the other, back toward the little hovel Dean and I are camping out in.

I squint, noticing a quaint stone cottage on the far edge of the community.

"We never visited there. Do you think they'll want to meet me?"

"I'm sure, but actually, I think Opal is the one you want to meet." Gregory forges ahead, passing our place and continuing to the cottage. "She's the other fae with spirit elemental."

"And by other one, you mean besides you?" Dean questions.

Gregory hums to himself. "Well, what I can do is linked to spirit, but it's nothing like what Hazel can do, or Opal for that matter." He points around the village. "All of this is protected because of her. She's the one who can keep us hidden. We'd be lost without her," his voice grows weary, "or more likely dead."

Our boots crunch against the snow as we head over. Nobody speaks. Finally, I can't help but ask. "What can she do?"

"It's something to do with memories and vision but I don't know all the details and I don't ask. Not my business. The little girl is… sweet. But she's also… a lot."

Girl? A little girl can do all that?

"This is where I'll leave you." He stops about a hundred yards from the house. "Good luck."

Umm, okay?

Dean and I cross the field, approaching the cottage with nerves flying.

"You sure about this?" he questions. He's always asking me that lately and I have to laugh.

"What?"

"Nothing, you're cute."

He frowns at that.

I shake out my hands and then ball them into fists to keep from fidgeting. "Yup, we gotta do this. We didn't come all this way for nothing."

I stare up at the cottage. It's adorable and made of stone and log, reminding me of a smaller version of Harmony's house back in West Virginia. The trees around the cottage twist in unearthly angles, spiraling in and around themselves. Sparkly white ice is crystallized across every surface, tiny snowflakes that don't melt when you touch them, not even for Dean. The flowers are like how they were back in the forest, a mix of beautiful pastels that look like they've been magicked to stay alive in the cold. We make it to the front door and knock.

It swings open right away.

Okay, first of all, this girl doesn't look like someone to worry about. Not at all. If she were human, I'd say she couldn't be more than thirteen or fourteen years old, but I know age works differently for the fae. She's an elf, with cute pointy ears and gold and silver earrings pierced up and down each one. Her skin is deep brown, eyes are sky blue, hair long and stick straight and white as the snow surrounding us. She's dressed in a midnight blue velvet dress and matching cape with silver embroidery around the edges. In a word, she's stunning.

She jumps forward, crushing me into a hug. It's so unexpected, I nearly fall backward.

"I'm so glad you're here," her wispy voice gushes. "I heard them talking about you in the village this morning when I went to get some eggs. Another spirit elemental! Finally! I've always been the only one, you know. Well, besides Gregory, but that man isn't exactly the most chatty with me if you know what I mean."

"Umm, hi." I peel myself out of her arms and smile brightly. "I'm Hazel and this is Dean."

Dean raises a hand.

"You're gorgeous." She gives him a wink and then another one to me. "Lucky girl. Of course it would be a girl that would bring him back out of hiding. You're the exiled prince aren't you? You are, I can tell."

Dean stiffens but doesn't move. She's the first fae to point out who he is and if she knows, it stands to reason others here might recognize him too. I wonder why nobody else said anything. Maybe they didn't know *what* to say.

"I was wondering if you could help me train." I take a deep breath and get right to the point. "I have spirit magic and can see the other realms but I can also turn into a spirit dragon, which is new for me. I don't really know what I'm doing but I have to figure it out like, yesterday."

She laughs. "Right. Well, we can start that part tomorrow." She pulls us inside her home as she keeps babbling. Her house is as cute as she is, small and cozy, with warm colors decorating the space. I catch a whiff of sage and immediately think of Harmony. "Today I want you to tell me all about the humans. You grew up in their realm, right? What's it like out there? I've never left this little bubble, you know? I have to stay and keep everyone safe. Can't leave." She lets out a breath. "Nobody else can do it. It's all on me." She grins again. "But I secretly love the attention."

I don't even know what to say, not that I can get a word in. Maybe *this* is why Gregory didn't want to join us. Not because there's something to fear about the girl but because she's got a huge personality for someone as quiet and broody as Gregory.

"I'll help you, Hazel," she babbles on, "but only if we talk first, okay? I have so many questions. I mean, you're from Spring I hear but grew up in the human realm which is wow, just wow. I'm not kidding, when I say I have questions, I mean I have a million and one questions. Maybe more!"

That makes me laugh. "You and me both."

TWENTY

KHALI

"SOMETHING ISN'T RIGHT," I WHISPER, leaning over the back of the couch between Terek and Maxx. We're in the queen's sitting room attempting to enjoy an afternoon tea service. Mother and Faros forced me to invite a handful of the higher ranking ladies and socialites to tea but I insisted on inviting my friends along as well. The food is as garish as the decor, with little cakes in every color, and the conversation is as fake as most of the company, but at least I have Terek's playful anecdotes to entertain me and get my mind off of everything. Thoughts of the arrival of the sorcerer and unraveling of my hidden memories pester me constantly. "I need to know why Aleeryrick is really here."

Terek looks at me sidelong underneath his dark lashes and raises an eyebrow. "Well, isn't that the understatement of the century?"

I need to go back to my seat soon but I can't help myself and lean in farther, quieting my voice even more. "Did something happen?"

The four other ladies are busy chatting with my mother but that doesn't mean some of them might not be trying to eavesdrop.

"Most people we've met aren't happy we're here," Maxx says. He takes an awkward sip of tea. His hand is twice the size of the delicate teacup and I almost laugh.

Mother shoots me a scandalized glare and I kind of want to slap her but she's right and I should sit down and be the good queen she taught me to be, but why? I'm so tired of the games. This is my life and she already got what she wanted, didn't she? I blame this sudden need to glare back at her on our old feelings. Or maybe on the fact that she's beginning to return to her old self now that father is doing better. Her and Faros insisted that only ladies be invited but I'm queen, aren't I? There's not a lot I can control at the moment but inviting my male friends is one of them.

"Why didn't Juniper come?" I ask. I thought for sure she'd take me up on the invitation considering she actually *is* a female and looks the part of a lady.

Maxx grumbles and sets his teacup down, folding his

arms over his chest and leaning back in his chair.

"Let's just say Juniper has been spending a lot of time with the little princeling." Terek waggles his eyebrows and my heart sinks.

"Oh." I don't have to ask, I know he means Bram.

"I don't know who's more upset about it, you or Maxx?" He grins.

I turn to my horned friend. "You like Juniper?"

His tanned skin turns the sweetest shade of pink and before he can answer, one of the more troublesome ladies pipes in from across the room.

"Are you enjoying your stay here at Stoneshearth?" The woman directs her question to Terek and Maxx. I take that as my cue to return to my chair.

The woman is older, closer to my mother's age, and I don't know her too well, though I've seen her flit about Queen Brysta often. I wonder if she even cares about the previous queen now that I've taken her place. Her name is Duchess Dasha. She's married to one of the more ambitious dukes in the kingdom and her daughter is the fifteen year old girl I saw kissing Silas before I ran away.

I give the woman a disinterested glower. I don't know if Silas is still having an affair with her daughter and I honestly don't want to know. Actually, I take that back. I hope they're still involved. Someone needs to keep him busy and *she* actually wants him.

Maxx and Terek answer the duchess's question in predictable fashion, complimenting the staff and the accommodations, but there's a resentful undertone to the direction of the conversation that worries me. Something is off but it's more than just hateful looks and snide comments. Most of the court aren't happy to have the fae here and they're even more upset by the sorcerer, but it's not these people that any of us need to be worried about.

It's Silas and his ambitions and his plan that are the problems.

Why would he be so welcoming to the fae? He never made the bargain to keep them around and well taken care of, that was all Titus. So what's Silas's endgame? Who's going to get hurt? Because someone always does…

"We've been talking with the king," Terek responds to some underhanded comment from Duchess Dasha about foreigners in the court. "He's invited us to bring anyone we know back home out of hiding to live in Drakenon."

I cough into my teacup. They all turn to look at me and I motion for them to carry on.

"Of course, that would take great time and a whole lot of convincing," Maxx adds with a sarcastic laugh. "Most of the fae don't trust dragons any better than the Occultists."

Terek clears his throat and the room falls into a moment of stunned silence. To compare us to them is a low blow.

But… I understand. Our peoples have been contentious for over a century.

"Well, I for one believe our king to be generous and wise." Dasha smiles through her thin lips and I'm pretty sure she's lying through her teeth.

"Generous is one way to put it," I whisper into my teacup but nobody hears.

My friends are smart enough to know they can't bring any more fae here, not with the Occultists closing in, and not with a king nobody can trust. I haven't told them that Silas is bound and determined to not only destroy the warlocks but to take over all of Eridas when he's done. There are so many things I want to warn them about but I can't with all these listening ears. So instead I ask Dasha, "Wouldn't that be nice to have so many more fae friends in our castle? They are such fun."

It forces another nod of agreement from the lady and I smile. *Liar.*

I inspect my friends. "But you ought to hold off moving anyone until you are sure they would be happy here." Happy is a synonym for safe.

"Oh but you must be missing them terribly," my mother interjects. She straightens her shoulders and brushes back a strand of dark hair. I eye her warily, hoping she's not back to her usual scheming.

"We do." Maxx nods.

"So why don't you leave and go back to them?" Duchess Dasha asks, sweet as vinegar.

"That's enough." I shoot her the kind of look that says she better be careful. Everyone stills. "I'm not feeling well," I cut off the conversation right there. "I'm going to take a walk alone to get some fresh air. Perhaps we can do this again another time?"

I stand, brush out my coral colored skirt, and hasten for the door. I don't give them time to argue or respond.

"Would you like me to join you?" my mother asks but it's more of a statement since it's not customary for queens to walk outside alone. Not that I'll be alone, I'm sure a guard will keep watch over me. They always do.

"Not today, Mother." I stroll through the door and out into the hallway. Really, I'm hoping my friends will follow me, but they don't…

Something is wrong. Something is wrong. Something is wrong, the mantra echoes through my mind.

I need to get out of this castle, out of these stuffy rooms

and echoing corridors. I haven't even been able to search for the dungeons yet, but I can go outside, can't I? There are no rules against that.

I don't have my cloak on me but I don't care. I pass a few people on my way out of the castle who give me little bows and curious glances but I pay them no attention. It's fresh air I need and nothing else. My breath starts to come out in little bursts and the walls begin to close in around me.

The winter air jolts me awake, snapping me from my worried thoughts, and I suck in a deep breath. Relief sweeps through my body. I head around the back of the castle to the gardens, my favorite spot. Not too far behind, the guards linger—ever watchful.

The garden is quiet this time of year, which I appreciate. In the warmer months it's always filled with people milling about, showing off their gowns, gossiping, admiring the floral smells and array of flowers. Last time I was here was with Bram, just over a week ago, but it feels like an eternity with everything that's happened.

I enter the labyrinth. The hedges are sparse but I know the maze well and it gives me something to do. The snow is hard and icy. It crunches easily under my boots. The guards wait at the entrance.

A few minutes into my walk, the sound of another's

footsteps stop me short.

I'm not alone.

Maybe the guards decided to follow after all?

Goosebumps crawl up my arms. I hold my tongue and stay as still as possible, listening. There are voices, two male, one female, but they're quiet, whispered, hurried. I can't tell exactly who they are or what they're talking about.

I take another step forward, so softly, and cringe when the snow crunches under my shoes. The voices fall silent.

I continue walking. This is ridiculous. I shouldn't feel afraid in my own garden. This is my favorite place and I'm queen now and I'll walk through this maze if I please. I don't need to skulk around and hide in the shadows.

"Who's there?" I demand. "Show yourselves."

"Khali?"

Bram steps out from around a nearby corner, Juniper on his arm. Her rosy cheeks and pretty blonde hair make my stomach twist but I force a happy smile anyway.

"It's nice to see you." I say. "Both of you." I clear my throat. "Together."

Now I'm the liar. What am I even saying?

Bram frowns and stares at me like I've hurt him and Juniper looks at me like she's been caught. "This isn't what you think it is," he blurts.

"Who were you talking to just now? I heard another man's voice."

Bram opens his mouth to reply but Juniper beats him to it. "Nobody else," she says sharply. "Just us."

Bram pales and then stares at me hard, like he wants me to say something, to challenge them. But what? Do I accuse Juniper of lying to me? Do I tell the truth, that I hate to see them together? I'm lost for words entirely because I'm sure, certain even, that they're keeping a secret.

"We'll be on our way," Bram says, giving me a sad smile. "Take care of yourself, Khali." Just as he passes, he whispers low into my ear. "Things aren't what they seem."

"Right." My voice is clipped.

And then I brush past them, pushing through the maze and as far away from the couple as I can get. My eyes water and my heart thuds angrily. Why are they lying? And who were they talking to?

I wanted to confess Silas's plans to them, like I've wanted to with Terek and Maxx. They all need to know that Silas is bent on taking over Eridas. I hate being the only one carrying this weight.

After a few minutes, I reach the center of the maze. I turn around in a circle, looking up at the sky. Some of the dragons are out training again, they swoop and spin, black specks in a sea of blue.

A man clears his throat.

I turn with a gasp to find I'm no longer alone. I don't know this man well. Growing up I was sheltered from most of the court, especially the people who had jobs to do and weren't interested with the frivolities of court life. This man, he's one of them. I only know of him, because everyone does.

General Cardos.

A fierce dragon shifter and earth elemental, and the head of the Drakenon Army—one of the most powerful positions in the kingdom.

"You were the one talking with Bram and Juniper, weren't you?" I say, keeping my voice low.

The general doesn't look at me. He stares up at the sky, hands pulling on his lapel, and clears his throat. "Yes," he answers, voice clear and honest.

Why didn't Bram just tell me that? Maybe it's stupid, but it hurts to know he's chosen Juniper as his confidant and not me.

"You were King Titus's right hand man," I continue. "And now you're Silas's..."

"Yes." His tone is flat. I can't read him, not even a little bit.

I study his profile, the salt and pepper hair, the broad shoulders, the relaxed way he crosses the expanse and sits down on the bench. I stare at him, right in his mossy green eyes. "What was the conversation with Bram about?"

He doesn't answer. Instead, he stares right back, and my limbs start to shake.

Is he loyal to Silas? My heart speeds because somehow I think he is not. Why else would he be sneaking around in here talking with Bram? Or maybe it's me he doesn't trust? But then again, I could be jumping to conclusions. I fold my arms over my chest, warding off the shivers.

"Do you know what Silas plans to do?"

His expression turns haunted. "Yes, I do."

"You know that he wants to take over all of Eridas?" I whisper, my voice barely a breath above the slight breeze.

He winces slightly and nods.

"And do you know how he plans to do that?"

The silence grows between us and he finally answers. "That, I don't know yet. It's what I'm trying to find out. He's been in talks with the merpeople but I don't know about what exactly. Perhaps it's the portal they are sworn to protect."

I freeze. "The portal to the human realm?"

His lips thin and he nods once. The news is so great, I'm forced to sit down next to him and collect my bearings.

"Do you know his plan?" General Cardos asks. "Why else could he be talking with the merpeople?"

The merpeople scare me to death and I hate that they're

another piece in the puzzle. I turn and hold his gaze. "Not yet. But so we're clear, I don't agree with my husband's desire to take over Eridas. I don't think dragons should rule over fae or anyone else. I have to warn you he'll do anything to get his way, hurt anyone, kill anyone. Do you understand what I'm saying?"

He laughs, his stoic facade breaking the whispered silence. "Believe me, I know."

I wonder how much King Titus told this man. Titus was strict and backwards in a lot of ways but he wasn't a tyrant. He'd never have done the things Silas is doing. But then again, he knew the truth about Owen's murder and tried to hide it. Titus may be dead, but he's to blame for a lot of what's happening now.

"You better watch your back." My voice is hollow.

His mouth hardens. "Yes. And you need to take the same advice."

I don't know if it's a warning or a threat but he strides away, shifting into his dragon and taking to the sky before I can ask. His dragon joins the other black specks that cut ruthlessly into the sprinkling of gray clouds against the blue.

I know I should be feeling many things in this moment, but all I can feel is a deep, deep jealousy of those dragons because I'm still stuck down here in the center of the hedge maze.

TWENTY-ONE

HAZEL

"ARE YOU READY?" OPAL ASKS, soft pink lips grinning from where she's perched on a bench made entirely of ice. She pats the open space next to her and I join her, trying to ignore the sharp cold of it. The padding of my pillowy black coat doesn't really help all that much.

I gaze out to the horizon, to the sun rising over the snowy field and the way it paints the sky blazing pink. If hope was a color, it would be this. And if someone would have told me a few months ago that I'd be learning how to control my abilities from an elf, I'd have laughed and said they were crazy. And yet here I am, sitting at the edge of a magically hidden supernatural village with a young fae elf who looks like she's about thirteen years old, but who is probably much older, and desperate for her to help me.

"I'm ready." I clear my throat and smile. "So where do we start?"

A dimple forms on her dark brown cheek and her blue eyes sparkle against the sunlight. "Why don't you tell me about what you do know about your magic?"

This still feels crazy to even think that I have magic, but here I am! And since Opal's the only one here with the spirit element, I've got to bite the bullet and at least try. I tell her about what I see, in both the human spirit realm and the supernatural one, and what I think it means.

She stops me. "But you said your mother is a faerie and your father is a dragon shifter, so why would you be so connected to humans?"

"Maybe because I grew up in the human realm? Maybe a distant ancestor was human? Or it could be something to do with the spell the Occultists put on me? I don't know."

"You're under a spell?"

I let out a long sigh. "An Occultist linked me to the dragon princess, Khali. Our magic reacts when we're around each other, she grows weaker and I grow stronger. And from what I understand, if I die, she will die. I can't help but wonder if the spell is what's making me who I am with all this"—I wave my hands around—"giving me access to multiple spirit realms and stuff."

She ponders on that for a bit. "It is curious. Maybe it is the spell that's given you that access or maybe the explanation is simpler than that. I think it's more likely that you have human blood in you. Could be a grandparent or some ancestor who's a full-blooded human. It's rare but it happens."

I nod but it's not like I have any clue. These realms are separate but it's not like it's impossible to crossover. People who have no business falling in love with each other do it all the time. I like the idea of one of my ancestors being a regular old human.

She smiles and twists a long strand of bright white hair around her finger. "Go on." She's got rings lined up on all her fingers, piercings up and down her pointed ears, and an energy about her that is so much more mature than she looks. It's different but definitely cool.

We spend most of the morning talking through everything that's on my mind. I'm anxious for action but I force myself to be patient—not an easy task. Finally she asks me to meditate, something I don't think I've ever done with any real effort.

"Clear your mind," she says, like it's the simplest thing in the world.

Yeah, right.

It's still hard to believe that I'm here. Lucky for us, the

ghost of Penelope had been the first of many keys to unlock the doors Dean and I needed to be allowed to stay in this adorable snowy sanctuary. Pretty much all I did yesterday was connect these fae who'd passed on and relayed messages. Some people didn't have their loved ones show up, but at least I could offer them the peace of knowing their person must have moved on to a better place. And then last night Opal and I had talked well past nightfall, becoming instant friends. We'd gotten up first thing in the morning to practice my magic, when she'd insisted I'd be stronger from rest.

"Do you see anything?" Opal interrupts. "Or perhaps feel anything interesting?"

"Uhhh…" My face reddens and my eyes pop open. "Sorry, I sort of got busy thinking about other things and forgot what I was supposed to be doing."

Opal rolls her eyes and giggles sweetly, and I'm suddenly so grateful that she is the one training me and not any of the others. She's kind but more importantly she's not intimidating. So many of the others are intimidating, older, war-torn, hardened… set in their ways. Opal is the opposite of those things. She's relaxed and fun, smart but doesn't take herself too seriously. Kind of like me.

"Sorry," I sigh. "I woke up this morning super worried about my friends and family. I've got to do what I came to do. I need to train and learn to grow my spirit abilities so that I can confidently shift again. I believe you about this meditation stuff, and about this realm being easier to work in than the human one, but my mind is struggling to catch up."

"I'm going to ask you something and you have to promise not to take it personally."

"Umm—okay." *This doesn't sound good.*

"Have you always struggled with self confidence?"

And now I feel like I'm talking to a therapist. "Well shoot, you don't hold back, do you? Yeah, I guess I've always had a hard time with it."

She clasps my hands into hers and stares me down with an arched eyebrow. "Forget about your past for a minute and give yourself credit for where you are." She motions around the village, with its frosted and enchanted coating over everything. "You're in Eridas. You're safe here with me. You are powerful and special. It's time for you to step into your destiny."

My eyes sting. "You're right. And I'm ready. I truly want to work my magic the way I see the other elementals working theirs, like Dean with his fire."

I glance over to where he watches us from a distance.

"And you can."

"But…"

"You're scared?"

I nod. "Yeah, I am. What if I fail? What if I can't control it? Or I hurt myself or others? Not everyone's magic works in the same way. Harmony was a seer…"

"Was?"

I blink rapidly, holding back tears. "Umm, yeah, Harmony kind of got herself into trouble. She's okay now. Safe. But her magic is gone. Wings, too. She sacrificed everything to help me."

Opal sits with that information for a long time, thoughts whirling behind her blue eyes. "What's done is done and what will be will be. You can only control right now, and right now, you need to give yourself a chance. Like I said, you're strong here in Eridas. If you meditate, you will connect with the land and your magic will grow."

I smile softly. "Okay, you're right. Sorry, I'm not great at doing something that feels like doing nothing, but *I know* it's not nothing."

"It will help you," she assures me. "There's so much magic in Eridas, more than you've ever had access to before. It's always helped me to clear my mind and let the stillness boost my magic."

"And your magic is?" I hold my breath.

She stares off into the distance for a while, as if trying to decide if she can trust me. A slow smile creeps across her face. "I can do two things. Mine is also connected to spirit. I don't see spirits as you do and I can't go to the other realm and talk to them. It's nothing like that."

"Then what's it like?"

"First of all, I can visit the past."

I tilt my head. "You're a time traveler?"

She snorts. "No, that's not real. I can see memories, that's all. Not many understand it."

Actually, I think I do because it reminds me of what Harmony did with blood magic.

"So try to explain it?" My voice is earnest and I want so badly for her to trust me. Maybe she wants the same thing. "Because I want to understand. Truly, I do."

"When I'm sleeping and sometimes when I'm awake, I leave my body and my mind is transported to someone else's life. I'm able to see their memories, but it's not like I just see them, I live them."

"That actually makes perfect sense," I say. "I've had that happen to me a few times. Once with a girl who died who showed her memories to me of what happened and again looking back at my mom's past to try to figure out some things we needed to know."

Her eyes go wide. "How did you do it?"

I hope that she doesn't judge me. "The first time the spirit showed me the things herself and the other times, well, we used magic."

Opal's smile falls. "Blood magic?"

I nod once.

"And I take it Harmony took the sacrifice to do that?"

"We all used our blood but…" I choke up.

I don't know what to say but I don't have to. "That's why you said she'd gotten herself into trouble. I remember her from when I was a small child but I barely have any memories left of her. Well, I guess I could go look." She shakes her head. "Is she okay?"

"Yeah, like I said, she's okay. She's alive at least." I don't have the courage to say the rest but I find it anyway. "She lost her wings, her magic, and she aged."

Opal nods in understanding.

"And what's the other thing you can do?" I ask. But I think I already know.

"The glamour over this place? That's all me. Gregory has spelled people to forget about us if they got too close. And I have a spell that uses my magic to glamour this place to an earlier memory of what it once was—an uninhabitable forest."

"Wow." It's the only word I've got!

Over the last two days I've sometimes wondered if these

fae feel an extra level of security because they have magic and a way to protect themselves. Or maybe it's that I have an extra layer of fear, worrying that I'm not strong enough and my magic won't be what I hope. Either way, I feel bad for Opal. I always thought my gift was a curse, but I prefer it to being trapped in other people's memories every time I go to sleep at night. I hated it the few times I've experienced it. And I'd hate to be stuck in one village for the rest of my life because people were counting on me to protect them.

"We're going to figure this out together," Opal says brightly, clapping her thin hands together. "My magic is connected to the spirit element just as yours is. If I can clear my mind, push out all the chatter, the pictures, the fear, the worries, I can control my gift. I can choose where I go, what I see, how long I'm in there for. What if it's the same for you? What if we get you centered and calm and trusting yourself, then maybe you wouldn't be so scared to shift again and maybe you'd actually be able to be in control of your gift?"

I laugh but smile, too. "That sounds like a great idea to me." Maybe it's all closer than I realize, maybe I do just need to trust. "My gift was spiraling out of control and then I turned eighteen and something happened to me. My magic got stronger but so did I. These last few days I've felt way more in control and I've never felt that way before. Being in Eridas has only helped, almost like this part of me has been set free."

She squeezes my hands and lets go. "Things become natural and automatic. Same as your lungs know how to breathe air without you putting any effort in."

"Geez, you're so freaking wise, for being what? Thirteen? Fourteen?"

She laughs and shrugs. "Sixteen. But I've been in a world at war for as long as I can remember so the only peace I've been able to count on is the peace I find inside of myself."

"This is exactly what I'm talking about! You're like a Greek philosopher."

"What's a Greek philosopher?"

"Umm—ages ago there were super smart and wise people who said a lot of super smart and wise things and humans still talk about them centuries later. I'm not kidding, there's whole classes dedicated to these dudes."

She rolls her eyes but I can tell she's pleased with the compliment. What must her life be like, stuck here in this tiny village? Maybe being able to travel through memories is what makes her feel alive. Maybe it isn't so bad, after all. Maybe she's traveled through my memories? That thought gives me pause. Wow, if anyone can understand what I've been through, it's this girl.

"So let's try again, okay? This time, I really want you to

focus on clearing your mind. Your dragon self, remember that she's already a part of you and always has been. Same with your spirit elemental. The only difference is now you're accepting of them, you're welcoming them, loving them, instead of pushing them away."

I nod, hoping she's right. She sounds right.

"Maybe this was always meant to be easy but you were the one making it hard."

"There you go again!" I pull her into a side hug. "You should write a self help book. We could call it, Spirit Magic: A Self Love Story." I laugh at myself.

"Self help?"

"Human stuff. We'll talk about that later." I wink. "Right now I need to meditate."

I breathe in the crisp air, close my eyes tight, and push out all the little thoughts, one by one. I have to block out memories, they come at me automatically, good ones like kissing Dean, bad ones like evil spirits I've seen. I get to the point where instead of trying to push them out, I let them come and then pass right by me, like feathers on the wind. I relax more and more, until nothing has any meaning. I'm just me.

Here.

Slowly, I'm surrounded by the white snow and then I'm surrounded by the white room of the spirit realm—on and on it goes. This time when I see a reaper settle next to me, I don't allow fear to enter. It can't hurt me anymore. It never wanted to.

"What happened to you?" I take in its red glowing eyes and stare at them, mesmerized. "Did the Occultists spell you?"

Yes, it hisses, *they spelled us to the human spirit realm. We were willing to do anything to be released.*

"Why did they spell you there?" The question echoes around me.

Because they wanted to go there and were attempting to use us as a bridge. They want to bring all the realms together. They want to make everything one.

"So they can rule over it all, right?" It's what we've known for a while. This is total confirmation.

"Can they do that to you again?" I ask. "Spell you?"

They're trying but it's not working, not since you set us free. Not since you're alive.

A chill runs over my entire body and I'm filled with a million more questions. It's like as soon as I get one answered, more multiply.

His raspy voice turns impatient. *I've got a lot of work to do.* He zips away, and I'm once again alone in the white room.

It makes sense he'd have work to do considering the reapers were parted from their duties for so long. Still,

I'm bugged that he left so quickly. There must be a lot of supernatural spirits that need to be moved to their appropriate destinations. I wish I could see whatever that destination is, could know with absolute certainty that whatever comes next is something good, something worth looking forward to, but for whatever reason, that knowledge must not be meant for me.

Every time I've been in this realm before I've been afraid. The human version and the supernatural one look the same and I'm still not sure how to differentiate between the two. Or maybe I really am a bridge somehow? Maybe that's why the Occultists want me so bad. I breathe it all in, letting myself accept the fact that there might not *ever* be someone who will be able to give me all the answers.

I'll find as many as I can on my own, even if deep down, I know I have to be okay with not knowing everything about the spirit realms or the spirit elemental magic. The control freak within me hates the idea but the bigger part of me, the real part, is actually okay with it.

I'm not afraid anymore.

I'm not afraid.

And with that final thought, I allow it to happen. I don't force it. I don't resist. I simply allow it to pour over me, the truth that I can trust myself, that it's *safe* for me to be powerful.

And all at once, I go from being Hazel the girl, to Hazel the little white spirit dragon with the great big life mission.

TWENTY-TWO

KHALI

IF THE KING HAS A secret passage from his room, it would stand to reason that the queen would have one as well. But I've been trying to find another way to the tunnels for days and so far I've failed. I can't keep sneaking into Silas's room without getting caught. Beyond our royal chambers, there are too many eyes on me, which means I can't go to the old entrance Owen and I used to use, even though much of that particular tunnel was blocked.

So sneaking through Silas's room seems to be my only option.

After breakfast, I dress in a simple white a-line gown and cover it with a matching cloak, then I wait until Silas is gone for the day. With one solid breath to bolster my courage, I slip through the shared family room and into his empty bedroom, going right for the bookcase. I slide my fingers along its edge until I find the hidden latch to unlock it. I'm more prepared this time with a lit candle to guide my way through the narrow tunnel and down the steep stairs. The darkness is thick but my eyes adjust quickly with the aid of candlelight.

When I get to Silas's underground study, I set down my candle and check the door. It doesn't open. If I had magic, I would try to break the lock. Bellflower Blossom wanted me to see something down here and whatever it is, it stands to reason it could be behind this door. I stop for a quick listen but there's nothing. I press my hands to the cool oak and I am met with a sharp zap. I scramble back, stifling a broken sob. Electricity burns through my body.

My palms are burned.

I hurry on, angry with myself for being foolish, with Silas for the ward, with everything.

The goal now is to get out of the castle altogether, not to run away but to go to the lake. I want to cool my hands off but also if Silas has been talking with the merpeople, they probably still have sentries near the surface for anyone requesting an audience. As the queen, and someone they've used as a pawn in the past, I'm eager to know what's going on. I don't know if they'll confess anything but maybe they'll talk. At this point, some information is better than none. I'm beginning to suspect Silas is rounding up as many fae species as he can to help take down the Occultists but knowing him, probably as part of his strategy to overpower their fractured kingdoms. He's playing nice right now, but he's not a nice man. He'll hurt them. Not if he has to, when he has to. It's only a matter of time.

The tunnels here are unfamiliar so I'm careful to memorize each turn so I don't get lost on the way back. Finally, I recognize a fork in the road, marked by a series of deep etches in the wall. It's the path Bram and I used to escape all those weeks ago. I'm slow, walking on soft footsteps, flickering light barely illuminating a few feet in front of me at a time. The walls are stone and dripping water. The ground is cold hard dirt, with puddled mud every few turns. Sometimes I hear people talking through the walls, or footsteps up ahead. Those are the moments when I hold my breath and move forward only an inch at a time.

Finally, just when I'm beginning to think I'll be lost down here forever, the little metal door to the outer wall appears before me like an answer to a prayer. I open it, pushing against the brushes that hide it, and scramble out onto the rolling fields of white snow. Glinting in the distance is the vast lake, mostly iced over from the winter. I tuck my hair into my cloak and hope that the white of my outfit blends in well enough with the snow. Dragons patrol these areas from above, but they're not looking for someone in a white cloak, they're looking for burgundy robes, they're looking for magic, for things in the sky, for things that don't belong.

I hurry to the lake's edge, my breath billowing out ahead of me as I run. The lake is enormous and so much deeper than meets the eye. The water elemental dragons have no problem training in here from time to time because of the treaty with the merpeople, but I've always hated the water. I was taken prisoner as a child by the merpeople. They used me as a pawn and even though things worked out okay in the end, I've never been able to get over my fear of them or their watery home.

Even the merwoman from the Summer Forest, the one who helped me find the portal there, terrified me. Her sharp luminescent scales and haunted milky eyes brought me right back to my worst childhood memories. Not to mention, she asked that I would repay the favor with an equal debt. I haven't seen her since and don't know that I will again on this dragon land, far away from that Summer lake. I may never have to pay that debt, though that seems like wishful thinking.

I trudge along the shoreline, nervous energy keeping me from stepping out onto the ice. As a child my elementals revealed themselves enough that I could breathe underwater but I can't do that right now. I notice a circle of blue up ahead and hurry to inspect it. It looks like someone took heat to the ice and forged a hole, which might have been the case, or maybe Silas used his lightning to bore the hole himself.

My palms still sting, but holding a bit of snow in each hand will have to suffice.

I daren't get too close to the lake but I hope if I stand near, someone will come to speak to me. The wind picks up, tossing my hood off my face and blowing my dark hair behind me. I hurry to fix it, trying not to shiver. The hole of water ripples. At first I think it's from the wind, but then a young man's head lifts through the surface. His skin is covered in pale blue scales. His eyes are acrid yellow, hair too, and he smiles with pointed teeth. I almost expect those to be yellow too, but they're stark white.

"Queen Khali." His voice is deeper than his apparent age. It sends a chill down my body. "Stay where you are. I'll let them know you're here."

And then he's gone.

I wrap my arms in on myself and stay put, making sure I'm not too close to the water that an arm could reach out and pull me in. A few minutes later the glassy surface ripples again and two new faces appear—a man and a woman. They're older and wearing identical crowns made of silvery gemstones and black pearls.

I step back and stand tall, recognizing them instantly.

They are Queen Talis and King Sentin, the monarchs of the community of merpeople, and the two people who stole me away as a child. Despite trying to block those memories, they now tug at me and I feel as if I'm being dragged underwater all over again.

I suck in a quick breath and bow low, forcing myself to be stronger than my fear.

"Queen Khali," Talis says, "we heard about your marriage and subsequent coronation." Her voice is dangerous, an ax cutting through steel. "Congratulations."

"Thank you."

"Yes," King Sentin adds stoically, "we look forward to working with you and Silas."

"My husband feels the same way," I lie and smile. "He sent me here to see if everything is in order."

It's a gamble, pretending I know why he came here earlier. But according to the general he did. And according to the general, these people are protecting a portal.

Talis cocks her head. Her eyes are deep purple and shine unnaturally in the sunlight. I don't think she comes to the surface very often. "Is that so? And what exactly does he want from us now?"

"I don't know what you mean."

"He already knows our terms but he didn't agree to them," she continues. "Perhaps you see reason? We can't very well turn over the portal to a sorcerer without adequate payment."

My stomach flips and I blink. *This* isn't at all what I expected.

"Yes." Sentin grins, his pointed teeth look like they could easily slice my flesh into ribbons. "And Khali, we've spoken with our cousin in Summer. We know that you owe her. She agrees our demands would satisfy the debt as well as what your husband has asked for."

"What demands?" I blurt out, then immediately chastise myself for revealing too much.

They exchange a bemused look, likely catching on that my husband and I aren't actually talking to each other about this *at all.*

"We want to return to land," Talis hisses.

"But you're merpeople." I frown, genuinely confused. "You can't."

"Some of us could if the treaty was amended," Sentin juts in. "Our ancestors walked on land but they're also the fools who agreed to keep our people locked underwater. We want to change the terms of our treaty. In exchange we'll give Silas what he wants and we'll consider your debt to our cousin in

Summer forgiven."

My heart thuds in my chest. "I don't have the authority to change the treaty." I step back, my stomach turning to a lump. This isn't good, especially knowing that Silas is trying to get access to the portal. "I'm sorry. That's not why I came here."

"So you came here only to demand answers? You wanted to know why Silas has asked for our help." Sentin's tone turns abrasive. "And what of your debt? It's time to pay it."

"I don't owe *you* that debt," I challenge. "It was an agreement I made with someone else." I'm quick to lose my temper and immediately regret it. What was I thinking, coming here alone? These people don't care about me. They used me once and would use me again if they could.

"We're one and the same." Talis rises slightly from the water, her fin long and slimy green, reminding me of a giant snake. "Unlike the dragons who have so many clans, merpeople people are one. We live in unison. We work in unison. We can communicate with each other through magic, no matter where we live. Do wrong to one of us and do wrong to all of us."

"I'm sorry." I shake my head. "I mean no disrespect. I shouldn't have come here."

As I turn to leave, a loud crack violates the quiet morning. The ice is breaking. Water splashes on shore, some of it hitting me, like wanting fingers. I whip around. Long ropes of seaweed fly toward me. A net!

I don't react fast enough. The icy net covers me, ropes digging into my skin, dragging me toward the water. I claw at the snow but it's too slick and my palms are still burned. I scream, crying out for help, my voice ripe with panic. I can't shift into my dragon to get out of the net. I'll drown. They don't know that I no longer have water elemental magic.

"Please," I beg. "You'll kill me within minutes. I can't go in the water!"

They don't listen. I'm sliding, closer, closer, closer. And I know, the moment I hit that water, I'll be dragged under. Sure as I know that the sky is blue and the snow is white and that the blue water will turn inky black down below, I know I am going to die.

TWENTY-THREE

HAZEL

I GAPE DOWN AT MYSELF, stunned by what I see and what I am. I don't know if I'll ever get used to this. My white scales glisten in the sunlight, blending in seamlessly with the snow. I stretch out my claws, marveling at the shiny pink tips. I take one of them to the ice bench, sure it's sharp enough to slice into it, but it slides right through. I'm in the spirit realm, then, unable to touch the physical even though they can see me and I can see them. I roll my shoulders back and my wings roll with them. Wings… I remember what it felt like to fly, how easy and natural it was for me. I want to do it again.

Opal observes calmly on the far side of the ice-bench, smiling at me with a knowing twinkle in her eye. I inch toward her and she stands, reaching out to pat my head, but like before, it slides right through me. "Amazing," she whispers. "This is unlike anything I've ever heard of before."

I peer around, noticing others watching in the distance, expressions of confusion and awe. Dean stands across the field, observing from the stoop of the little house we've been staying in, his arms folded over his chest, a giant smile on his normally unreadable face. He's giving me space to do this, but he's not willing to let me out of his sight, which is actually pretty sweet.

I turn back to Opal, wishing I could speak to her right now and explain that when I'm a spirit dragon, I'm in two places at once. But then again, I'm pretty sure she's already figured that part out. My eyes adjust and on top of the physical world are the spirit realms, both the supernatural and the human. Everything is layered on top of each other and they call out to me, begging to be explored. I could go. Right now, I know I could go.

But… my wings twitch. The urge to lift off and soar into the wide open sky grasps me again, stronger this time. The temptation of it is so unbearable, I have to force myself to stay put. I don't know how far the magicked border around this little village goes and I need to keep control. I would never forgive myself if I put these people in danger. They're already taking a huge risk by letting Dean and me stay here.

Stop thinking about flying.

Focus on something else.

"Clear your mind," Opal says again. "You can do this. *You're* in control."

And I try, but the light of the spirit realm, it grows and grows, brighter, whiter, wider—so so beautiful. Before I can stop myself, I step toward it, and then I'm no longer in two places at once. The living world is gone and I'm wholly in the spirit realm—nor am I alone. I gaze at the people here, realizing I'm in the supernatural spirit realm. A few of the dead people I saw yesterday are here again, eager to reconnect with their family again, they surround me, some talking, some sending images. Elves and faeries, mostly. There's a gorgeous centaur, with bright azure eyes, black hair and body, who stands far back, ever watchful and guarded. A few pixies dash past, chasing after each other, oblivious to me.

A black dragon flies in and I already know by his blue eyes and the swift movements that it's Owen. He lands right in front of me, nuzzling his head against me in a sort of hug, and the others leave us.

It's good to see you again, he says through the dragon link. *You have no idea how happy am I to see you've shifted again. I've been waiting and waiting for you to come talk to me.*

I smile to myself. *And where have you been? I haven't seen you in a while.*

He releases me and stretches his wings out. They're so strong, so real, so *here*. I almost can't believe that he's dead. It's different when spirits visit me in the other realms; they don't have this solidness to them. It's hard for me to understand why I get to be here with a link back to real life and they don't, but then there are so many things I don't understand, so what else is new?

I've been watching Khali. I'm worried about her. Owen's voice is strained and almost accusatory.

Dean and I are worried about her, too.

Could have fooled me… His tone turns sour.

What? What do you think we're doing in Eridas? Ever since Silas took her away we've been trying to find the safest way to get to her. Well, and Cora and Macy, but Owen doesn't have to know that.

Well you're not trying hard enough. A low growl rumbles through his body.

I'm stunned. Is he kidding me? This is the first time I've ever had Owen be rude toward me and I don't appreciate it. I don't know how to respond with only words so without much thought, I shift into my regular self and fold my arms over my chest. He can talk to me face to face if he's going to have an attitude.

He shifts too, but it's not a crappy attitude I find staring back at me, it's fear. His hair is a wild mess around bloodshot eyes.

"Owen, what's going on?"

"Look for yourself." He points into the white vastness and an image appears.

It's Khali. She's on a shoreline, caught in a net, screaming for her life. Someone is pulling her toward the water. Are those mermaids? They don't look like the pretty versions human idolize, these are terrifying, with pale sickly scaled skin, unearthly eyes, and razor sharp teeth. Khali screams again, her eyes wide with horror and rimmed in red.

"She's in trouble," Owen presses. "She's lost her magic. She lost it the day she turned eighteen. And now the merpeople are going to drown her!"

My chest burns hot and then cold. I want to help her, to save her, but I'm also wondering… how is it that my magic grew and hers was lost on the same day? It must be the spell. I've finally found myself and I don't want to let that go. But another part of me, the bigger part, wants to fix her magic and save her from the scary mermaids. We're connected. I have to help.

"Go to her." Owen points at the image. "You can walk right through that and go to her now. You don't have to stay in this village."

I nod and fill my lungs with a long, slow breath. He's right, of course. I know this is true, that this is part of my abilities. Like spirits, I can basically teleport from this realm to the people I love. So why am I so afraid? I could check on Mom and Harmony. I could go to Cora and Macy and make sure they're okay. Just the thought of them and more images pop up around me. I glimpse Harmony and my mother in our kitchen, cooking breakfast. They have false smiles and worry in their eyes. I could go to them, tell them I'm okay, and then come right back here.

But what if it doesn't work? What if I got stuck there?

No, I shouldn't risk it.

I turn away from the vision of them to find the one of Cora and Macy. I cry out, the image of my friends sending me reeling. They're asleep and alone in a barren and dark stone room, laying on tiny straw beds, dressed in tattered gowns. Relief hits me because at least they're not dead, but it's short lived and quickly followed by guilt. Are they locked up in that room? How much do they know about where they are? I want so badly to go to them and ask a million questions, to make sure they're okay, to get them out of there and back home.

But again, what if I can't come back? Or what if I can only travel through the portals like the other living dragons and faeries. What if it's not that easy like it seems to be for the spirits? Owen is right, I have to go to Khali, she's in mortal danger.

She needs me *now.*

My voice cracks. "What if I fail?"

"You need to do the right thing," Owen snaps, running his hands through his sandy hair and staring at me with the clearest blue eyes I've ever seen. "Go. Go help her now."

"Okay." I suck in a breath. "But I can't leave Dean here. And I'm training. I'm not prepared to deal with the dragons and whatever comes next."

"Don't you get it?" Owen growls. "Dean can't go to Drakenon! He'll be executed on sight. And my people are running out of time—all of them, especially Khali! *They don't have the luxury of waiting.*"

He opens his mouth to speak again, but a flash of black swoops between us and cuts him off. The reaper is so fast and swift that we barely scramble out of the way.

"No," Owen growls, turning on the reaper. "I'm not ready yet. I haven't said goodbye. I haven't made sure they're safe—"

The reaper stretches out a bony hand toward Owen anyway. "It's your time, Boy."

"No!" I scream and dive on top of Owen, dragging him away from the reaper.

The white room disappears in a flash and we're right back to where I was in Winter. This time, Owen is with me, but he's taken on that ghost quality again. I'm the only one who can see him.

I'm solid, back to me, and my heart is racing. I pant and little puffs of steam flit into the cold morning air.

"Are you okay?" Opal asks. Her eyes are wide pools of blue and her dark complexion has gone pale.

"Yes," I groan, but really, I'm not. And Khali, she most definitely *isn't* okay. I might already be too late as it is. I shoot Owen's spirit a charged look and a nod before turning back to Opal.

I spot Dean across the field, still watching all of this. He's abandoned his spot on the porch and is jogging toward us.

"I'm okay," I whisper to Opal. "But I have to leave you. Today. Right now."

Her face falls. "So soon? Are you sure? There was more I wanted to do."

I nod and rest my hands on my knees, still trying to catch my breath. "Me too but I'm sure. I have people that need my help right now."

Owen nudges me, his expression growing even more impatient. "Not to mention a dragon spirit who's going to haunt my butt until I do what he wants."

Owen laughs and growls at the same time and the sound cracks through some of my fear.

Opal stares at me like I've lost my mind, but she nods anyway. "Well alright then," she says brightly, pulling me into a quick hug. "Let's go tell Dean."

Owen shoots me another annoyed glare. "There's no time for that."

I know he's getting impatient. I hope that Khali is okay, that she's fighting the merpeople off, but he's right. I can't keep thinking about this, about her, I have to go. *Now!*

I look back to Dean and wonder if I should leave him here where he'll be safe. Drakenon isn't going to be kind to him. What if they kill him like Owen says they will? What if they don't even give us a chance to try to get him pardoned for his stupid "crime"? But deep in my gut I know that if I ditch Dean right now, he might find a way to follow, but he may never forgive me for leaving him. There's no reasoning with that boy when he's got his mind made up about something; he and I have that stubborn trait in common.

He catches up to us across the snowy field and wraps me into his warm arms. "You did it," his breath tickles my ears. "Good job. I'm so proud of you."

"Well I hope it's good enough," I groan.

"It will be."

"It has to be now." I step back and give him a cheesy smile. "Cause guess what? Your dead brother is insisting I go to Drakenon *right this second.* He says our friends are out of time. They need me. Khali's in big trouble with the mermaids."

His expression turns stony.

Owen is busy pacing behind us. His blond hair is a disheveled mess and he looks about ready to explode. *Okay, Dude, I get it.*

"And this next part is going to be hard for you to understand." My voice wobbles and I have to force myself to hold his gaze. I breathe in his smoky rain scent, take in his coal fire eyes, his warmth and goodness, and try to cage it in my memory. "But I need to go alone."

"What?" Dean hisses. "No way!"

"I can go directly to Khali using my gift and Owen will be there with me."

"What the hell is Owen going to be able to do for you? No way, Hazel. It's too dangerous. You don't know these people. You don't know how ruthless they can be."

"Which is exactly why you can't come," I beg. "They exiled you!"

"Don't do this," Dean pleads. He's gripping my wrists so tight. His eyes are so wide, so pleading and desperate. My heart aches but I have to do this. I have to. For him.

"I love you," I whisper the words for the first time. This wasn't the situation I imagined saying them in but I can't go without telling him how I feel. "I love you so much and I'm doing this because I love you."

He's speechless and my heart breaks a little.

"But I really have to go, Khali is running out of time. I have to find her. Please, don't follow."

I rip myself away from him and shift, immediately jumping into the spirit realm. Owen is already there. He shifts too. Praying I'm doing the right thing, I follow the dragon into the unknown.

TWENTY-FOUR

KHALI

THE TINGY WHOOSH OF A blade slicing through the air precedes a quick snap. The net goes limp and I scramble to push the heavy wet net away. The merpeople yell but I can't focus enough to listen to what they're saying. A strong hand grabs hold of my upper arm and heaves me to my feet.

Flannery, my centaur friend, holds me against his hard chest. In his hand, the golden spear glints. My heart leaps with gratitude. "Where have you been?"

"No time," he says gruffly. "Jump on my back and hold tight to me and the spear. We have to go."

I don't quite understand but I do as he says, climbing onto his horse back and reaching my arms around his broad shoulders and wrapping one hand around the spear. He holds on to it as well, never once letting go as he charges through the snow and away from the lake, toward the neighboring forest. Bits of snow and mud fly all around us and the merpeople are still yelling in the distance. It won't be long until the dragon army is here, demanding answers. Once we're in the cover of trees, Flannery slows to a stop and I climb off his back.

"You saved my life." I'm on the verge of crying. I throw my arms around him for a hug. "Thank you. I owe you."

And then it all comes tumbling out right along with the stupid tears. I confess to my magic being lost, to my hopelessness, and explain how everything went wrong after we parted ways with him at the border. I cry as I talk about our hostage Occultist betraying us and the wedding to Silas and Bram killing his father and finally about how the merpeople would have drowned me if he hadn't shown up. Flannery watches me in that steady way of his until I'm finally done. I wipe away the tears and apologize.

"No need to apologize," he offers simply. "You've been carrying a lot on your shoulders."

I nod and release a cathartic laugh. "I just don't get it. How did the Occultist get away from us? We had a deal. Everything should have worked out."

"You can't make deals with the Occultists." His voice goes flat. "I tried to warn you. Their blood magic ties them to a bond that nothing else can break."

I let out a shaky breath and gaze up into the pine trees heavy with snow. Flannery is bare chested just as the day I met him, but he doesn't seem to mind, he doesn't even shiver. His blood must run hotter than mine because I'm freezing.

"I've been traveling to new places and learning about the Sovereign Occultists for years," he says. "But it wasn't until a recent conversation where I learned that not only does their blood magic make them strong because they offer so many sacrifices to it, but there's so much more that goes into it. A strong blood bond like that is powerful enough to resist other kinds of magic, even the agreement you two made."

I stomp my boot into the snow, angry. "Okay, so how do we stop them?"

"Break the bond."

I roll my eyes. "Okay, but it seems like nothing can break it."

"Something must."

"And what would that be?"

Flannery frowns. "If only I knew."

"So, okay… what else is their magic capable of? Let's start there."

He shakes his head and grimaces. "I'm afraid it's capable of far more than we realized. It's cursed the fae who are left to slowly turn into animals, which I don't have to remind you about."

And it's linked me to Hazel somehow… but I don't want to explain that right now. "And it caused the reapers to attach to my father and Bram, leading to King Titus's death."

"Yes."

"We have to stop them."

"Yes," he says again. "And soon because they're working on bringing Drakenon's borders down entirely so not only will their strongest be able to pass through but their weakest too. All of them are planning to invade you. They've been at the ley line portals trying to get through there as well but it hasn't worked, they simply don't have the right kind of magic, so now they've refocused on Drakenon. And what do you think they'll do to you if they catch you, Khali?"

"They'll kill me." I swallow the hard lump in my throat. It's still hoarse from screaming earlier. "And they'll use my death to strengthen their bond even further."

"Exactly. But you're the most powerful elemental alive in Eridas right now. It could make them strong enough to do anything, strong enough to pass through the ley line portals, strong enough to regain control of the reapers. Khali, if they do get through before you figure out what's going on with your magic, you can't let them find you."

"But my magic is gone, remember? What good am I to them?"

"Are you certain of your magic's disappearance?" He questions, raising his eyebrows. "Or is it spelled away to make you *think* it's gone so that you're extra weak when they come for you."

I blink, the truth of his words settling in. "You're brilliant, do you know that?"

He laughs, the sound hearty and solid. "So I've been told."

"How do you know they've spelled my magic?" I never told him about Hazel.

"The Occultist talked about it when he was with us, remember?"

I let out a breath. "Okay, so how do I get my magic back?"

"Unfortunately I don't have any ideas." He ponders each and every word. The breeze catches his hair and blows it off his shoulders, making him appear even more intense. "You'll have to figure that one out for yourself. But here." He hands me the golden spear. When my fingers wrap around it, I have to swallow down a gulp of panic. "This spear is one of the last magicked objects left in Eridas. It was forged by my people centuries ago, passed down from chief to chief, and is magicked with the gift of invisibility. It will help you survive the coming battle."

"I knew it!" I laugh, feeling the heaviness of the spear and marveling at its beauty and power. "I knew Bram and that Occultist couldn't see you when we were traveling."

"It only makes you invisible to those you don't want to be visible to at the time." He shrugs. "I didn't want them to see me, so as long as I held it, they didn't."

I switch the golden spear from hand to hand, admiring the intricate detail of carved vines and flowers. It's heavier than it looks. "Which is why you had me hold onto it too when we ran from the merpeople. Are you sure you don't need this?" I can't imagine how hard it must be for him to part with something so special.

"Of course I need it." He smiles and his eyes sparkle knowingly. "But you need it more. And besides, you must promise to return it to me when this is all over."

"If I'm not dead," I grumble.

"I have faith in you." He stares straight on, meaning what he says, and something about his words boost me up.

"Thank you. And yes, I promise."

The weight of his incredible gift presses down on me. I'm grateful, but I'm also scared I won't be able to live up to his expectations. I have to find a way to get to Hazel because I'm sure now that she's the only one who can help me get my magic back. It's that damned spell linking us together. I need to break it.

Well, that and I have one other idea of what I need to break…

"There are very few of my kind left," he says, cutting off my thoughts. "My wife and child are hiding in the Winter Kingdom. They're safe for now but I fear for them every day. I haven't been to see them in many years."

His confession cuts me to the core.

"Are you sure you don't want this back?" I frown at the spear. "You could use it to go to them and take them somewhere safer."

"There is nowhere in Eridas safer for them than where they are." He shakes his head, and then his demeanor lightens. "I already told you." His smile quirks. "I'll get the spear back when this is all over and you've defeated the Occultists. But until then, you must be brave."

I want to make a self-deprecating joke but instead I just say thank you again. This is the nicest gift anyone has ever given me and despite everything working against me, his confidence in me gives me the boost I've been needing. Before I can talk myself out of it, I rush forward and wrap him in yet another tight hug. He hugs me back and I can't help but smile against his warm chest. His heartbeat thumps against my ear. His hind legs kick at the dirt. And he feels—

so solid—so real. And he believes in me. The stakes just got higher but I also just got stronger thanks to Flannery. I'm not going to fail him. I'm not going to fail anyone. At least, that's what I'll keep telling myself.

TWENTY-FIVE

HAZEL

I FOLLOW OWEN THROUGH THE white light and into the portal that will lead us to Khali. Time seems to slow, fraying at the edges, and then speeding up as I'm transported from the spirit realm to the castle. I'm back to me, no longer a dragon, standing in a room of stormy gray stone and detailed dark wood carving all the accents.

Wait… this isn't the lake where we saw Khali needing our help. So why on earth did I pop up here? And where did Owen go?

The rugs are plush and the furniture velvet and everything is medieval looking, like something from a European museum. It's actually pretty neat—too bad I'm freaking the freak out! I feel like I'm in a storybook and should be dressed in a princess gown, but instead I'm in head to toe black with tight jeans, fitted puffer jacket, and snow boots. I'm so wholly out of place, it reminds me of when I went to a Halloween party in middle school dressed up like the Wicked Witch of the West, complete with green body paint. Yeah, I'd missed the memo that dressing up wasn't cool anymore. Fun times.

I gaze around, looking for Owen, but he's still gone. Unease crashes over me. *What the heck? Where is he? And where is Khali? Does this mean she's okay? Does it mean this is actually where she was last or something else?*

I suck in a gulp of stuffy air and muster up the courage to find Khali. All I can figure is I must have lost time because it's no longer a bright morning sun casting through the windows at the back of the room. In fact, it's a dark starry night that greets me. I hope she's okay, but right now, I need to make a decision.

There are three doors—three choices.

One on either side of the room and one on the far end. I'm reminded of a gameshow and I've got to pick the right door to get my prize: door number one, two, or three, which is it?

"Okay, here goes nothing," I whisper and go for door number one on the side of the room.

The cool brass handle presses into my palm and I push it open, peering into the room. I don't find Khali. Actually, I don't find anyone. The room is empty except for a large four-poster bed, as intricately carved as the other wood accents, and wardrobe, and a bookshelf. But it smells decidedly male in here and I know at once this isn't where I'm going to find Khali.

"Nevermind." I turn on my heels but run right into a hard male chest and stumble back. He catches me by the forearms.

"Ah." The boy smiles proudly. "I've been wondering when you were going to show up."

My voice catches and panic zips down my body. "Silas."

He's almost as I remember him, with memorizing eyes, a winning smile, and white blond hair. But his clothes are completely different. Gone are his casual human clothes from that night at the party and in their place are the kind of clothes that match this place. I don't know what they're called, but they're exactly what a medieval prince would wear. Again, he's out of a storybook and I'm out of place.

"Like what you see?" he laughs.

"I'm sorry," I mumble. "I was looking for Khali."

"My wife is busy at the moment." His voice goes sour.

When he calls her his wife, my heart hurts. "Busy? Does that mean you saved her?" I can only hope that she was rescued from those freaky mermaids.

He frowns for a second. "She's fine. I just had dinner with her." He tightens his hands on my forearms and shoves me forward. I trip over my own feet and he hauls me against him, marching me farther into the bedroom.

"What are you doing?" I gasp.

"You need to come with me."

"Where?"

"Well, we have options." He chuckles low. "I could kill you now or I could deliver you to the sorcerer and he can kill you later. Hmm… "

"If you kill me, you'll kill Khali."

That stops him for a second, a mark of frustrating realization passing over his pretty features. "Didn't she tell you about the spell?"

He's silent and I let out a laugh. "You don't know."

He shoves me against the wall. My wrists sting and I brace myself for another impact. I'm suddenly certain he's going to hurt me. He fiddles with the bookshelf until it opens, revealing a secret passage into a dark tunnel. It looks so cool, reminding me of a million fantasy books I've read, but being in the situation myself, being forced to go into that dark tunnel with a bad guy and no light? Yeah, not so cool.

I cry out for help and he covers my mouth with one hand and twists my arms behind my back with his other hand. He's taller and larger than me on every count, and when I try to bite him or shove back, I don't get anywhere. It seems to make him even more excited.

"Come now." His voice is pure metal. "Don't you want to see your friends? What were their names again? Oh, I forgot, I don't care enough for mortal humans to remember their names. But I do appreciate that bringing them here got you to follow."

I go limp, thinking of Cora and Macy, and stop fighting. I let him lead me through the cold darkness. I can't see a thing. He must know these tunnels well though because he has no trouble navigating the turns and steep stairs. He holds on to me the entire time. My magic churns within, but it's weakened from traveling through the spirit realm, and anyway, it's not like I'm going to shift right now, not when he's taking me to see my friends. He says Khali is fine so she must have gotten away from the mermaids and this is my chance to help Cora and Macy. I hope they're okay and don't hate me. I'd probably hate me if I were in their shoes. My life is so insanely complicated and those complications have put them in this position.

Silas said he was considering killing me. Now that he knows what it will do to Khali, I'm praying he believes me and doesn't follow through with it. Still, I can't know for sure, so my heart is racing a million miles a minute, my palms are sweating, and I'm pretty sure I'm like two seconds away from having a full-blown panic attack.

We come upon a torch hooked into the wall, and what little light it's fire gives soothes my panic just a enough for me to get ahold of my wits.

"I'm going to let go of your mouth now," he says against my ear. "If you scream, nobody will hear you."

Somehow, I believe him.

I do as he says, keeping the panic inside when he lifts his hand from my mouth and grabs the torch off the wall. He carries it, still holding my wrists, and the deeper we go, the darker and colder it gets. We pass a few doors and eventually Silas leads me into one of them, using a key to let us in. As we stride inside, I force myself to go willingly even though it's still too dark to make out anything. The air is damp and the cold is a deep freeze, even with my coat on. It looks like I haven't escaped winter even though I left the Winter Kingdom. Why couldn't this dragon castle have been the one stuck in eternal summer or spring? Heck, I'd even take autumn at this point. After this crap is all over, and assuming I make it out alive, I'm going on a beach vacation!

We continue to walk for a while and then eventually a brighter torchlight flickers up ahead. My eyes adjust. We're in some kind of dungeon. *Oh, crap!*

"You locked them all the way down here?" My eyes water

and anger burns deep.

"I needed to keep the fact they were here from making it to the court gossip," he replies simply, not the least bit defensive. "They don't know about my recent escapades into the human realm and I'd rather like to keep it that way. I don't need my army deserting me right when they're actually going to be needed to do something for once in their pathetic little lives."

I hold back my tongue and all I can think is that this guy is awful and his people probably hate having to deal with his snotty attitude and selfish ways.

When we find them, at least they are together, at least they're clothed and have beds and blankets—at least they're okay. But their dresses are dirty and thin, their eyes are tired and worn, and when they see Silas, they scramble back. When they look closer and realize I'm here too, they blink with surprise and confusion and relief and pain.

I rush forward, my hands gripping the barred window on the door that locks them in. Silas stands right behind me, hands on my shoulders.

"Are you okay?" Tears run down my cheeks.

"Hazel? Is that really you?" Macy asks in that sweet soft voice of hers.

Cora sighs with relief. "Please tell us you came here to save us?"

"Yes!" I gush. "Of course I'm here to save you!"

Silas barks out a laugh and uses that moment to open the door and throw me into the cell. He slams the door shut with a clang just as the three of us run at it.

A wind forces us back, slamming us to the far wall. The air is cold and choking, piercing my lungs. *I can't breathe!* I scramble to locate my own magic and inner dragon but she's not there. Where is she? Is this it for me? Is he going to kill us after all that?

But the wind stops abruptly and we all gasp and sputter for breath.

"You will stay here," he growls through the bars, "until I am ready for you."

"You can't hold me!" I threaten.

He smirks. "Elemental magic won't work with that necklace on."

And then he's gone.

Necklace? My fingers fumble to my neck and locate a cord. It's tied tightly enough that I can't get it off. A pendant rests at its end but it's too close to my skin for me to see it.

"It's a dragon," Cora says. "Of course it is. Because nothing makes sense anymore and apparently dragons are real."

"I can't get it off," I growl. "I think it's magicked to stay tied." My eyes fill with tears again and I drop my head into my freezing cold hands. This isn't what I came here for; it wasn't supposed to happen this way. I left Dean. Owen is missing. Khali doesn't even know I'm here or was coming. Nobody knows we're down here.

"Hey." Macy scooches in closer and rests her head on my shoulder. "It's okay, Babe. Don't cry."

"It's… not… okay," I mutter between sobs. "This is my fault."

"Yeah, it's not okay." Cora lays her head on my other shoulder. "But we'll figure it out. Don't worry too much."

Her tone doesn't match her words in the slightest and I know she's just as worried as I am, if not more so. I wonder how long they've been down here. Have they been treated okay? Are they hungry? I wish I had food but I lost my backpack when I left it back in Winter.

A wave of exhaustion greets me and suddenly all I want to do is sleep. And what do you know? There aren't just two beds in here, there are three. Silas was waiting for me to show up and I played right into his plan.

Stupid!

I crawl to the bed and climb under the heavy blankets, not even bothering to remove my puffer jacket. It's too cold to take it off anyway. "I just need a nap," I whisper to my friends. "Getting here took everything out of me. Let me sleep for an hour and then we can come up with a plan."

They exchange nervous glances but I'm way too tired to ponder their meaning. No way can I think another coherent though, let alone hold a conversation right now. It's all too much. My eyes flutter closed and I drift off within seconds, only to be met with nightmares.

TWENTY-SIX

KHALI

I CAN'T SLEEP. I LAY on my too-soft bed, staring at the shadowed ceiling, my mind racing as I categorize the events of the day. It appears that the merpeople went back to their watery home after I ran off this morning because I haven't heard a word about it. I hope nobody else saw me, which seems too good to be true, and I worry that Silas already knows what I did. But at dinner tonight, he didn't mention it.

After Flannery gifted me the spear, getting back into the castle proved easy—being invisible made sure of that. But finding a place to hide the magicked item? Not so easy. I couldn't disappear for long without an alarm being raised so I had to find a place for it. Right now it's stashed under my bed but I know that I can't leave it there. One maid or another cleans every nook and cranny of the room almost daily, and besides, I don't want this spear near Silas. My parents are still being watched and I'm not sure that I can trust my mother right now, so I can't take it there. My fae friends already don't feel safe here so hiding the spear with them could put them in even more danger.

I peel myself from the bed and retrieve the golden artifact, enjoying the weight of it in my hands and deciding that Bram is the best choice to look after it. He's the type to have stacks of books and relics in his chamber, not to mention he has a huge locked chest in his study. He might even be able to hide it in plain sight. Part of me doesn't want to see him after catching him and Juniper with secrets. That hurt me. But a bigger part of me wants to see him more than anything.

Using the item's magic to shield me, I steal through the castle's corridors, sneaking past the guards, and slipping into his chambers. He's reading, as usual. His nose is in a huge book and he's so engrossed in the text that he doesn't care about the way his hair is standing on end, probably from running his hands through it one too many times. Nor does he seem to notice the fire burning in his hearth is nothing more than a pile of glowing embers. A small oil lamp glows from the table beside him, lighting the planes of his face and the gold of my spear.

I'm invisible but I let my guard down, revealing myself.

At first, he doesn't move or seem to notice me. But then his voice comes out in a scratchy whisper. "I didn't think I'd ever see you in here again."

I step forward and lay the spear at his feet. "It's a gift from a friend and I need a place to hide it."

He doesn't seem surprised by the magicked item itself, more awed than anything. He takes it into his hands, examining it, turning it as the light catches every angle.

"Careful. The tip is sharper than it looks. Can you hide it for me?"

His eyes flash to mine. "Of course."

He stands and strides to his bookshelf, opening a book at random, but it's not random because there's a little brass skeleton key inside. He uses it to unlock the trunk. He pulls out a silvery blanket and turns on me with a sheepish smile. "After I walk you back to your room, I'll return the spear here and wrap it in this blanket. This chest has been warded and can only be opened with this key"—he holds it up— "so your spear will be safe here. You're the only other person who knows where to find the key and I promise not to tell anyone of what you've entrusted to me."

He worries his bottom lip between his teeth. "Thank you for trusting me."

We stand staring at each other for a long moment, the

space between us is small but right now it feels impassable. "What secret are you keeping from me? I have to ask."

He stills. "It's not my secret to tell."

"Bram—"

"I shook on it, I'm sorry." He grimaces. "But I promise it's to protect us from Silas and you'll know about it soon anyway."

I have nothing to say. I want to trust him, and actually, I do trust him more than anyone. But I can't help from feeling left out, rejected, my heart a little bruised.

And then, I think I know. "Is it the portal? The one the merpeople guard?"

"So you know…"

"Walk me back," I say. "I'm ready to be done with this conversation."

But he doesn't make a move. He just continues to stare at me, the emotions behind his eyes charged with wanting. It's the same wanting I feel low in my stomach.

"We can't," is all I say and he understands, the burning expression on his face fading into coolness. And that makes it even harder, makes me want to go to him, to kiss him again, to not go back to my rooms but to stay here with him tonight instead.

But I was right and I've been right. We can't. I'd rather

hurt him than do something that would end up killing him. I didn't have a choice in this, not really. I've already decided I wasn't going to endanger him, I've already risked that with the spear and I won't do more.

"How was your day?" he asks, startling me with the typical question.

Truth be told, after hiding the spear under my bed, the day felt pointless. This? Taking care of Bram's safety, asking him for help, being with him, even seeing just him and breathing the same air as him? This feels like purpose.

"Well, getting this spear was quite the story."

He raises an eyebrow but I don't elaborate.

"I had to entertain more ladies in the queen's rooms in the afternoon," I sigh sarcastically. "So that was fun."

I don't mention that I had to suffer through dinner with Silas that evening as he discussed war strategy with his army generals. I'd looked the part of a doting wife and said all the right things, but a deep sadness had fallen over me like a dark cloud. Maybe because I didn't know how I was going to get my magic back and was starting to believe I never would. Maybe because Flannery's spear made this so real, and I was feeling a little guilty for accepting it in the first place. Or maybe because Aleeryrick was popping up everywhere Silas was lately and I hated that King Titus bargained my first daughter away to be that man's apprentice. Everything had become such a mess and each time I tried to make a plan or move forward, I had failed. Again and again, I was failing.

"Are you doing okay?" Bram steps closer. Too close. My mind flashes back to the kiss we shared in this very spot and I'm overwhelmed with impatience.

"I'm fine." It's not true.

He must see it because he frowns. Then he picks up the spear, disappearing from view. I suck in a breath, and when his hand brushes my cheek, I hold it.

"Nobody can see us, Khali."

And that's all it takes for him to save me.

Our lips collide—a fervent prayer—and every ounce of fear and sadness and frustration is washed clean with passion and love and *choice*. We stay like that until we're panting and burning for more but it's time for me to get back because if we keep going we won't be able to stop.

True to his word, he uses the magicked spear to escort me back, stealing more kisses along the way. When I slip inside my room and he leaves, I plop down on the rumpled bed, and go back to staring at the dark ceiling, but this time, I don't feel so awful anymore.

It doesn't last long.

I should sleep and give myself a break, but I couldn't even

manage to. Tears bubble, hot and demanding. A heaviness presses in on my chest and I can't help but cry, trying to breathe through the pain. I love Bram. I do. I don't care if he's not Dragon Blessed or if he's not my husband or not the best mate for me. I can't change whom my heart wants. And that realization is a wound to my soul. Our relationship is only the top of a mountain of problems I'm facing. I squeeze my eyes closed and pray to the Gods. *I need help. I can't keep doing this. Please.*

Muffled shouts snap me out of prayers and I bolt upright. The noise is coming from Silas's room. It's dangerous for me to go check it out but I can't help myself. I spring from the bed and tiptoe into our shared family room, pressing my ear to his bedroom door.

"You're wrong." Silas's voice is prickly. "I did the right thing. If I hadn't done it, Drakenon would've been doomed to fall to the Occultists because you'd never had agreed to my plan."

There's a moment of silence before something slams to the ground. "No!"

More silence.

Then a quieter "I'm sorry" from Silas, two words I don't think I've ever heard him say. He clears his throat and a quick sob escapes followed by another sorry.

What in the world is going on in there?

"Queen Khali." The voice is deadpanned but it makes me jump and spin around. My response catches in my throat and my breath evaporates as I stare up at the sorcerer. "Spying on your husband, are you?" He holds his magicked wooden staff in one hand and I can't help but stare. It glows brighter than ever before. Colors of green, blue, red, and yellow swirl within the wood and the inlaid gemstones pulse. It's mesmerizing but also terrifying, and I take a step back, pressing myself into the hard door.

I don't have a chance to answer him. The door swings open and I stumble into Silas's arms.

"Khali?" he questions, voice throaty. "What are you doing awake?"

I turn to him. His eyes are bloodshot. He's obviously been crying.

"You woke me up with your yelling," I lie. "Who were you talking to in there?"

Silas sighs and steers me to one of the chairs in our shared sitting room. He deflates into the chair next to mine and Aleeryrick joins us, as if none of this is odd, as if we do this all the time.

"Did it work?" Aleeryrick asks Silas. His face is unreadable behind his white beard and steely eyes.

Silas nods.

"So that's all of them." He smiles, satisfied.

"All of what?" I ask. Worry unravels in my stomach.

"All the elementals," Silas says. He releases a slow breath, running his hands through tangled hair. "Khali, you heard me talking to Owen and my father. They appeared to me in spirit form."

I blink, disbelieving. "How?"

"I found a way to harness spirit magic," he says, a little flicker of pride dancing on his upturned lips. But there's a restless sadness in his eyes still. So he had to face the twin he murdered and the king he replaced? Good. I hope they haunt him for the rest of his miserable life.

"So you have all the elementals now?" I can't believe this. "All of the elements for what purpose? I don't understand. And how could you get spirit? And fire is nearly as rare as spirit is."

Does this mean he's like how I was? Or is he talking about something else? These questions stir in my mind, an ocean, each drop unable to separate from the rest.

Silas turns away from me, refusing to answer, and my stomach hardens. I look to Aleeryrick and his staff. I haven't forgotten that Silas told me he has a plan to trick the sorcerer and the very thought of it makes me sick.

"What's going on there?" I point to the staff. "Why does it look like that?"

Silas shakes his head. "That sorcerer's staff is what's going on here, Khali."

"This is how your kingdom is going to beat the Occultists," Aleeryrick adds. "The blood magic is strong, and the bond grows stronger every day, but this magic"—he slams the end of the staff into the rug—"is far more powerful. Combining all the elements together makes us unstoppable."

I scoff. "And what's in it for you? Why would you help us? Is this all for the staff?"

Silas drops his gaze and Aleeryrick smiles ruefully. "You'll see." He turns back to Silas. "The army is ready?"

Silas nods. "They're in position."

"And everyone else?"

"Yes."

"Good. We can begin." His muddy brown eyes glisten. "By this time tomorrow we will have succeeded."

"I still don't understand," I whisper, but nobody is talking to me or listening. I'm a spectator now and that is all.

Silas reaches out and grips the staff that Aleeryrick still holds tight. A new color appears, mixing in with the others—a bright and relentless white. It must be the spirit magic Silas somehow managed to procure. I rack my brain, trying to focus on what I could be missing, but my palms are sweaty and my heart is racing and I can only stare at the magic staff as the colors grow brighter, shifting, twirling, blending together and then spreading apart.

"Do you feel that?" Aleeryrick asks Silas. "Feel all that magic?"

Silas nods. His eyes are no longer bloodshot, they're clear and sure.

Aleeryrick glances at me. "Do you want to experience this kind of power?"

So badly. More than they could ever know. Maybe it would bring my magic back. Or maybe it would make me like them…

I stand, shake my head, and edge back toward my bedroom door.

"The wards will be gone by morning." Silas gazes up at me. The colored light from the staff reflects off his face and hair, and his eyes, they're darker than normal. Excited. Nervous. Prepared. "Get some sleep. Tomorrow is the big day."

TWENTY-SEVEN

HAZEL

MY EYES FLUTTER OPEN AND I bolt up with a gasp, everything coming back to me. I have no way to tell what time of day it is or how long I've been asleep. The torchlight from the tunnel outside the room still flickers through the barred window. Cora and Macy are fast asleep. I climb from the bed and pad toward the door, peering out into the hallway. There's nobody there.

"Don't bother." Cora's quiet voice startles me. "There's never anybody there except sometimes the hot boy king or that creepy old dude."

"Creepy old dude?"

"I don't know who he is," Cora continues, "but he looks like a wizard or something. Carries a wooden glowy staff with him and has a white beard and everything."

"How stereotypical." We both laugh softly but it rings false. "I'm so sorry."

Macy sits up on her bed and gazes over at me through bleary eyes. "Hazel, are you going to tell us why we're here? We were kidnapped and taken by dragons. If I had been alone, I would have for sure thought I'd gone crazy." Her voice cracks like she's about to cry. "Sometimes I still think I'm crazy."

I go to her and wrap her into the biggest and tightest hug I can. "I'm so sorry." I say it again. I could say it a million times and it would never make up for what has happened to them. But what I can do is explain and so I do. I answer all their questions and they readily believe every word I say. Considering where we are right now, I'm not surprised. If I'd told them all this back at Westinbrooke, I don't know if they'd have believed me. Probably not.

But now they're—we're—living it. And unfortunately, they may be living it for a while. I just hope that they can survive this place. Now that Silas has got me here, what use does he have for them? He may kill them and get rid of the evidence.

"I'm going to get you out of here," I finish with a promise. "We're all going home. But right now we need to figure out a way to get this necklace off. If I can't use my spirit magic then I can't get out of this room, but if I can, then I can travel through the spirit realm and go find help."

They blink at me, as if they're caught in a dream. Maybe we all are.

It's strange but I haven't felt an ounce of my spirit magic since Silas put this thing on me. It's everything I'd hoped the obsidian necklaces would do. This thing really works. A few months ago I would have done anything to get my hands on this necklace, but now that I have it, I'd do anything to get it off. I don't feel the electric pulse I've had ever since I turned eighteen when my dragon self manifested and I definitely don't see any spirits. It's not as if I see them all the time but I feel it deep in my soul that they're gone from me. I am completely shut off from the spirit realm. Is this what it's like to be normal? It's what I've always wanted but now that it's here, I kind of hate it. I'm too empty.

Cora and Macy take turns trying to undo the knotted cord but it's impossible—the necklace doesn't want to budge. We don't have anything sharp to cut it off but even if we did I don't think it would work.

"It's hopeless," I declare. I try to calm my breathing but I'm starting to hyperventilate. This wasn't supposed to happen. And Dean? Dean is going to come after me. I'm sure of it. *I know him.* He doesn't have any idea where to find me all the way down here. He'll be executed.

The room goes ice cold. A little snap sounds and the

necklace falls to the ground. "What the...?"

Macy and Cora stare at the necklace, dumbfounded. "How?" Macy asks.

But I'm not staring at the necklace anymore, it's the three spirits standing in front of me who've caught my attention. One is Owen. Another is a reaper, his scythe shining like liquid silver and balancing between skeletal fingers. And the third spirit is an old version of the Brightcaster boys, most resembling Silas.

"Sorry that took so long," Owen says in an annoyed tone. "I had to find a reaper who would agree to cut that thing off of you." He points to the necklace and my mouth drops open. "Hazel, I'd like you to meet my father, King Titus Brightcaster."

The man doesn't say anything, he just stares at me like I'm some sort of deformed creature. This guy is unnerving and totally intimidating. He's tall with impossibly broad shoulders and long blondish hair. His eyes are bluish purple and dance with untapped electricity. He wears kingly attire and even a golden crown on his head.

"Woah..." is about all I can manage to say.

"Hazel, what's going on?" Cora asks, "What do you see?" But I can't answer her, not now, not yet.

At the back of my mind, I still wonder if I should fear the

reaper. But they're not my problem anymore. They're here to help, not to harm.

Owen turns on the reaper. "I'm almost ready. Soon, I promise."

The reaper hisses and disappears in a cloud of black smoke.

"Come on," Owen says, reaching out to me. "We're running out of time."

"Time for what?"

"Time to save Khali," the king says, his deep rich voice catching me off guard. "And the rest of my family. Silas is…" His voice trails off. "He's dangerous. And so are the others."

I swallow. "The others?"

"The wards have been down for hours. The Occultists are almost here."

A fear unlike anything I've ever known crawls over my skin with icy fingers.

This is happening.

I turn back to my friends, hoping they'll understand. "I'll be back, I promise, but for now you're much safer down here."

"What's going on?" Cora demands again. Macy stands frozen, tears in her eyes.

"We need to go, Hazel," Owen says, voice growing more urgent.

"Some really bad guys are here," I say. "And I have to go stop them before they kill everyone." My friends' eyes go wide and their faces pale. "Step back, okay? I'm going to shift."

I don't think I can hurt them considering my spirit dragon is part of two realms and they'll be able to see me but not touch me—still, I can't risk it. Macy and Cora press themselves against the far wall and I shift into my dragon form. I'm small enough to fit in here but just barely. The last thing I see are the mystified expressions on my best friend's faces before I'm hurling myself from this dingy prison cell and into the relentless white of the supernatural spirit realm.

This time traveling through the spirit realm isn't nearly as exhausting as the first time. Maybe because I'm already getting the hang of it or maybe because I'm not going far, but time doesn't slow like it did earlier. I follow Owen and Titus through the white and to the image of Khali. She's pacing in her room, dressed in the type of a-line green princess gown that I'd expect for Drakenon. Her hair is pulled back into braids on the top of her head. She's dripping in red rubies and her eyes are painted with some kind of smudgy eyeliner. She's beautiful, but she's sad.

I have to help her.

I jump through the image, landing in the physical room beside her. I'm panting, like I've finished running a mile, but at least I'm in my human form.

"Hazel?" Khali gasps and wraps me into a tight hug. She's shaking and thinner than I remember her. "I'm so glad you're here!"

She's never hugged me before. Actually, she's stayed away from me, since touching me has hurt her in the past. But I hug her back and my magic doesn't react.

"Where's Dean? He's not here, is he? Silas will kill him!"

"No, he's not here. He's somewhere safe for now. What about you? Are you okay?"

"Yeah," she sighs. "No."

"What's going on?"

She releases a heavy breath. "Well, the wards are down meaning the Occultists are going to be here any minute. Silas has a plan to stop them but I'm pretty sure it's going to create an even bigger problem. I have to get to Bram. He has something I need… " Her voice trails off.

"I know all about the wards. Owen and Titus told me."

"Owen and Titus? You saw them?" She stops short, gaping at me.

"Yeah, but we can talk about that later. Where's Silas?" I take in the room, and yeah, she's the queen alright. This room is gorgeous, but that also means her vile husband could be near. "I don't want that jerk to catch me and lock me up again."

Her face pales as she releases me from the hug and steps back. "He locked you up? When?"

"Last night," I say. "He's got some of my friends down there too."

"Oh no." She starts to pace again. "Your friends are down there? For how long?"

"Maybe a week."

"That must be what Bellflower Blossom was talking about."

"I don't know—"

"And *that's* how he got the spirit magic. He took it from you."

"He did," I growl, "but I'm fine now. I got it back." I swallow down the fear about what I'm about to tell her. She needs to know. "Khali, you need to know the truth about the spell between us." Her eyes hold mine. "If I die, you will die too. That's why they did it. They're trying to kill you. They thought they'd hold me prisoner as a baby and keep me until I was eighteen when they could sacrifice me, but my mom got us out and raised me in the human world."

"Well, that explains a lot…"

"We have to stop the Occultists," I say, "and I think we have to do it together."

Her pretty round face sets into a look of sheer

determination. "Okay, but first we need to go get my weapon from Bram."

I raise a brow. "And what might that be?"

She smiles for the first time since I've found her, her unusual eyes twinkling. "A really sharp spear with magical powers."

I can't help it, I smile too. "Sign me up! Let's go get it."

TWENTY-EIGHT

"THE SPEAR ISN'T HERE." MY panic is a frantic punch in my gut as I look around Bram's library, skeleton key in my hand and empty chest at my feet. He's not here either. "No, no, no, this can't be happening."

"Hey, it's okay," Hazel says. She tries to sound calm but worry slips in the cracks between her words. "We'll figure something out."

"This *was* my something." I fall to my knees and rest my head against the edge of the wooden chest. Just last night Bram had locked Flannery's spear in here for me. Did he take it? And if he took it, why would he break his promise to me?

"We can fight without it." Hazel sounds confident but she doesn't know about my lost magic or exactly why the Occultists want to sacrifice me. "Come on. It's going to be okay. We need to go out there though." She points to the window and I stand on shaky legs to peer out. Beyond the city wall, lines of black lethal dragons are readying to fight. "That's where the action is going to be so that's where we need to be."

My throat goes dry. *No, no, no!* How am I supposed to fight? I need to tell her the truth. "Hazel, there's something you should know—"

A chorus of dragons roar, interrupting me. It's not just the dragon army preparing themselves for battle anymore. I squint, making out Aleeryrick and Silas among the crowd. There are others with him too. I catch the sun shining off Juniper's blonde hair and Maxx's ram horns. Someone turns and I'm sure it's Terek's face glancing back up at the castle. They're all dressed in armor.

They're here because I brought them here.

"What is it?" Hazel asks.

"It doesn't matter right now. You're right. Whatever is going on, it's not happening in this castle." I thought perhaps Silas would keep his guards on me or lock me up in my chamber, knowing that my magic is gone, but he hasn't. In fact, I haven't seen him all morning. Everyone who can fight has joined the battlefield. And now it's our turn.

Nerves wash over Hazel's face and I give her a stiff nod

and speak the words we're both probably thinking but afraid to say. "Okay, let's go."

I LEAD HAZEL THROUGH THE tunnels. She tells me this is where Silas has been keeping her human friends and where she spent the night. It immediately makes sense as to why Silas was able to talk to Owen and Titus last night and why Aleeryrick asked him to pass some of the spirit magic onto the staff—the necklace.

"Did he put a necklace on you?" I already know the answer.

"Yes!" Her voice grows angry. "It took my magic away."

"It didn't just take it away," I say, wishing I didn't have to tell her the rest. "Anytime you tried to use your magic, it was syphoned right to Silas."

She shakes her head and fists her palms. "Son of a—"

"I'm sorry, I know, he's horrible." I peer at her over the flicker of the oil lamp's small flame. "But when this is all over, I promise to help get you and your friends home."

"Thank you." She sucks her bottom lip between her teeth and thinks for a while. "I hope you can make good on that promise, Khali."

"Believe me, so do I." What am I doing? I shouldn't be

making promises. Truth is, I'm probably not going to survive this. If she knew I didn't have magic, she wouldn't be putting her trust in me right now.

We continue on through the narrow tunnel, the little flame as our guide through the darkness, and fall into silence. My mind returns to when I hugged Hazel earlier. I'd hoped that it would trigger something within me, that maybe my elementals would return, but nothing happened.

Nothing.

I'm certain that whatever the Occultists did to spell us together as babies meant that when we turned eighteen she'd fully develop her powers but I'd lose mine. Now they just need to kill one of us, right? I shudder to think what that would mean.

She tells me about her parentage and even though we're both Dragon Blessed, we're not closely related. All I can think is that the warlocks had to find a dragon child who was born on the same day I was for their spell to work and they caught wind of Hazel's mother's pregnancy and somehow spelled her to give birth the day I was born.

As we walk, she confides in me more about being half faerie and half dragon, and explains how her dragon actually manifests in between realms.

"Your gift sounds very unique," I supply. "Don't take it for granted, okay? Promise me you'll work hard on developing it."

She looks at me sideways but agrees.

I hate that my four elements are nowhere to be found. But despite the openness of her eyes and the honesty in this conversation, I keep my secret locked up tight.

It's killing me.

It's probably literally going to kill me very soon, but if I told her the truth now she wouldn't want to go out there with me. None of them would want me there for the battle. I can't have that. I need to be part of this, I need to fight, to do something. I won't stand down any longer. The Occultists have taken nearly everything from me. If we can defeat them, we can defeat their spells as well. It's the only way I'm going to get my magic back. I have to try.

With each step forward, I've realized something about myself. I always thought I needed to get away from this place, to fly and to be free on my own. I thought I needed freedom to be happy and I wanted to avoid my duties as Drakenon's future queen. But it turns out, what I thought wasn't actually true. To be happy I need to help the people I love and do the right thing. Standing up for myself has never been a problem, but what about all the other people who need someone to stand up for them? What about the fae who are left to hide away? And Bellflower Blossom who died for nothing? What about Bram and people like him who aren't Dragon Blessed?

I'll die today to save my people if I have to… and I'm at peace with that.

Because I'd rather die than live as a coward. It's an odd feeling, knowing this will likely be my final day of life. I wonder if Owen will be there for me on the other side and what King Titus will have to say about my choices. I can only hope Bram and my parents and so many others will make it out of this fight alive. And I hope that they can have a better life, without a tyrant for a king, and without the zealous warlocks bent on destroying them.

We finally make it to the end of the tunnel and step out from the hidden trapdoor in the wall, scrambling through the thicket of bushes and blinking against the midday sun. I'm hit with a caress of gentle wind. It brushes the hair from my face, almost to tell me that everything is going to be okay.

I know it won't, but still, I allow myself to hope.

I squint and look around. Most of the snow has melted. The ground is rock hard in some places and muddy in others. The smell of fresh winter and metal armor and bridled fear dance on the breeze.

"This isn't going to be easy, is it?" Hazel sighs.

"I'm afraid not."

"Hmm…"

"Stay away from Silas," I say quickly, grabbing onto her hand. "And don't touch the sorcerer's staff. There's something dark going on there with those two. You shouldn't get any more involved than you already are. Let's just focus on keeping as many people alive as we can and fight off the Occultists."

"Easier said than done, right?" She chuckles with self-deprecation and rolls her eyes. "But sure, I'll do my best."

Bootsteps squash against mud to our right and we turn to find several of the Dragon Blessed army approaching. Some are already shifted into fearsome dragons but most are still men and women, dressed in heavy leathers. They're the same leathers Hazel and I stole to put over our clothes on the way out of the tunnel. No guards were left in the castle. It was easy.

Was it too easy?

"Queen Khali," a man says, "Silas has requested you to join him."

A sinking feeling comes over me because yes, it was far too easy. Maybe Silas wanted me to follow him down here. What if this is a trap?

I glance at Hazel, holding her gaze for a long second, wishing I could speak to her through the dragon link. "Stay here."

"Both of you," the man adds, his voice clipped.

"Well, then…" Hazel sighs. A strand of her wheat colored hair catches in her mouth and she pushes it back up into her hair tie. "Let's get this over with."

We follow the army men and women over to King Silas. As we approach, I look to Terek, Maxx, and Juniper, who all seem excited by the prospect of a fight. These are people who've probably trained for something like this, or maybe they're just ready to get vengeance on the Occultists. They're dressed the part, with swords and bows in their hands, and determination on their faces.

One by one, they see me, and they startle. They know it isn't safe for me to be here. Terek opens his mouth to say something but Maxx pulls him back. Juniper just stares, her face draining of color.

And Silas? The man is beautiful in his battle clothes, there's no denying it. He looks every part a dragon king, with his blond hair tied back and a small crown perched on his head. The black battle leathers look good against his muscled arms and legs and he stands like he has everything to gain. But the way he watches us approach is anything but beautiful. It's terrifying. And I want to look away but I don't.

"I see you've found my prisoner." Silas's electric eyes land on Hazel.

"Keeping her locked away is a mistake. She's an asset to this fight," I challenge.

He frowns at that, and then his eyes linger on her neckline. "Where's the necklace?"

"Destroyed," she growls back, shoulders tensing.

"I made it myself," Aleeryrick says, stepping forward. The sorcerer looks older in this light but then again he's immortal so there's no telling how old he really must be. The magicked staff glows beneath his palm and his brown eyes narrow on Hazel. "It can't be destroyed. It's impossible."

"Not with a reaper's scythe it isn't," Hazel barks back.

The group falls silent for a tense moment. I worry about what they'll do but Aleeryrick only smiles curiously and Silas laughs like this is an amazing new development.

Not what I expected.

"What do you think?" Silas turns to Aleeryrick. "Can we still do it?"

Aleeryrick's hand tightens on his staff. "We can."

"They're here!" someone yells.

It happens so fast. Black tendrils of smoky magic curl around us out of seemingly nowhere the very same moment a line of endless Occultists appear on the horizon. Within seconds, people start to fall, their bodies being eaten alive by the smoke. Blood seeps from their eyes and mouths in a gruesome scene. Chaos erupts.

"Charge!" a man yells and the dragons shift, taking off in flight toward the enemies. Earth rattles, wind roars, water from the nearby lakes shoots through the air, a fire burns— all the elements are at play here, meaning all the best of the Dragon Blessed are fighting. It's an amazing sight to behold. The black smoke retreats just as quickly as it came and I think that maybe we will stand a chance to beat them.

Hazel grabs my hand. "Ready to shift?"

She thinks we're going to charge in there and take them on together. She still doesn't know my problem. I take a step back, my mouth dropping open and a soft "I can't" tumbles from my lips. She stares at me, dumbfounded.

"Now," Silas says. He grabs hold of Aleeryrick's staff and the pulsing colors swirl through it like they did last night. The men slam the end of the staff into the hard ground, and when they do, all my friends fall.

Juniper falls.

Terek falls.

Maxx falls.

Hazel falls.

"What?" I scream, rushing forward to yell at Silas. "What are you doing to them?"

But he doesn't answer. I whip my head around, frantic,

and that's when I notice my friends aren't the only ones who have fallen. Many of the dragons are on the ground too.

And color, like the black smoky magic only in color, is seeping from them and traveling to the staff. Browns, greens, reds, oranges—every color is joining the staff, power radiating off it.

"What's going on?" I scream at Silas again.

Still holding one hand on the staff, he pulls a pouch from his pocket and dumps a plume of sparking gold dust on the staff.

"The pixie dust I promised," he says to Aleeryrick.

My heart drops to my stomach as guilt and anger take over. He got that from Bellflower Blossom! He killed her for it! I shove at the men, careful to stay away from touching the staff. They don't budge but at least my angry shoving seems to get their attention. "What are you doing?" I scream again, pointing to all the bodies writhing in the snow and mud. "You're killing them!"

"Then so be it!" Silas glares back at me. "This is what it takes to beat the Occultists, to take their magic as our own."

As our own? "No!"

"All this elemental magic in one magical object," Silas continues, his voice growing mad with power. "It's worth the sacrifice."

"It's not your sacrifice to make!" I scream but my words fall on deaf ears.

Aleeryrick laughs. "Yes, it's quite perfect." He eyes Silas with glee. "And you still think you're going to betray me. Didn't you ever wonder if I'd be the one to betray you?"

Silas blinks, the madness clearing from his eyes. "Wait…"

Aleeryrick shoves Silas off the staff and he falls to the ground, immediately convulsing like all the others. An electric blue color floats from his body, joining the staff. The crown atop his head pops off and rolls to rest against my leather boots.

"You can join me, Khali," Aleeryrick speaks with a casual tone though I know he's anything but casual, "or you can die."

I'm speechless.

"Just as well," he cackles. "This way I'll take what they wanted."

I can only stand there. Stunned and angry and not knowing what to do. He must take that as a no because he shrugs and nudges the staff toward me. That's all it takes, a simple nudge. Searing pain envelopes my entire being from the inside out, so terrible that I can't even scream, my throat won't let me. My limbs go numb. I hit the ground with a thud and my vision goes from white to black to white again.

And then there's nothing else.

TWENTY-NINE

HAZEL

MY BREATH HITCHES, JOLTING ME awake. I'm in a vast white room—the spirit realm. My heart pounds. My ears ring. Something about being here this time feels different. I'm more solid somehow, but also the opposite of that, like my body is weightless.

Isn't there somewhere I'm supposed to be right now?

I blink and gaze around, noticing the images of my loved ones floating in space. I reach out toward the scene of Harmony and my mother decorating a tall and skinny Christmas tree. Mom's wings are back, they glisten silver in the light of the multicolored lights as she hangs a vintage ornament. She was waiting until I got home from school so we could go to the tree farm and decorate it together, but that was before everything changed. I can't believe I'm going to miss Christmas but even more startling is that I forgot about it entirely over the last few days. How does someone like me, someone obsessed with the holidays, forget about it?

I'm trying to remember—to put all the pieces together—but my mind is foggy.

I catch sight of another image, one that makes me scream and rush forward, until I'm no longer in the white room. I'm standing on a patch of white snow, reaching out for Dean. He's bloodied and bruised, his black hair hanging around this face, as he struggles to stand. On each side, two Occultists hold onto him, keeping him up right.

"No! Dean, why did you follow me?" I cry.

And then I remember it all—and how I got here.

Nobody hears me. And the Occultists, they look eerily similar and ageless, with glowing lustful red eyes and deep burgundy robes caked in water and mud along the bottoms. Their hoods cover sickly white bald heads and they chant together, their voices somehow rearing a black smoky magic that rumbles and pulses along the ground.

"Dean?" My voice squeaks. Tears burn my eyes. "Can you hear me?"

But I already know that he can't. And when I put my hand out to touch him, my fingers pass right through him. I scream again and look out over the expanse of the field, spotting the sorcerer with the staff, and my own body laying there among the carnage.

I'm not using my spirit magic right now. This isn't a normal shift and travel between realms. This is death.

I've died.

My lungs pulse, holding back a scream, but the battle scene around me is replaced with the white room before a sound escapes my throat.

This time I'm not alone.

Owen is here and King Titus, too. And also so many others. Too many. People I don't know on a name basis but who I recognize from the battlefield, dressed in the dark leathers that the Dragon Blessed wore into battle.

I find Khali standing aimlessly and my heart plummets. "No," I whisper. My death must have meant hers, too. *Unless…*

"Where are we?"

Her question interrupts my thoughts and I meet her fearful eyes with a simple nod of my head. I wish I could lie to her but I can't. "This is the spirit realm."

Her face pales. "Does that mean…?"

"I'm afraid so, for me too." My voice breaks as I try to get the words out. "I'm so sorry."

I pull her into a hug and she's solid to me, real, and even

though we're dead and we've failed, we're still in this together. My heart aches for everything and everyone we're about to leave behind. Knowing what I know, being who I am, I've had a lot of time to think about death. And I know this: I'm not going to stick around this waiting place. I want to move on. I can't be the ghost who won't let go of the life she lost, sad or angry or desperate to send a message to the living. I already know my mom won't be able to see me, nobody will, so why would I want to see her pain? And there's nothing I can do to help Dean without a body. All I can wish for is that everyone I love survives this attack and goes on to live wonderful lives, and one day when it's their time, I'll meet them on the other side.

It's strange, I already can't wait for that reunion but I also want it to be a long time away.

I'm crying. I didn't even realize it at first but the tears are unstoppable, hot and wet and burning. It feels like someone has stuck a dagger in my heart which they just keep twisting and twisting. This hurts so bad. It wasn't supposed to be this way.

"Khali?" a deep voice comes between us, filled with confusion and regret but also love and joy. Khali and I turn to find Owen standing before us. He's so, so beautiful. He's dressed in his princely attire again and has a mischievous glint in his bright eyes but also something else, something only reserved for Khali, something unmistakable—love.

In an instant she's out of my arms and burrowed into his, sobbing. They hug for a while and whisper to each other in hushed tones. I hear "I'm sorry" and "my fault" and "I love you" and "it's going to be okay" but then Khali suddenly steps back and says forcefully, "no."

"I am not leaving," she says vehemently, "I can't give up."

"But you're dead." Owen's sky blue eyes are sad and pleading. "You can't go back. Believe me, I've tried. It doesn't work that way."

She shakes her head again, settling into denial like the stubborn girl that she is. I guess it takes one to know one.

"I knew I was most likely going to die today," she says, "but not like this, not so quickly, and not before I made a difference. We have to stop the Occultists first. And now we have to stop Aleeryrick and Silas."

"Silas is dead, too."

Shock races across her expression and she's left without words.

"You saw it happen."

Her hand covers her mouth. "But I didn't realize that's what was happening."

King Titus pops in out of nowhere, startling us all. His

eyes are frantic and overbearing as he looks around the white room, witnessing the growing number of people who have appeared here. He grabs Khali and hugs her hard against this broad chest. She sputters with surprise. "I'm so sorry," he says. "This is my fault. I should have never made you marry Silas or trusted the sorcerer in the first place."

He lets her go and stares into her eyes, like whatever he has to say next is of utmost importance. "But there's still a chance for you. And if you go back, all your vows and bonds and spells will be broken. You will start fresh."

"What?" Her voice cracks with disbelief. "How can I go back though?"

"Bram," he says simply, his face filling with pride.

"And Juniper." One of the fae steps forward, a handsome one with golden blond hair, catlike eyes, and an easy smile. "Maxx just disappeared," he says, his voice excited. "And Juniper isn't here which might mean what I think it means."

I don't quite understand any of it but his words light Khali's eyes and she jumps from Titus's arms and into the fae's. "Terek! Are you saying there's a chance?"

"I think so!"

"A chance for what?"

They turn on me. "Juniper is a healer," she gushes. "She might be able to bring us back."

My eyes practically pop out of my head as hope burns bright in my chest. "But if I'm dead, then you're dead. The Occultists or that sorcerer should already have your magic."

"Not if I died first," she muses, "the spell only works if they kill you first, remember?"

"Listen to me, girls," Titus says gruffly, taking both our hands between his large rough ones. It's strange, but also comforting. "This is important. Don't forget what I'm about to tell you."

We nod, all ears.

"The Occultist's blood bond works through sacrifice, strengthening their bond each time someone dies, but it also leaves them weaker because if their master is killed, then they will all die." He grins. "Don't you see? By spelling you two, they revealed their weakness."

"How do you know this?" Khali questions.

"We've been able to visit them because of Dean," Owen adds, "we can go visit our living family and he's with them now. He's with the master. They're going to sacrifice him to the bond once they get to the portal the mermaids are protecting."

"I love my son," Titus says, "I love all my sons. I have failed them. But you might have a chance to save Dean. He needs you."

Owen interjects. "It was only in death that we learned the truth of the blood bond but now we know—we know the truth—and so do you. They never could have anticipated this."

I nod, because they're both right. And I'm determined to save Dean, to save us, and everyone I possibly can.

"Juniper is close," Khali says, her eyes fluttering shut and then opening again, landing on Owen. "I have to leave you."

Something light and feathery tugs at my conscience, and Owen and Khali hurry to say their goodbyes. The edges of my vision start to fade to black and my body grows heavier and heavier, but I don't give into the fear. Rather, I fall into the void. I'm being given another chance. It feels exactly like a miracle.

THIRTY

KHALI

IT'S ALEERYRICK'S BLOOD CURDLING SCREAMS that wake me before anything else. "What have you done?" he bellows. My eyes flutter open. "Now you're all going to die!" He screams again, vengeful and determined. Fuzzy thoughts cling to my mind but his words wake me. I scamper to my feet, the haze of death clearing in seconds.

"Bram… " His name is a balm, soft on my lips, and my heart speeds to find him. Standing with Flannery's golden spear in one hand, Bram is covered in dirt and sweat and blood. His emerald eyes are zeroed in on the wizard with complete determination, his jaw set in a sharp line. I gasp. At their feet are the two broken ends of the Jeweled Forest staff. All the color and magic that was being held there has vanished.

"You okay?" Juniper asks. I almost forgot she was at my side but I nod. She's holding my hand and I didn't even realize it. She squeezes it once and then runs over to where Hazel is sprawled out. Thank the Gods for Bram and Juniper. Bram for being brave and smart. And Juniper for her healing magic, which must have saved her first and now she's saving each of us, one by one, attempting to heal us before we're fully lost.

But the sorcerer's staff is broken so whatever it was meant to do, it failed. The black smoke from the Sovereign Occultists has also vanished but I'm certain that won't last much longer. The charge of the magic still lingers in the air. They'll realize whatever was stopping them has failed and come back at us, and with more force than the first time. I blink across the expanse of the field and see them, still lined up, still chanting, still very much alive.

No. I won't let them win.

Aleeryrick yells again and raises his fist to Bram, his arm readying to swing. I lunge forward. Magic bursts through my body, the four elementals filling every last crevice, and tears spring to my eyes. Titus was right! My magic has returned because all vows and spells were broken when I passed through death and joined the spirit realm. I've returned stronger than ever.

I use air to send a gust of wind to push Aleeryrick away from Bram, flattening him to the ground. "You will pay for this!" I use the earth elemental to have the mud around him suck at his limbs and pull him under. *I will bury this traitor alive if I have to!* His eyes flash to mine, fear crossing his features. *Good—he should be afraid.* I'm not going to let him get away with this. He thought he could take my first daughter, thought he could work with Silas to steal our magic, then turn on us.

"Please," he gasps, as if I can be swayed to take mercy on him. I can't.

A savage anger burns molten within me, hotter even than my fire elemental rising to the surface. Fireballs flicker to my fingers and grow into flames, taller and taller and taller. And hot, hotter than anything I've ever felt before. Aleeryrick is half under the earth but the fire wants to take a crack at him, too. And who am I to stop it? The rage is all encompassing. Maybe I should stop the anger; maybe I should take pity on the man. But I don't. Immortal doesn't mean he can't be killed, just that he won't die of old age. Well, I think he's lived long enough.

"Please stop!" he begs.

"You claim to have lived more than a century," I snarl. "That your magic kept others from entering Drakenon."

"I can explain."

"Your time is up!"

"No!" he bellows, squeezes his eyes shut, softening his expression, and then... he completely disappears.

I blink, confused. He's gone? "What? How? Where is he!"

The staff still lays broken beside where he was and I direct the fire at that instead, burning it until it is nothing more than ash. It hisses and resists, but my magic is too much for it.

"I need to find that sorcerer!" I scream, the anger still raging inside me.

"We have other things to worry about," Bram's voice is sure and soothing, quick to temper my flame. He steps forward and pulls me into a hug, kissing the top of my head. I melt into him.

My Bram. Thank Gods my Bram is alive.

We survey the battlefield. So many are dead. Silas, included—he still hasn't gotten up from where he lays sprawled out and bloodied. Juniper runs from person to person but steers clear of the young king. Maybe I should direct her back to him, maybe I should have pity on Silas, forgive him, but I don't. Seeing Owen on the other side and saying goodbye didn't give me the peace I thought it would. It only made me sad. His death was unnecessary. So much of what has happened shouldn't have happened. But it was at Silas's hand and there are more who would have died because of him. My fae friends, some of the dragons, Silas was in on this with Aleeryrick and he was willing to sacrifice even more lives to get the power he wanted—the Occultist's power.

Being king of Drakenon wasn't enough for him and it never would have been.

He was willing to kill whoever necessary for his selfish ambitions. I don't know what kind of fate Silas will meet on the other side, or who he'll have to answer to, but I'm not going to stop righteous judgement from happening. He deserves the death he got, the betrayal he walked into. He chose it with his actions.

And Bram is right. I have other things to worry about right now. Namely the plume of crawling black smoke that is billowing toward us and the hordes of Occultists floating in our direction from the other end of the field. Their chanting grows louder with every passing second. Whatever break in the battle this was, it's over.

"Keep going," I yell to Juniper. "Bring back as many as you can!"

Then I turn, frantic to find Hazel, but she's already beat me to it. She's awake again, human again, and charging right back toward the Occultists, her blonde hair streaming behind her, her legs pumping her forward.

"Come on!" she yells at me. "They have Dean!"

My heart seizes. *No, please not Dean, too…*

Bram releases me from the hug. "You can do this," he says. He's so sure. His face, his eyes, everything about him is positive that I'm capable of success. He believes in me, more than I believe in myself, and that gives me the strength to do what needs to be done.

"Keep using that!" I point to the spear. "Stay hidden!"

Then I shift, my dragon form taking over like a second skin, and vault into the air, flying after Hazel. I catch up to her and she shifts as well. Her white dragon is half the size of mine, and not quite solid, but she's fast. And she's able to be in multiple realms at once, to see this place and the spirit realm, and for a moment I wish I could see it, too.

But I have my own magic to wield—magic I'll never take for granted. Not ever.

The battle begins with a roar, louder than I expected, and the action moves fast. My body takes over, knowing exactly what to do. I blow fire when I can and use my other elements to cut down the enemy. They're quick to dodge me and fire back with their black magic. It hits me a few times, sucking the life out of me before I can get away. I'm growing weaker with each hit but I don't let it deter me. And I'm not alone in that. The expanse of snowy field transforms into sheer hellfire and magic and black death and powerful elementals—and best of all, dragons.

We're everywhere.

These are *my people* and I love them. I'll fight to the death for them. And I'll never ever *ever* run away from them again. As I fight alongside them, defending who I can, letting them defend me, roaring with sadness and anger when one goes down, and triumph when one of ours takes one of theirs, I realize this is exactly where I am meant to be. We call to each other through our dragon link, our thoughts instantly communicated to the group, and it turns us into a ruthless and united force. It's our own kind of bond, and it's not made of blood sacrifice. It's made of centuries old magic, of friends and family, of being who we were born to be. And now, finally, I get to be one of them. I get to lead. To prove myself. To do all the things I've dreamed of doing.

The fae join us. Terek shoots arrows. Maxx cuts through the enemies. Juniper heals the fallen, as many as she can get to in time. Over the crest of a nearby hill, others charge toward us. Not dragons. Fae of all kinds, here to fight, led by a gorgeous bronzed centaur—Flannery. They send out a battle cry as they come at the warlocks from behind.

With their help, we're surrounding the warlocks on all sides. They seem to be moving toward the lake's edge, to get at the portal no doubt. The merpeople appear, cracking through the ice, spears at the ready. They snarl and hiss, determined to defend their territory. It's the warlocks against every other kind they have wronged and maybe, just maybe, we can win this.

I catch sight of Hazel. She's right near Dean, so close to breaking him free from the two warlocks who hold him. I screech and fly forward to help, dodging black magic as I zip through the frosty air. I blast the men who hold Dean with a torrent of ice and they lose their grip, trying to fight off the impenetrable cold. That one small moment of freedom is all Dean needs. He shifts into a roaring dragon and pours judgement upon their heads, lighting them like torches. They fall and he cuts away from the warlocks, quick to team up with Hazel.

The two of them take on the world together, moving in tandem, as if they are of the same mind. He shoots fireballs and rips the enemy apart with his teeth, and she's right there with him. I'm not entirely sure what she's doing, but she must be doing something with her spirit elemental as she sweeps through the crowd, because there's a determination leading her little white dragon body, something that speaks of ancient magic.

I don't have time to wonder about it, I have to keep moving. Keep fighting. It's kill or be killed. There are simply so many warlocks, countless more than I ever thought possible. And they just keep coming. They don't fight with swords or fists, it's that black magic, and it's growing more and more with each passing second. I knew the Sovereign Occultists had years to build their cult, decades, maybe longer, but I never knew it was this big. Maybe that's a good thing that I didn't know because if I had, I would've had a lot more fear coming into this fight.

Bram is out here with the spear and even though part of me wants to make him go back, he's too vulnerable, I have to trust in the magicked spear to keep him alive. Flannery brandishes a mighty sword. He seems comfortable with the weapon, crazed by the fight—by revenge—as he screams a gutteral battle cry and charges into a horde of the evil men, cutting each opponent down in seconds. His bare muscles move in a strange kind of grace as he fights, it's dazzling. I wish I could fight like that.

But then… he falls too.

Juniper sees it happen at the same time I do. I swoop toward him and she sprints forward, falling to her knees at his side. She puts her hands out to heal him. I shift back to my human form so I can talk to her.

"Is he okay?"

"He's not waking up," her voice is strained. She keeps her hands pressed to him while life gushes from the wound at his abdomen. "The blood should be stopping by now. The wound should be healing itself." Her eyes grow frantic. "Why isn't it working?"

Flannery's eyes flutter open, staring into nothing as if they're trying to focus but they can't. "Tell them…" he whispers, "tell them I love them."

Then his entire body slackens.

He's gone.

The black plumes of the Occultists' blood magic crash over us, swallowing us whole. I can feel their bond coiling through me, heavy and powerful. It's stronger than I ever could have imagined, a condensed magic unlike anything I've experienced in my life. Juniper is here with me in this magic, both of us lost to it. I reach out to her but find nothing. I'm alone and all I can see is inky, endless black. My lifeforce is sucked away as my body weakens. I crumple to the ground—it too, is an endless darkness. One thought centers in my mind: there's no coming back from death this time.

THIRTY-ONE

HAZEL

MY WINGS CARRY ME AS if I'm weightless, the inertia of flight creating an awesome sense of purpose. It's indescribable! If I wasn't in the middle of an epic battle that could be straight from a fantasy TV show, I would be able to appreciate it more. As it is, I'm just trying to keep Dean alive. My thoughts are all my own but my body is still new to me, this dragon self who feels like an old friend. I'm untouchable when I'm her—nothing can hurt me. No magic. No enemy. It's the most freeing feeling I've ever experienced.

I'm straddling two realms like it's my natural state of being. I can see the physical world and the spirit realm at once, but that also means I can't touch either of them, almost like I'm a ghost, visible to all.

They can't touch me. And *that* is the only good thing about this because there is blood, so much blood, everywhere. And there are cries and screams. And the smell of burning flesh and blood and sweat and magic and snow and mud and so many things I can't even begin to describe.

I follow close as Dean charges after the enemy, attacking without hesitation. I swoop in and around him, awed as he fully awakens to his powers in a way he's never shown me before. He's ruthless, leaving no warlock alive in his wake of raw power, claws and teeth and fire.

Why did you leave me? His accusatory voice juts through my mind. It's the question he asks me again and again since we reunited. And I don't know what to say… This dragon communication is far more amazing and capable than what humans can do. I can hear the dragons calling out to each other as they work to bring the enemy down, but I can also clearly hear all my own thoughts, and Dean and I can speak to each other without others listening in if we want.

But now, because of this shared intelligence, I have to answer to Dean. I can't keep putting this off.

I didn't want you to get hurt, I relent. *I still don't.*

That wasn't your decision to make. I was prepared to see this through to the end.

Well, I see you followed me anyway, didn't you? And let me guess, that's how you got caught. The village wasn't compromised too, was it?

Suddenly I imagine hordes of Occultists converging on the cute little Winter village and my gut turns. I don't know what I would do if the hidden fae village was found out and people were hurt.

They're fine, Dean responds. *I left the village to come after you the second you took off, but many of the fae demanded to come with me. The Occultists caught me at the border. The other fae got away, thank Gods.*

They were going to sacrifice you, weren't they? As I ask the question, I know without any doubts that this is true and my heart aches at the possibility.

Yes. Eventually.

Dean follows his answer by cutting down another warlock. The man bellows in pain, his eyes crazed and glowing red as he drops to the ground. His body changes, ages, and within seconds he's dead. I watch as a reaper appears and overtakes on him, dragging him away to whatever hell is waiting. This is how it is with each warlock, whether the death is easy or hard, the reapers are here, swarming, ready to take them. It's nothing like so many others I've seen, where the reapers give the dead time to decide they're ready to move on. Not anymore. They just act, grabbing hold of them in the spirit realm and disappearing into a portal of black.

So in a way, I guess they are making it through portals, just not the kind of portals they were hoping for. Karma, right? They deserve it.

When I think the battle is starting to sway toward the dragons' favor, the thick black magic from the warlocks multiplies tenfold. The men chant together, loud and clear, in that ancient language that makes my toes curl. The black wraps around the entire battlefield, like a cloud of death. Dean, Khali, the fae, all the other dragons, everyone is lost to the darkness.

And we've played right into their plan.

They wanted this, sacrificed many of their own for this, because now we're all in one place. They'll suck the life from all of us and that will be the end of it, the royals, the army, everyone will be dead. The rest of Drakenon will have no choice but to surrender.

I continue to fly, the black magic unable to hurt me in this form, horrified that I have to watch these people die and I can't stop it. I blink, looking for Dean, but he's gone. I can't see anyone anymore, it's too thick. *Dean? Khali? Where are you?* Nobody replies. The communication is gone. All of it. I roar, the noise rolling over the too-quiet field.

This can't be happening. No!

If my dragon could cry, she would be crying right now,

but she can't. And the only people I can see are the ones popping up in the spirit realm, dragons and warlocks. I can't save them if they end up there. I don't have Juniper's power. I don't know where their bodies are.

The reapers hover around, waiting for more warlocks.

One turns to me. *What do you see?* he asks. *You have the sight.*

I shake my head.

We can't see mortal realms, he continues, *not unless we possess a mortal body. We can only sense you and feel what you feel. That is how we find you.*

How are the warlocks doing this? another one asks, swooping in. His voice is a slippery hiss. But I'm not afraid of him or any of them anymore. They don't feel scary, they feel wise and even compassionate.

I gaze from side to side, trying to make sense of what they're asking me. *There's black magic,* I think through the dragon link, hoping they can understand.

What does it look like? a third reaper says, coming in closer than the rest. *Describe it.*

It's black, swirling, cloudy, kind of like smoke and magic. I don't know.

Look closer, he presses, *use your spiritual eyes, see what we see.*

He reaches a skeletal hand out and places it on my dragon shoulder and suddenly, the fear and anger and pain, everything clears and I can focus in on exactly what he's talking about.

It's not just black magic. It's so much more.

And I understand that the reapers were the key to everything all along.

For a while I thought they were the problem, but they were only being used for evil by the Sovereign Occultists. The warlocks wanted so desperately to cross the portals and when they couldn't do it by manipulating elemental magic, they forced a spell on the reapers to try to take their abilities for themselves. The only problem was the reapers were never meant to travel from the Eridas spirit realm to the human realm and the ability never transferred to the warlocks, it simply pushed the reapers to where they didn't belong. So that's why they became sick. They're not sick anymore. They're here to help me. Not just me, countless others. All the supernaturals. All the fae, the dragons, the merpeople, anyone who belongs to Eridas also belongs to them after death.

But the Occultists? They *are* sick. They *are* evil. And it is of their own choosing. The magicked bond they share is forged by blood magic, by countless unwilling sacrifices. It's made them powerful but King Titus is right, it's also made them too dependent on each other and vulnerable. I can't only feel the weighty magic of the blood bond coming from the Sovereign Occultists as they work in tandem to destroy, I can see it.

It's the sight my father tried to tell me about!

The black smoky magic in the physical world is how it manifests to the eyes, but to my spirit eyes, it's far more than smoke. It's alive and intelligent… but it's also dead in a way. It's a thing riling against itself, rotting and grotesque. The more it grows, the sicker it becomes, sick with power, sick with death, sick with tainted magic.

Today, I will end it, even if it means I end, too. This isn't a power I want to see in my human world, let alone in Eridas. It has to go.

Where does it lead? a reaper asks. *Show us. Take us to the master.*

I study the magic, trying to make sense of what they're asking. At first it's as I saw it before, a black pulsing smoke, but then it's as I see it with the spirit eyes, sparkling and interconnected, but also broken, the magic full of fissures. It rolls in on itself, leading back to one direction—the source. Could that be the master? I take flight again, following the direction in which the magic is sucking the life from the fallen and syphoning to the blood bond. The reapers follow close behind me, nipping at my wings.

They may not be able to see everything that I can see but they can see me. And that will have to be enough.

I force myself to ignore fallen dragons and fae on the battlefield, pushing onward until the black magic converges to a single point, like the eye of a hurricane. And there stands the master.

He's not what I expected.

He's not as ageless as the others, as well built or tall.

He is older and smaller, and his face is deformed on one side, the bone concave. Still, he has those glowing red eyes, those endless orbs dripping with death. He stands with his legs and hands apart as the others around him chant. They surround him on all sides in a wall of protection. From his outstretched hands flows the black magic, and right back into his hands flows the sparkling intelligence. It's like he's feeding this entire thing and being fed by it, too.

And that, that right there, *that's* the blood bond.

Kill him, a reaper hisses, *kill him quickly. Show no mercy.*

A shock of pure terror runs through me. I'm supposed to kill him? How? I can't touch him in this dragon form.

"Ah," the master speaks, voice low and reverent. "The spirit elemental is near." He smiles. "We've been waiting for you."

I can't fight him. I'll die.

But I have to try. I'm almost out of time as it is. Dean needs me. Khali. My mom. Harmony. This is it, this is my destiny. I might die, but if I die, he's going down with me.

And with that thought, I shift.

I'm human. Vulnerable flesh and blood. And I'm standing a mere foot away from the master.

"There you are."

He lunges.

Something metallic flashes to my right. As I'm taking the leap to dodge him, a reaper tosses me his scythe. I expect it to be heavy. It's not. It barely weighs anything—the ethereal made manifest. The blade arcs effortlessly as I swing it forward with all my strength and cut right through the master's frail neck.

There's no time for him to react. His body falls the same moment I turn away, screaming as hot blood sprays.

The same reaper swings into action, immediately taking his spirit away. I use the scythe, hacking away at the black magic. I don't know what makes me do it. Fear? Anger? Hope? The black magic screams and sizzles, dying almost as fast as it sprang to life.

The smoke and haze clears. I'm surrounded by the men in robes. They're ageing, dying with the loss of the blood bond, their bodies decaying instantly until there is nothing left but brittle skeletons littering the muddy snow. My stomach roils and bile rises in my throat. I turn away and run, glorious satisfaction lifting a smile to my face, lifting my heart, too. With my spirit eyes, the reapers are attacking the warlock's spirits, taking them away with swift vengeance. There's no coming back from this. It's over for them.

The smoke clears and I search the battlefield. There's so much death. Bodies are everywhere. The snow is red with blood. I try to find Dean and Khali, but I can't make them out amongst the carnage. What if I'm too late? What if they're already dead?

THIRTY-TWO

KHALI

TIME, THOUGHTS, PEOPLE, MY BREATH, my heart—it all moves in slow motion. The deadly smoke magic clears away and I'm left to see who is still alive and who didn't make it. Juniper is faster than me, up and moving, quick to heal whoever she can. I'm sure it's going to be impossible for so many to come back from this, they'd have been dead too long, wounded beyond even what her healing magic can repair. We're bound to have casualties and I can't bear to look just yet.

Flannery is dead.

I crawl over to him, taking his strong lifeless hand in my own and kissing it once. "I'll tell them," I whisper, my voice growing ragged. "I'll tell them that you love them." His long hair is matted and bloodied, and his warm eyes stare off into an unseen distance. Flannery's sacrifice meant his death. His family is waiting for a father who will never return home and my heart aches as I realize the repercussions of their loss. The centaurs have been said to be extinct. To lose this incredible unique man is a terrible blow to all of Eridas.

I rest his hands against his chest and softly push his eyelids closed. Then I muster up the courage to look around. The warlocks are nothing but bone and dust among fallen robes, but they're not the only ones who are gone. Bellflower Blossom already died because of this mess. Silas is dead and so many of the people he hurt along the way are never coming back. And now there are more, so many more. I force myself to wipe away the blurry tears threatening to fall and stand on weak legs. I need to be strong. The ones who are left, they will need me to be strong for them, to lead them into something better—they deserve better. The wind brushes against my cheeks as I survey the battlefield, glad to see that more people and dragons are getting up. At the lake, the merpeople are wailing over the death of their Queen.

I will have to reward them for helping. Despite everything, they did their duty and protected the portal below the lake. They want to walk on land again. Silas and his ancestors wouldn't grant that but maybe I will find a way to make that happen and keep my people safe.

I turn away and a flash of bright blond hair catches my

eye. Juniper is draped over a body, her sobbing voice high and desperate. My heart breaks all over again—what if it's Bram? I run after her, tripping on my own boots as I go.

But it's not Bram I find in her arms.

It's Maxx.

I pull her against me as she sobs. "He's g-gone. And I-I never got to t-tell him how m-much I loved him."

"I'm so sorry." It's all I can say.

She caresses his face, his horns, his arms… all lifeless.

Across the field, I spot Hazel and Dean and Terek, and my heart swells with relief. And then it's Bram standing just feet away from me, bloodied and bruised, but very much alive. And it's my turn to burst into tears.

I let Juniper go and run to him, no longer caring who sees the love on my face. It's Bram—he's it for me. Blood and dirt mar his beautiful face. He staggers with a pained limp, the spear dragging behind him. Our gazes collide and his hold me in their emerald focus. He's always been so focused, this man of books and intellect and observance and sacrifice. I watched him grow from a pensive boy into a loyal man and I feel blessed to see him for who he really is.

When I reach him, he drops the spear, no longer invisible to anyone he wishes. We're truly exposed now but I don't care. I wrap my arms around his shoulders, my fingers trailing along his curled hair, and stand on my toes, pressing my lips to his.

He doesn't hold back.

He returns the kiss, deepening it. Others must be watching but none of that matters right now. It will soon, very soon, but right now, all that matters is this exact moment, this kiss, and this perfect boy.

"DO WE REALLY HAVE TO do this?" My voice, my spirit, my thoughts—everything is heavy, and sad, and relieved, and exhausted, and delighted and simply ready to be *done*.

"The remaining court demands an audience," Faros says, hovering over me as she brushes my hair into long loose curls. I stare at myself in the mirror, every bit of me feeling numb. My eyes are red around the rims, proof of the sadness in my heart. I hate my eyes in this moment, I hate the two colors and what they're going to do to me just as they have always done to me. Because this is it, isn't it? This is the moment the court demands I remarry someone other than Bram. Because they can't imagine someone save for a Dragon Blessed as their king, and they'll want a king. They'll demand one right away.

I won't do it. I'll refuse.

"Are you going to be okay?" Faros asks. She stares down at me, worried.

I shrug. "No… but does it matter?"

"To me it does."

"But what about the rest of them?"

She doesn't have an answer to that.

It took hours to clean up everything after the battle yesterday. The dead were carefully wrapped up in linen and we're planning to begin funerals tomorrow. There were simply too many pyres to build to have them right away. And I refused to have mass funerals. I want each and every fae and dragon that fell to receive a proper send off into the afterlife.

The bloodied snow was washed away and once all was said and done, everyone went home, hardly believing what had happened. There should have been feelings of celebration, because we'd finally won, but how could we celebrate when so many were dead? Impossible. What little was left of the Occultists was burned immediately and we at least praised the Gods for that.

The clean up? The death? I could handle all that. It was hard, but I was stronger than I knew. It was *okay*.

But this right now? This demand to present myself to the court? This, I can't handle this. I'm not strong enough anymore to deny my feelings for Bram or let someone else choose my future.

I'm back to being scrubbed and primped, dressed up like a pretty doll, a crown placed atop my head, as if everything in my life didn't just change forever. The metal digs into my scalp as Faros adjusts the silver, rubies and emeralds and diamonds sparkling against the morning sunlight. I glare at the crown because I don't know if I want it anymore. I mean, I do, I want to be Queen, but as *myself.* The cost of being Drakenon's Queen as the woman others want me to be has always been so high.

But…

But maybe this time, things could be different.

No matter what, I don't want to be a queen to someone who isn't Bram. Because I love him. I do. And now what? I'd give up my crown for him but I also don't want another person like Silas to reign. So then I'm stuck, aren't I?

I haven't even seen him since our passionate kiss on the battlefield. He took the magicked spear after that and disappeared, hiding it again until we can return it to Flannery's wife. He said he took it from the chest in the first place because he was bringing it to me, but I'd already left my chambers by the time he arrived. That's when he knew he had to take it to the battlefield himself. I'm so glad it worked out that way, that he had it, that he used it when we all needed it most. My heart shudders to think of what would have happened if he hadn't been there to break the sorcerer's staff.

I long to see Bram again, to go to him right now. And my heart aches with what he must think now that Dean is back.

Oh, Dean…

I won't let them kill Dean. No way. And now that he's here maybe he'll want to be king but I saw the way Hazel looked at him and I can't take that from her. I don't think he would want to do that either. It's obvious they're in love. Would he give up love to be king?

Maybe… but I don't think so. Actually, it's the other way around. That man would give up just about anything to be with Hazel.

"You are stunning." My mother lets herself into my room. She's Lady Alivia Elliot by the looks of it, taking on that air of sophistication and poise that she has used so well to her advantage over the years. "Come on," she says, reaching out to pull me from where I'm slumped on the chair. "I'm going with you."

I don't bother to say anything in return.

My gown is fitted, golden with red adornments and as beautiful as anything else in a queen's wardrobe. My hair is a pile of perfect curls cascading down my back. Faros put all the right makeup on my face to hide the puffiness from crying and lack of sleep. I look the part of Drakenon's Queen but I don't feel it. I don't feel much of anything.

"Snap out of it." Mother places her arm through mine as we walk down the castle's long empty corridor. "If we're going to pull this off, you can't go in there moping."

"What?"

Before she can answer me, we're swept into the throne room.

It's not a room I've spent a lot of time in since the coronation. But today must mean business because it's filled with every surviving member of the dragon court and they're all looking at me like I'm the most wonderful creature on earth.

What?

Their respect is the second biggest relief to killing off the Occultists. I can breathe, finally. I can breathe. The peace that is met with it rings through me like a church bell, filling every crevice of my soul. Maybe everything is going to be okay, after all.

They bow and curtsy to me.

Hazel is here with her two human friends. The fae are here, too. Everyone watches me, like they know what is about to happen, like they're excited for the show.

And in the back stands Bram, leaning against the far wall, eyes locked on me and filled with pride.

When I take my seat in the throne up front, I don't choose the smaller one next to the king's. I choose the bigger one, the one normally reserved for a Brightcaster King, and take it for my own.

The energy in the room shifts, growing charged.

The doors swing open. Dean strides in, dressed head to toe in the princely attire I remember so well. I expect whispers to erupt, as that's how these things usually go, but today they don't. Or maybe some of these people will yell and try to get their word in, demanding his execution, but nobody does. It's quiet, calm, again it's like everyone has a shared understanding except for me.

What is going on here? My eyes narrow and my spine goes stick straight.

Dean reaches the front of the room to stand before me. His black hair hangs across his molten fire eyes and a little smile flickers at the corner of his lips.

Seriously, what is going on here?

Could it be...

He motions to the members of court, to all the people I grew up with, many of whom are my friends. "We gathered this morning before you were asked to come here," Dean says coolly, "and we all agreed on one thing."

My heart pounds. Is he going to ask me to marry him? I don't think I could handle that. But I also… don't think he will ask such a thing of me. For so long Dean was all I wanted but now I wouldn't be able to accept him, not with Bram in the back, watching me like I'm the only person in the room—the only girl in the world. His green eyes have so much love in their depths. I risk a glance at him, my heart dancing when he runs a hand through his disheveled brown hair, a stray strand letting loose, and he smirks reassuringly. All I want is to go over there and fix his hair and bring those knowing lips down on my own.

"And what's that you agreed on?" I force myself to refocus on Dean.

"That you should be our queen."

I laugh, not quite impressed. "I already am your queen."

"Let me rephrase." His smile hitches at the corner and turns into a full-blown grin, a rare sight for the broody Dean I know so well. "That you should be the sovereign queen, the ruler of Drakenon, in your own right. *You* and nobody else."

My face drains, lips popping open. "Me alone? Which means… "

"That you're going to start your own royal line with

whomever you choose? That your husband, whoever that may be"—he winks knowingly—"will be your partner and not your ruler. Yes, that's exactly what I mean."

I blink, dumbfounded. One by one, the members of the court stand and bow, calling out "Gods save the queen."

Nobody protests. Not even one.

I stand, finding my words one at a time. My dragon leaps joyfully alongside my elements. "Thank you." My voice cracks and tears fill my eyes. "I promise. I will not let you down. I will do my best to be the queen you deserve. I'll take care of us and put the needs of the kingdom before my own. We will learn and grow stronger from our past mistakes and become the best version of Drakenon we can be."

I've walked forward by this point to be among my people. I turn to gaze back at the thrones. I never did like them. How they're raised above everyone else. How one throne sits higher than the other. That's not the kind of monarch I want to be.

The decision comes easy.

I draw the fire to my palms and throw it at the thrones, smiling wide as they catch the flames. That gets more than a few gasps but I don't let it stop me. The thrones burn quick, embers rising into the room. I use my magic to fling open the windows, releasing the smoke. And then I call on my water elemental to extinguish the flames. There's nothing left of the thrones besides ash and embers which is just as well. It's time for something new.

I turn back to the crowd, letting the steam rise behind me.

"I am not above you. I am your queen, but I am here to love you and guide you, not to lord over you. I want to be a part of this kingdom but most of all I want us all to be one. United."

They stare at me, shocked, but also eager. They must want the same thing.

"We're one," I say. "We're Drakenon."

"We're Drakenon!" They call out in unison and the room erupts into rapturous applause.

I catch Bram's eye from where he still lingers in the back of the room and return his knowing smile. No matter what happens next, he's the man I'm going to marry. He will be my husband. And this time, it'll be my choice—the right choice. And the best part is that I have no doubt he'll choose me back, not because of my status or my magic or what I can do for him, but because he loves me.

And that is its own kind of magic.

ONE YEAR LATER

HAZEL

"ARE YOU READY TO GO?" I hitch my backpack over my shoulder and wink at Dean. "This isn't too much luggage, is it?" I'm standing at the entrance to Dean's house with my little roller bag at my feet. It's packed full of everything I could possibly need to visit Stoneshearth, excluding the medieval gowns I'll wear once we get there. I seriously can't wait for that part. Dressing up like a storybook princess is super fun and I'm about to do it for a whole week.

He raises an incredulous eyebrow at me. "Yeah, I'm ready. What do you have in that thing?" He points to the suitcase.

"I've packed presents for Khali and Bram, mainly in the form of chocolate and books. Maybe a plushie or two... or three."

He laughs and zips the suitcase and backpack into his

massive waterproof duffle bag. That thing is ridiculous, but he can lift it up like it weighs nothing. Mom is going to meet us at the portal in an hour and then once we get through the freezing cold water—always the worst part—we'll be on our way to Drakenon. I could just jump through the spirit realm and skip the water but I don't know, I kind of like doing it all together. It's sort of our own little Polar Bear Plunge.

"So what books are you bringing Khali this time?" He eyes me with feigned interest. I know he doesn't really care about the books, fiction isn't his thing, but I love him for humoring me.

I got her hooked on Harry Potter when we visited over the summer and it turns out she actually appreciates the amazingness that is my all time favorite book series. Sometimes when she gets a break and can visit me, I'm going to whisk her away to Universal Studios and blow her mind. For now though, we'll work our way through the rest of the best fandoms one at a time. The girl is busy, what with being queen and all, but she loves reading for entertainment as much as I do, so it's fun to share that common interest. "Next I'm getting her into Twilight—Go Team Edward!" I mumble to myself. "Actually, I was Team Jacob until the weird baby thing happened and then I didn't really know what to think."

"I have no idea what any of that means."

"Don't worry!" I pull him into a hug and plop a kiss on his cheek. "When we get back, we'll have a movie marathon, and you'll know exactly what this Edward versus Jacob rivalry is all about. Prepare to be entertained!"

"Twilight has movies, too?" He doesn't sound so excited.

I laugh because he has no idea the amount of eye-rolls that are in his future and this is going to be so much fun.

"You're sure you want to go?" he asks, "We really can just do the entire Christmas break in Ohio, or split it between here and there. No homework for a month. It sounds pretty good to me."

Yeah, right. I know he wants to go visit his home just as much as I do.

"And miss the opportunity to experience Yule in Drakenon?" I pout. "No freaking way! We'll be back to my Mom's place by the 24th, and Harmony is going to join us there, so we can have the best of both worlds."

And it really is the best of both worlds.

Dean and I are still attending college and living in the human world, but we travel to Eridas often. Usually it's to hang out in the Fae Forest and work on our magic. It's nice to get that little recharge. But sometimes we travel over to Drakenon to see his old friends, his mom and brother, and of course Khali. I tend to fly with him, even though I could go through the spirit realm portals. It just depends on the mood I'm in but I don't love how the portals lose time and the whole day is just "poof" when I travel those long distances. I'd rather experience the thrill of flight as a dragon and have Dean at my side.

Dean kisses me softly before opening the front door. "Let's go to our other home."

We shuffle out into the icy morning air and wait for Macy to arrive. She should be here any minute. Good thing she's agreed to give us a ride. A hired driver might question why we want to be dropped off on the side of a forested highway in the middle of winter.

"Oh shoot!" I pull my phone out of my back pocket and frown. "I forgot to put this away." We can't take any electronics with us to Eridas because they'll get fried.

"I'll go put it in my safe with my computer and phone."

"Thanks, Babe."

He takes it and runs back inside, leaving me to wait on the front stoop. The wind picks up a notch and then settles into complete silence. Eerily, so.

"Wait a second." My eyes narrow as I take in the mysterious man sauntering up the drive. "I know you."

It's the angel Elias. He looks the same as that night he appeared to me at that seedy motel. His blond hair is pushed back off his chiseled face and his amber eyes are so bright, they almost look like fake contacts. He wears a tan wool trench coat—no wings visible today—and his hands are hooked into deep pockets.

If I wasn't head over heels in love with Dean, I'd be all sorts of swoony right now.

"And I gotta be honest," I say as I go out to greet him. "I never thought I was going to see you again."

His smiles hitches. "I'm here to thank you."

"Well, you're welcome, but please don't warn me of some new threat. I don't think I can take on another battle anytime soon."

"There will always be threats to the humans." His voice is surprisingly playful. "Good thing too, or I'd be out of a job."

This makes me laugh. I get to see the angels doing their tasks sometimes, but they're not like the reapers and they don't talk to me. Elias is different though. He's got to be some kind of hybrid because his wings aren't brilliant white, he's not freakishly tall, and well, he's flesh and blood and bone standing right in front of me.

"So what are you doing here?"

"I told you, I came to thank you."

"Is that really all?"

He sighs. "I have to leave this place. I'm being transferred to another," his voice tapers off. "Well, anyway, I came to let you know that you won't be seeing me again. I need you to promise you'll keep the spirit realms protected as best as you can."

"Well, yeah, sure, but nothing has happened in a year."

He nods once. "And I hope it stays that way but the thing about supernaturals is they can get… greedy. There may come a time that you will have to take action again and I need you to promise me that you won't hesitate to protect the humans."

"Okay, this is weird, but fine. Sure."

He's acting strange, like he doesn't want to leave, and I wonder if this man has been watching me and the other supernaturals around here more than he's willing to let on. But he's an angel and he said himself he's not allowed to travel to Eridas, that his job is limited to humans, so I guess it makes sense. Maybe this meeting really is just his way of bidding me goodbye.

"Can I give you a hug?" I ask. "You look like you need a hug."

His eyebrows shoot up and his mouth turns down. "No." He steps back, adamant. "I'm leaving now."

And then he disappears into thin air.

Well, okay then.

"Who were you talking to?" Dean returns. No way I'm going to keep this from him. So I tell him the whole thing, still keeping Elias's name to myself, and by the end, Dean is as confused as I am, if not a little nervous. "Well, he's right that supers get greedy and it's smart to be on the lookout."

We don't talk about it again.

Before long we're with my mom and the three of us are flying over the Summer Forest on our way to Drakenon. I can't wait to tackle Khali in a huge hug. We've become good friends now and dang, is that woman rocking it as queen or what?! Seriously it's like she was born for diplomacy and grace and all the things a monarch should be. Not to mention she's all shacked up with the hottie Bram now. Those two are so adorably cute together that it's borderline gross. Like I thought Dean and I were a little too much PDA at times but those two can't keep their hands off each other. No doubt there will be a wedding and then little dragon babies running around the castle soon. And thank heavens for that because I don't know what I'd have done if Dean had chosen that life over the one he has with me.

And I love my life.

I love school. Him. My friends. We brought Cora and Macy home as soon as we could after the battle. It was difficult at first for them to process things and move on, especially since their parents were pissed that they "went on vacation without permission", but eventually everything went back to normal between all of us. Macy declared her major as exercise science and wants to become a personal trainer and Cora has decided on a double major with political science and business, she even has a boyfriend now and it's been fun to watch her fall in love this year. She's always been such a tough cookie but Julian brings out her soft side. They're super cute.

Mom went back to work as a nurse, and now that she knows who she is, she's able to use her own glamour to cover her wings out in public, but she's also able to help people heal. Her ability is a lot like Juniper's, though it's quite tempered from all her time in the human realm. It's pretty telling that she was able to figure out her calling in life, even before the memories returned. She visits me in Westinbrooke and travels to Eridas a lot now so she can grow her abilities. I don't mind because I love spending time with her. She keeps talking about moving down here and I bet within the next year she lands a job and can make it happen. Who wouldn't want to hire an amazing nurse like her?

And fortunately for me, Harmony came back to Westinbrooke and reopened The Flowering Chakra. She doesn't do readings anymore because she can't, but I do medium readings and enjoy the time I get in the shop. And I *love* working with her. She's the perfect mentor for me. I never thought I'd be able to embrace my gift and stop calling it a curse, but I have. I'm able to help people move on after death, both on this side of the veil and the other, which is kind of remarkable. I keep saying I still want to go to vet school, but more and more often, I'm feeling like that might change. At least I have time to figure it out since I'm only nineteen. So much can happen in a year or two, or even a month or two, so who knows what's next for me. All in all, things are magical—as cheesy as that is to say. I don't know what the future holds, but I know I get to have Dean in it, I know I get to live between all the realms that I love, and that's enough for me.

Mom is slower than Dean and I, so we don't make it to Stonehearth until well after dark. The sky sparkles with stars and the castle below is lit up with candles in every window. More dragons join us as we veer toward the roof, calling out happy greetings through the telepathic link. We land and shift, Dean dropping the duffle bag at our feet, just as Brysta, Khali, and Bram burst through the doors.

"You're here!" Khali squeals and runs toward us, hugging us both and planting a friendly kiss on Dean's cheek. "Oh, I'm so glad you made it. You're going to love Yule!"

We're ushered inside and laden with gifts and food and so many welcomed greetings. It's the first night of what is going to be a week-long celebration and I seriously can't wait. My dragon is stronger here, my magic and my family too. I love this place!

Growing up, I always felt like I didn't belong anywhere. I struggled to make friends and never fit in. I didn't know my ancestry and certainly didn't have control over my gift. But now that's all changed. I've been able to say goodbye to my dad and make peace with my past. I have my mom and Dean, and now Khali and so many others who love me.

I have my home in West Virginia, the spirit realms to explore, and now this magical place to call my own. I realize now that I was never meant to fit into one kind of place or only connect with one type of people. Harmony once told me I was a bridge and at first I didn't understand what that meant or why it was a good thing but now I get it and I'm thrilled to be the bridge between all these amazing people and places.

"Are you happy?" Dean whispers low into my ear and laces his fingers with mine. His touch still sends a flutter of butterflies in my chest.

"Yes," I respond first with the words and second with a kiss. In fact, I never thought this kind of happiness could exist.

"Are you happy?" I ask the question right back.

His eyes bore into mine, dancing flames lighting up around the coal irises, and he smiles. "Thank you," he whispers.

"For what?"

He nods toward where his brother and mother are sitting on the nearby sofa, laughing at something so loudly that tears stream down the older woman's elegant face. Khali stands at the window nearby, not gazing out longingly, but with peace on her face. My mom stands at her side, chatting with her about the upcoming festivities.

"For putting my family back together," he says softly, his lips a brush against mine as he speaks. "At least, as much as possible."

I kiss him again. Just once. Quick. "We did that. Both of us. All of us, actually. But you're welcome."

Now that we know what we've got and how fleeting life can be, we won't ever take it for granted again. Not even for a second.

THE END

ACKNOWLEDGMENTS

THANK YOU FOR READING. I appreciate your support. If you enjoyed this book, please consider leaving a written review and telling your friends. I can't do this without you.

Thank you to my husband for always supporting me, to my cover designer Daqri Bernardo, my paperback formatter Molly Phipps, my editor Kate Foster, and my proofreaders Sarah Mostaghel, Ailene Kubricky, and Kate Anderson. Thank you to all the readers, friends, and family who continue to champion my books—I LOVE YOU ALL!

ABOUT THE AUTHOR

NINA WALKER is a *USA Today* Bestselling author. She lives near the beautiful red mountains of southern Utah with her family. She writes across multiple genres and loves metaphysical magic systems, forbidden love interests, and unexpected plot twists. She takes pride in publishing books that both teens and adults can enjoy. You can learn more at WWW.NINAWALKERBOOKS.COM or find her on social media to join in on the fun!

www.ingramcontent.com/pod-product-compliance
Lightning Source LLC
Chambersburg PA
CBHW032203180726
48284CB00001B/167